It's cold in Hell, too. So cold.

That thought threatened to tip me over into howling madness, so it vanished. Swept under the rug. Hey presto.

My skull was still there. Hard curves of bone, tender at the back. I let out a sob. Held my hands out, flipped them palm-up. They shook like palsied things.

Branches. Like branches.

But the image fled as soon as it arrived, mercifully. My forearms were pale under the screen of filth. On my right wrist, just above the softest part, something glittered. Hard, like a diamond. It caught the moonlight and sent back a dart of brilliance, straight through my aching skull. The sight filled me with unsteady loathing, and I shut my eyes.

Start with the obvious first. Who am I?

The train's rumble receded.

Who am I?

Praise for the Jill Kismet series:

"Saintcrow is a visceral writer who keeps the plot going at a frenetic pace."

—*RT Book Reviews* (4-1/2 Stars)

"Loaded with action ~~and starring a kick butt heroine.~~"

~~...~~s.com

BOOKS BY LILITH SAINTCROW

Dante Valentine Novels

Working for the Devil
Dead Man Rising
Devil's Right Hand
Saint City Sinners
To Hell and Back

Dante Valentine (omnibus)

Jill Kismet Novels

Night Shift
Hunter's Prayer
Redemption Alley
Flesh Circus
Heaven's Spite
Angel Town

As Lili St. Crow

The Strange Angels series

Strange Angels
Betrayals
Jealousy
Defiance
Reckoning

ANGEL TOWN

LILITH SAINTCROW

www.orbitbooks.net

This book is a work of fiction. Names, characters, places, and incidents are the product of the author's imagination or are used fictitiously. Any resemblance to actual events, locales, or persons, living or dead, is coincidental.

Copyright © 2011 by Lilith Saintcrow

Excerpt from *The Iron Wyrm Affair* copyright © 2011 by Lilith Saintcrow

Orbit
Hachette Book Group
237 Park Avenue
New York, NY 10017
www.HachetteBookGroup.com

First Edition: November 2011

Orbit is an imprint of Hachette Book Group. The Orbit name and logo are trademarks of Little, Brown Book Group Limited.

The publisher is not responsible for websites (or their content) that are not owned by the publisher.

Printed in the United States of America

10 9 8 7 6 5 4 3 2 1

OPM

To all the survivors.

Acknowledgments

Thanks are due first of all to Maddy and Nicky, my twin reasons for enduring. After that, my endless gratitude goes to Miriam Kriss and Devi Pillai, for believing in Jill—and in me—even when I did neither. Thanks are also due to the long-suffering Jennifer Flax, and to the usual suspects: Mel Sanders, my bestie; Christa Hickey, who teaches me how to be brave; and Sixten Zeiss, for love and coffee.

Last but not least, dear Reader, I shall continue to thank you in the way we both like best: by telling more stories. Come in, sit down. I hope you like this one...

An army that continues to fight on regardless of the outcome must be considered a well-trained army, whether it is well led or not.

—John Mosier, *The Blitzkrieg Myth*

Decensus ad Infernos

Descent into Hell

In the shifting wood of suicides that borders the cold rivers of Hell, what is one tree more or less?

They are a mosaic, those trees. Every shade of the rainbow, and hues humans cannot see. Every color except one, but that has changed.

There is one white tree, a slender birchlike shape. Instead of a screaming face hidden in the bark, there is a sleeping woman carved with swift strokes. Eyes closed, mouth relaxed, she is a peaceful pale pillar amid the cold shifting.

For Hell is frozen, a chill that burns. The trees shake their leaves, roaring filling their branches.

Under the spinning-nausea sky holding dry stars of alien geometry, something new may happen, might happen, will happen…

…is happening now.

Pinpricks of light settle into the white tree's naked branches. She has not been here long enough to grow the dark tumescent leaves every other tree shakes now. The screaming of their distress mounts, for these trees are conscious. Their bloodshot eyes are always open, their distended mouths always moving.

The pinpricks move like fireflies on a summer evening, each one a semaphore gracefully unconnected to the whole. They crown the tree with light, weaving tiny trails of phosphorescence in the gasping-cold fluid that passes for air. They tangle the streamers, and the storm is very close.

Hell has noticed this intrusion. And Hell is not pleased.

The trails of light form a complex net. The other trees thrash. Takemetakemetakeme, they scream, a rising chorus of the damned. Their roots hold fast, sunk deep in metallic ash. The river rises, white streaks of foam clutching its oilsheen surface. Leaves splatter, torn free, and their stinking blood makes great splotches on the dry ground. A cloud of buzzing black rises from each splotch, feeding greedily on the glistening fluid.

The net is almost complete. Almost. Hell's skies are whipped with fury, the storm breaking over the first edge of the wood as screaming thunder. Maggot-white lightning scorches. The pale net over the white tree draws close, like a woman pulling her hair back.

Long dark curling hair, spangled with silver.

The storm descends, ripping trees apart. The souls of the damned explode with screams that would turn the world to bleeding ice, if the world heard. The ashes of their destruction will sink into the carpet of the woods, each separate particle growing another tree.

For there is always more agony in Hell.

The net collapses, silvery filaments winding themselves in. It shrinks to a point of brilliance, and the shadows this light casts are cleansed. They etch themselves on the ash, *and under the wrack of the storm is a sound like a soft sigh.*

The light winks out.

A few tiny, crystalline-white feathers fall, but they snuff themselves out before they reach the heaving ground.

The white tree no longer stands. It is gone.

And Hell itself shakes.

I: Anastasis

Resurrection

*B*uzzing. In my head. All around me. Creeping in. A rattling roar, filling my skull. Crawling into my teeth, sticky little insect feet all over my face, feelers probing at my lips. They move, hot and pinprick-tiny, and that sound is enough to drag me screaming out of...

...where?

Dark. It was dark, and there was no air. Sand filled my mouth, but the little things crawling on me weren't sand. They were *alive*, and they were droning loud enough to drown out everything but the sounds I was making. Terrifying sounds. Suffocating, it was in my mouth and my nose too, lungs starved, heart a suddenly pounding drum.

Scrabbling through sand, dirt everywhere, the buzzing turning into a roar as they lifted off me. The insects didn't sting, just made that horrible sound and flew in disturbed little circles.

I exploded out of the shallow grave, my screams barely piercing the rumbling roar. Little bits of flying things buzzed angrily, flashing lights struck me like hammers and I fell, scrabbling, the wasps still crawling and buzzing and trying to probe through my mouth and nose and ears and eyes and hands and feet and belly.

They were still eating, because flesh had rotted.

I had rotted.

I scrubbed at myself as the train lumbered past. That was the light and the roaring. My back hit something solid and I jolted to a stop. The wasps crawled over me, and when I forced air out through my nose it blew slimy chunks of snot-laced sand away.

I collapsed against the low retaining wall, breath sobbing in and out. My head rang like a gong, I bent over and vomited up a mass of dark, writhing liquid.

The stench was awesome, titanic, a living thing. It crawled on the breeze, pressed against me, and I vomited again. This time it was long strands of gooey white, splatting. Coming from nowhere and passing through me, landing in twisting runnels.

Just like cotton candy! a gleeful, hateful voice crowed inside my head. The eggwhite was all over me, loathsome slime turning the sand into rasping dampness.

I squeezed my knees together, bent over, and whooped in a deep breath. The wasps crawled, and other bits of insect life clung to me. Maggots. Other things. Of course— out in the desert, the bugs get to you. Especially in a shallow grave, when there's been trauma to the tissues.

I grabbed my head. The sound was immense, filling me to the brim, the roaring swallowing my scream. Gobbets of rotting flesh fell away, the wasps angrily swarming, and the train rumbled away into the distance.

Leaving me alone. In the night.

In the *dark*.

I tore at the rotting flesh cloaking me. It peeled away in

noisome strips, and under it I was whole, slick with slime. I retched again, a huge tearing coming all the way up from my toes, and produced an amazing gout of that slippery eggwhite stuff again.

Ectoplasm? But—The thought floated away as the pain came down on me, laid me open. Skull cracked wide, bones twisting, everything in me creaking and re-forming. My knees refused to give, my short-bitten nails dug through the cloak of rotting and found my own skin underneath.

I scrambled along the retaining wall. The grave yawned, leering, crawling with disturbed insect life. I fell on sand, grubbed up handfuls of it, and scrubbed at myself. I didn't care if it stripped skin off and left me bleeding, didn't care if it went down to bone, I just wanted the rot *away*.

Under the mess of decaying flesh was a torn T-shirt, rags of what had been leather pants. At least I had some clothes. I was barefoot.

I collapsed to my knees on the sand, looked up.

A full moon hung grinning in the sky, bloated cheese-yellow. The hard, clear points of stars glittered, and steam slid free of my skin.

Whole skin. Clear, unblemished, scraped in places. But not rotting.

The pain retreated abruptly. My questing fingers found filthy hair, stiff with sand and God knew what else. The wasps were sluggish—it gets cold out here at night. Everything else was burrowing to escape the chill.

It's cold in Hell, too. So cold. That thought threatened to tip me over into howling madness, so it vanished. Swept under the rug. Hey presto.

My skull was still there. Hard curves of bone, tender at

the back. I let out a sob. Held my hands out, flipped them palm-up. They shook like palsied things.

Branches. Like branches.

But the image fled as soon as it arrived, mercifully. My forearms were pale under the screen of filth. On my right wrist, just above the softest part, something glittered. Hard, like a diamond. It caught the moonlight and sent back a dart of brilliance, straight through my aching skull. The sight filled me with unsteady loathing, and I shut my eyes.

Start with the obvious first. Who am I?

The train's rumble receded.

Who am I?

I tilted my head back and screamed, a lonely curlew cry. Because I didn't know.

1

I shivered, pushed the door open. My feet left bloody prints on faded blue-speckled linoleum.

The diner was deserted. Long white lunch counter with chrome napkin holders, pies under glass domes, and the smell of industrial coffee fought with the reek around me. The night wind had scrubbed the worst of the stink away, but I still felt it like a cloud breathing from my skin.

Why I was worried about that when I was dripping with sandy, crusted filth, bare- and bloody-footed, and wild-haired in the rags of leather pants and a T-shirt was beyond me. Still...it bothered me. Something about my hair bothered me, too. I felt completely naked, even though all my bits were mostly covered. I was too scrawny for there to be much to look at anyway. Pared down to scarecrow bone, muscle wasted away, my elbows bigger than my biceps, my knees knobs.

The diner sat alone off the highway, its windows glowing gold with warm electric light. Two ancient, spaceship-shaped gas pumps stood outside in a glare of buzzing fluorescents. No car was visible for miles in any direction. In the distance, the glow of a city rose, staining the night. I'd been heading for that glow for a slow, stumbling eternity, reeling drunkenly on the blacktop because the shoulder was full of pebbles and other things. Broken glass. Cigarette butts. Nameless, random trash.

I was just another piece of refuse, blowing along.

The booths marched away, all covered in blue vinyl. The tables were spotless, their chrome edges sharp-bright. The window booths even had sprays of artificial violets in tiny mass-produced white ceramic vases, the kinds with pebbled sides and wide mouths.

For a moment I had a memory, but it slipped away like a catfish in muddy water. I stood there on an industrial-grade rubber mat that used to say WELCOME in bright white paint. The *E* and the *OM* were scuffed into invisibility by God alone knew how many feet.

The place probably did a land-office business during the day. Maybe.

"Justaminnit!" someone yelled from the kitchen. There was a sizzle, and the heavy sound of a commercial freezer slamming shut. "Be right with ya!"

Yeah, great. I don't even have any money. There was a phone in a booth outside the front door, but who the hell would I call?

I didn't even know my own name.

"Well, good eveni—gooood gravy *Marie*!" The man hove into sight, two hundred fifty pounds if he was an ounce, most of it straining to escape his white T-shirt and the stained apron slung loincloth-style below his considerable belly. Despite that, he looked hard, and the lightness of his step told me he could do some damage if he wanted to.

If he had to.

But he simply stopped and stared at me. "God*damn*, girl, what happened to you?"

How the hell did I know? I'd just clawed my way out of a goddamn grave. I opened my mouth, shut it.

The door opened behind me. Instinct spiked under my skin; I jerked to the side. My bare, bleeding feet slapped down, braced for action. I ducked, my hand blurring up in a fist.

But broad, warm fingers closed around my filthy, naked upper arm.

He set me on my feet. Taller than me, stoop-shouldered and wiry, his dishwater hair laying close to the skull, and a shadow of acid-melt scarring over the lower half of his face. I stared, a sound like rushing water filling my head, and his ruined lips twitched. You could see where the scars had been really bad, but they were... were they?

Yes, they were retreating. I knew it because I'd seen him before. The black curtain over whatever had happened to me didn't part, but I *knew* him.

"You," I whispered.

"I'm about to call the Authority." Apron Man crossed his beefy forearms. "What the *fuck* is—"

The scarred man looked up. His eyes were bright blue, and that was wrong, too. Something shifted under the skin of his face, and his mouth opened slightly. No sound came out on the slight, soft exhale, but the fat man shut up.

"Well, why'n'tcha *say* so?" he mumbled. "Nobody ever *tells* me nothin'. Coffee, comin' up."

Blue Eyes looked down at me. Then, as if it was the most natural thing in the world, he raised his other hand, indicating the booths. Like he was asking me where I wanted to sit.

Those eyes. They'd been filmed before, gray cataracts hooding them. And the scarring had been much, much worse, in runnels and pleats like the flesh had been re-shaped with acid. He'd worn gray coveralls, and the name tag had been a snarl of faded thread.

"I know you." My voice cracked halfway through. "How do I know you?"

He shrugged a little, and indicated the booths again.

Great.

Well, there wasn't anything else I was doing. I picked a booth along the wall, since the windows made my nape prickle and I needed to see the front door.

Why? Why do I need to see it?

I just did, that was all.

He let me choose my side, slid in across from me. Fine threads of gold glittered in his hair under the lights. There were fluorescents in here, too, but over the door and the window booths were incandescent bulbs. It made the light softer, actually—fluorescents are hell on everyone.

Sand fell off me. The scrim of eggwhite goop in my mouth tasted of ashes. My skin prickled with insect grime. Bloody footprints tracked in from the front door, and now that I was sitting I felt just how filthy and exhausted I was. Every part of me had been pulled apart and put back to-gether by someone who had no fucking idea what they were doing.

I stared at Blue Eyes. He regarded me mildly, his ruined mouth curving up in what could have been a small smile. Strings of dirty hair fell in my face, and it seemed wrong. I tried again to think of what my hair *should* look like. Got exactly nowhere.

We sat like that for a while, until Apron Man brought

two heavy, steaming china cups and plunked them down. He gave me an incurious glance and walked away, his heavy shoes blurring two of my footprints.

What the hell?

Blue Eyes cupped his hands around his mug. Looked at me.

I figured I could ask, at least. "Who am I?"

Blue Eyes shrugged. It was a very expressive shrug. Now that I was sitting down, the shaking started. It began in my feet and worked its way through my bones one at a time, until I was shivering like a junkie. The neon OPEN sign in the window buzzed, and Apron Man began to sing as something sizzled on the grill. An old Johnny Cash tune, "Long Black Veil."

How could I know that, and not know my own name?

My stomach cramped. "You know me," I hazarded. "But you can't talk?"

Another small shrug, this one different than the last.

"You *won't* talk."

This earned me a nod.

Well, great. "How am I…Jesus. You…I…" I looked down at myself. The trembling threatened to rob me of words. "I know you somehow."

Another nod. Then he made a slow, deliberate movement, reaching under the table like he was digging in a pocket. Faint alarm ran through me, tasting like copper through the ashy sludge in my mouth.

He laid the gun on the tabletop, its barrel carefully pointed away from either of us. I stared, my mouth hanging open as he picked up his coffee mug, deliberately, and drank.

It was a .45, custom-built. A nice piece of hardware,

dull black, a real cannon. I knew what it would feel like if
I picked it up. I knew the heft and the pull, knew exactly
how much pressure to apply on the trigger. I could *feel* that
the butt was reinforced as well for pistol-whipping.

"My gun." I sounded like all the air had been punched
out of me. "That's mine. I have a gun." *Or I had one. And
you're returning it.*

Blue Eyes nodded. He set down his mug with a decisive
little click, then edged the butt a little closer to me with
one fingertip. A faint breeze touched my face. His mouth
opened as if he would say something profound, but then he
shut it tightly and shook his head. *Sorry, Charlie. No can
speak.*

"You're going to have to help me here. Give me a verb,
or something." The shaking started tapering off. Sand slid
off my clothes, pattered on the bench and the floor. The
thought of a shower filled me with sudden longing. Maybe
some food, too. A bed to sleep in, because I was so, so
tired.

Dead tired.

Nausea cramped under my breastbone again. Blue Eyes
was fiddling around under the table once more. This time
he came up with something very small. A tiny metallic
sound as he laid it on the table, his palm covering it.

A gun, and something else. I looked up.

His face changed. With the cataracts over his eyes peeled
away, those eyes spoke for him. Right now, they burned
with pure agonizing sadness. The expression drew his mouth
down, and I found out the scarring *was* retreating. It shrank
on his face a little, the skin smoothing out. I blinked.

His hand lifted.

It was a ring. A simple circle of silver, and my heart

leapt like a landed fish inside my chest. Scruffed up and obviously worn, I knew that if I picked it up I would see the etching on the inside. Tiny scratches of Cyrillic, the only thing I would ever know how to read in that alphabet, because someone had shown me a long time ago.

Do svidaniya, it said. "Go with God."

The other meaning: "goodbye."

Bile whipped the back of my throat. I picked up my mug with dream-slow fingers. It was too hot, but I took a searing gulp of the acrid coffee anyway. It tasted like it had been on a burner for a while, but it was better than the eggwhite crap.

Ectoplasm. It was ectoplasm. Something's happened.

Hot water filled my eyes. A tear rolled down my cheek, and Blue Eyes nodded. He pointed at my right hand, and I knew without asking what he meant. I set my mug down and turned my hand over, looking at the thing embedded in my right wrist. Just in the softest part, above the pulse's frantic tattoo.

It was fever-hot, a glittering, colorless, diamond-shaped gem set in my skin. Its edges frayed, like it had been surgically implanted and then pulled around a bit. It spasmed and settled like a shivering little animal. That tiny twitching tremble communicated itself up the bones of my arm, settling in my shoulder with a high hard hum.

Fear whipped through me, and a bald edge of anger like smoking insulation.

"What the fuck is *this*?" I whispered.

His lips moved slightly, and the flesh on his face crawled. Like there were bugs underneath. I pressed back into the booth, my torn heels sending up a shriek as I shoved them into the floor, my right hand darting for the

gun with scary, instinctive speed. Fingers curling, my arm
tensing, the barrel trained unerringly at his head.

Familiar. Done this before, too.

He pointed again at my right wrist. His lips moved
slightly. The words slid into my head, interlocking puzzle
pieces of meaning.

When you're ready.

One moment he was there, solid and real. The next,
there was a *pop* of collapsing air, and the booth was empty.
Another breeze feathered against my face, touching the
crusted strings of my hair. I flinched, the gun lowering as
I scanned the entire place.

Empty. Except for Apron Boy, who came shuffling out
from the kitchen. Quick as a wink, I had the gun under
the table. My left hand scooped up the ring, and the feel
of cool metal sent a zing through me, like tinfoil against
metal fillings.

Apron Boy held a steaming plate, which he plopped
down in front of me along with silverware wrapped in a
paper napkin. "Nice guy," he said. "Paid for your breakfast, at least. You eat right on up, honey." He looked
expectantly at me, expecting some kind of conversational
volley back.

I cleared my throat. "Yeah. Thanks."

That seemed to satisfy him. He hove away, moving side
to side like a walrus shouldering up onto a rocky beach,
but lightly, his feet planted with care. The plate held ham,
scrambled eggs, hash browns.

It looked good.

Eat while you can, Jill.

A klieg light went on inside my head. "Jill," I whispered. "I'm Jill."

I tucked the gun safely away. The ring fitted securely on my third left finger. Was I married?

A pair of dark eyes, silver-scarred hair, and fluid grace. He half-turned, reaching for something beside the stove, and the clean economy of motion made my heart skip a beat.

As soon as the image came, it vanished. I shook my head. More sand slipped free in a hissing rush, but none of it fell into the food. I was suddenly hungry. Not just hungry.

Famished.

A gun. A ring. And whatever that thing was on my wrist. And vanishing blue-eyed mutes. Whoever I was, I was certainly *interesting*.

Well, as long as the food was here, I'd take it. I'd worry about what to do afterward.

I hunkered down, stripped the napkin off the stamped-metal knife and fork and spoon, and started shoveling it in.

2

By the time I quit, Apron Man had refilled my coffee twice and brought out two more plates. I couldn't get full, felt like a pig. At first the food just vanished into the huge hole in my gut, but after the second plate I slowed down a bit. I was in the middle of the third before I began to feel halfway satisfied—biscuits and gravy, sausage patties, a mountain of wheat toast dripping with butter, a smaller plate of huevos rancheros with a side of rice. It was enough to put a grown man in the hospital, but it looked good to me. I did my best, but the yawning emptiness in me suddenly filled halfway through the eggs. The plates looked like something feral had been at them, but Apron Boy didn't say a word, just took them as soon as I pushed them away, then came back with the coffee pot and a slice of coconut cream pie.

I didn't even know if I liked coconut cream pie. I sat there and looked at the piped decorative cream and the little shaved bits of toasted nutflesh and felt sick. Then I wondered if chocolate cream would've been worse. Or cherry. Or...

How could I know about pie and not know who I was?

The gun's heavy weight rested against my side. *Jill. You're Jill, and you're armed. Focus on that, the rest will take care of itself.*

"Sure be glad to close up early tonight." Apron Man shuffled back with another cup of coffee. He wedged himself into the other side of the booth with a sigh. "Get off my old dogs. I'm going into town, give you a lift."

Another one of those silences, and I figured out he was waiting for me to say something. "Really? That's . . . nice." My voice was a papery husk. "Town?"

He shrugged. "Santa Luz. The bad old lady herself. You'd have to walk a fair ways. Told your friend I'd give you a lift, since he was goin' elsewhere."

Was he, now. I'll just bet. I picked up the clean fork, cut off the tip of the pie slice. "Nice of you." Awkward, like the words were sharp edges and I had to hold them just right.

"Yeah, well. Got to do what we can to he'p each other. You got somewhere in town you're goin'?"

I don't even know my name. Just how to hold this gun. And that if I wanted to, I could be across this table with this cheapass fork stuck in your carotid in a hot half second. It played out in vivid Technicolor inside my head—spurting blood, the greenstick crack of a neck breaking, the things I could do. "No. Just the city limits will do."

He gave me a dubious look, but his attention was snagged by the pie. "Is it gone off? I wouldn't think so, ol' Onorious brought it in this morning."

Onorious? "It's good." It was a lie, I hadn't tasted it yet. But the rest of the food was good. I slid the plate over into the middle of the table. "Want to share?"

His face lit up. "Boy howdy!" And wouldn't you know it, he had a spoon. He must've been waiting for me to ask.

I put my forkful in my mouth, studied his wide walrus face. He looked…kind. But something bothered me. I barely tasted the pie, but it was okay. I could get to like coconut cream. "What are you doing out here?"

He shrugged, chewing vigorously. Swallowed in a rush, took a gulp of coffee. "Landed here a while ago. Get a fair amount of business. People drive, they get hungry. And here I am. Gas pumps still work, but mostly it's the phone and the cookin'. People come in for the phone, and it smells so good they want to have a bite."

I nodded. My right hand came up, I offered it across the table. The gleam on the underside of my wrist sent a small rainbow winging across the Formica. "Jill."

He grinned even wider. It was a nice smile, broad white teeth with not a trace of food clinging to them. The corners of his eyes crinkled up, and for a moment something golden moved in the depths of his eyes.

You could see where he had been handsome, once.

His hairy paw closed over my filthy, smaller hand. "Martin. Martin D. Pores, atcher service. Honor to meetcha. Now, what do you say we finish up this here piece of pie and get movin'? Dawn's a-going to break afore you step over that limit, miss."

Dawn? But I was past questioning by then, really. A great wave of exhaustion crashed over me. My stomach was full, I had a gun and the ring, and that was all that was important right now. "I'm tired." I sounded like a cranky child.

He considered me for a long few seconds, and if I'd been less tired I might've been concerned about the things moving deep in his gaze. "I'll bet you are. You want to visit the ladies' while I get this all closed up?"

* * *

The car was a 1975 Mercury wagon, faded fake-wood paneling and handling like a whale. The engine had a slight knock to it, one I caught myself trying to suss out. For all that, it was comfortable. There's just something about a piece of American heavy metal when you can stretch your filthy battered feet out and watch the miles slip away like silk under the wheels. The ribbon of white paint running alongside the freeway reeled us along just like a big silent fish on a hook.

Martin kept it five under the speed limit, and he drove like an old granny. It didn't matter. There was nobody else on the road at this hour. The stars were hard clear points of light, each one a diamond, and the moon was low.

"You like music, Miss Jill?"

I thought about it. Did I? Didn't everyone? I decided on a good answer. "Yes."

"Well, that's good. Music's a good thing." He twisted the shiny silver knob and caught what must have been an oldies station, because Johnny Cash was singing about shooting a man in Reno just to watch him die.

I shivered. It couldn't have smelled good with me in the car, so I'd rolled my window down. Fresh, cold air poured over me, the roaring of the slipstream almost making words. I propped my filthy hair against the back of the seat and sighed.

Martin kept both his beefy paws on the wheel. He hummed along as Cash turned into the Mamas and the Pa-

pas, singing about nobody getting fat but Mama Cass. My eyelids were suddenly heavy.

Stay alert, Jill.

But there was no way. I'd had a hell of a day. Night. Whatever.

The hum of the engine and the song of the wheels were both soothing. With a full stomach and the heater finally blowing warm air into the car, I fell asleep to Martin's tuneless humming.

Just like a newborn baby.

3

I drove the knife into the sand next to me. Picked up the gun. Hefted it, and looked at him.

If his grin got any wider, the top of his head would flip open.

I pointed the gun at him, and smiled. The expression sat oddly on my face. He hissed, Helletöng rumbling in the back of his throat.

I almost understood the words, too. A shiver raced down my spine.

"You can't escape me." The rock groaned as his voice lashed at it, little glassy bits flaking away. They plopped down on the sand with odd ringing sounds. "The fire won't last forever, my darling. Then I'll step over your line in the sand, and you'll find out what it means to be mine."

"Think again." I bent my left arm. Fitted the gun's barrel inside my mouth. My eyes were dry, my body tensing against the inevitable.

Comprehension hit. Perry snarled and lunged at the banefire. It roared up, a sheet of blue flame. Twisting faces *writhed in its smokeless glow, their mouths open as they whisper-screamed.*

I glanced down at the slice on my palm. Still bleeding. It was hard to tell if the black traceries were still there. For a moment, I wondered.

Then I brought myself back to the thing I had to do. Stupid body, getting all worked up. What the will demands, the body will do—but it also tries to wriggle, sometimes.

Not this time.

"Kiss!" *he howled.* "You're mine! MINE! *You cannot escape me!"*

I saw Saul's face, yellow and exhausted, against the white pillow. I smelled him, the musk and fur of a healthy cat Were. I saw Galina's wide green eyes and marcel waves, Hutch's shy smile, Gilberto's fierce glittering-dark gaze. I saw them all, saw my city hunched on the river's edge, its skyscrapers throwing back dusk's last light with a vengeance before the dark things crawled out of their holes. I saw Anya perched on Galina's roof with her green bottle, staring down at the street and wondering if I had the strength to do this. Wondering if she would have to hunt me down, if I failed here.

And I heard Mikhail. There, little snake. Honest silver, on vein to heart. You are apprentice. Now it begins.

I love you, I thought. *I love you all.*

"You cannot escape!" *Perry screamed, throwing himself at the banefire again. It sizzled and roared, and the rocks around me begin to ring like a crystal wineglass stroked just right. If this kept up they might shatter.*

Wouldn't that be a sight.

"Do you hear me, hunter? You cannot escape me!"

Watch me, I thought, *and squeezed both eyes shut. The*

*banefire roared as he tried again to get through, actually
thrusting a hand through its wall, snatching it back with
a shattering howl as the skin blackened and curled. It was
now or never.*

I squeezed the trig—

—up from the concrete with a southpaw punch, bone shattering as my fist hit. My foot flicked out, heel striking
sharply in the second man's midriff, and I was beginning
to wake up. The alley tilted crazily, both sides leaning toward each other like old drinking buddies, and the rotting
refuse in choke-deep drifts along its sides smelled about as
horrible as I did. Faint grayish light seeped in through the
crack of sky showing above. The sky was weeping a little,
a diseased eye.

There were two more of them, one with a chain that rattled musically as he shook it. Cold fear and exhilaration
spilled through me like wine.

Gutter trash, Jill. Not worth your time.

But my body wasn't listening. It knew better than I did,
and I was suddenly across the distance separating me from
Chain Boy, my knee coming up and sinking into his groin
with a short meaty sound. He folded down, and I had the
gun in my right hand, pointed at the last man. He fetched
up like a dog at the end of his tether.

A chain's only good if you can use it. It's also only
good for a very short distance, shorter than you'd think.

For a moment I wondered how I knew that.

The fourth man was actually a boy. A weedy little boy
with greasy lank hair and a lean, sallow face, a leather
jacket that creaked like the cow was still mooing and
hadn't missed it yet, and pegged jeans that looked dipped

in motor oil. The switchblade made a small clatter as it hit the concrete, dropping from his nerveless hand. My finger tightened on the trigger.

He's just a kid. Come on.

But that kid would've followed his buddies in raping and possibly killing me if I was what they'd thought I was.

Wait. What am *I?* It said something that even sleeping like the dead, I kept hold of a gun.

I didn't see the Mercury. Martin D. Pores, nice guy and granny driver, had left me in an alley. Nice of him. Why was I surprised? Of course he would, it was the way things were going.

Pay attention! A sharp phantom slap, my head snapping aside, and my right foot flicked out again, catching sneaky Guy #2 in the knee. *Crack* like well-seasoned firewood when the axe split it, and he folded down with a rabbit-scream.

Must've hurt.

The boy in the motorcycle jacket just stood there and shivered. I don't know what he saw on my face, but it gave him some trouble. Maybe it was the mismatched eyes, one blue, one brown, that I'd found staring at me in the diner's restroom mirror. Maybe it was the gunk smeared all over me.

Maybe it was even the gun.

"Go home," I rasped. My voice didn't want to work quite right. "Go to school. Get a job and stop hanging out in alleys."

His head bobbed, lank hair falling forward in strings. He reminded me of someone, but I couldn't say just *who.* Someone with a flat, dark stare, someone I knew because...

...it was gone. Just for a second, I had it. Then it retreated, maddeningly.

He turned tail and ran, his sneakers whispering over concrete and kicking aside random bits of trash.

I spun, slowly, in a complete circle, marking every fallen body. The gun swept like a searchlight, tracking by itself to cover possible hiding places before I even thought of it. An easy instinctive movement, just like breathing. Whoever I was, I'd spent a lot of time doing this.

Training, milaya. A gruff, harsh voice, the words freighted with a foreign accent and cut off short and sharp. *It gets into bones. Run all the way deep.*

Who was that? My right hand jerked a little, as if the gem set on the inside of my wrist was twitching, pulling me.

He'd trained me well. The guys were down and moaning, except for the first one—the one I'd punched, his cheekbone shattered and bits of white tooth flecking the wet hole of his twisted-open mouth. He lay utterly still, with his head at an odd angle.

Oh, Christ, did I kill someone?

The sudden certainty that it wasn't the first time poured down my back, ice cubes trickling. Nobody who handled a gun like this could be innocent.

I backed up two steps, bare feet on cold concrete. At least I wasn't bleeding anymore. Maybe I was toughening up.

You clawed your way up out of a grave. I'd say that's pretty damn tough. The question is, what do you do now?

I had a full belly. But I needed shelter, and some more clothes wouldn't be amiss.

A quick search of the two moaning men produced rolls of cash as thick as my forearm. Plus little plastic baggies full of illegal smokable stuff, switchblades, and two guns—a .38 and a 9mm. I tossed them down the alley so the boys didn't get any ideas, and considered the guy I'd punched. After a second or two of thought, I found another roll of cash as well as more baggies on him. He was still breathing, the air bubbling through the bloody mess of his mouth. I'd broken his cheekbone and quite a few of his teeth. My hand didn't hurt at all, and how had I blinked across space to take out Chain Boy?

The gem on my right wrist glittered, colorless, a hard dart of light as dawn strengthened and spilled more illumination through the crack serving as the alley's ceiling.

You don't know your own strength, girl.

"I guess not," I muttered. "Jesus."

I got the hell out of there.

4

The crackling plastic bags on the tiny room's colorless bed gave up a black V-neck T-shirt and a pair of jeans that were a little too big, but I hadn't been able to try them on. It was bad enough waiting in the shadows for the gigantic Walmart a mile away to open. By 9 a.m. when the doors whooshed wide, I was a bundle of exposed, dirty, and vulnerable nerves.

I shouldn't have worried. Those employees don't bat an eye. I guess no matter what I looked like, they'd seen worse. After getting an eyeful of the crowd waiting to scramble on in and get their cheap shit even cheaper, I won't exactly say I was heartened—but I was feeling a little more anonymous.

I remembered my shoe size, at least, but the sneakers felt weird, too light and flexible. The holster for the .45— I'd stuck it in the waistband of my ruined leather pants while shopping, just like a good American—didn't *quite* do it, but a little duct tape fixed that right up. The .45 ammunition had been reasonably cheap, and as soon as I put it in my basket I'd felt soothed.

Whoever I was, I didn't like being unarmed. Or short of ammo. I was hoping the modifications on the gun hadn't made it unable to fire a basic clip, but there it was.

I found a place on the edge of the barrio. Some clear instinct warned me not to go any further into that tangle of streets, so I just picked a likely-looking hotel and paid for two nights. Cash up front, no ID requested or given. It was the kind of place usually rented by the hour, and after about 2 p.m. it started doing a brisk trade. Footsteps, soft cries, some screams, doors opening and closing. I didn't listen too close. It was bad enough that my hearing was jacked up into the red, and I could smell every single person who had ever used this tiny room.

Sirens. Jackhammers. Traffic.

At least the shower worked. It was tepid, but there was decent water pressure. The drain almost clogged, sand and gunk sliding off me in sheets. I didn't bother with the towels. Who knew what vermin they were carrying? Instead I wrung my hair out and air-dried. The wheezing air conditioner didn't help very much against an egg-on-the-sidewalk sort of day, a glare of heavy sunlight golden against the barred window. It was like being in prison, only with a door that locked on your side.

Which meant it wasn't very much like prison at all.

Once I was dressed and the gun was checked, cleaned with a just-bought kit, and set on the flimsy bolted-down nightstand, I lay down on top of the cheap chintz bedspread and let out a long sigh. The ruined, filthy clothes were in a plastic bag; I'd dump them elsewhere. Something told me it was best to leave no traces.

My hair was already drying, raveling up into dark curls. I was pale, and the face in the mirror was nothing special except for the mismatched eyes. Long, thin nose, mouth pulled tight and thin, bruise-colored shadows under said eyes almost reaching down to the prominent cheekbones. I looked half starved. I was hungry again.

Who the hell am I?

Evidence: one silver ring with Cyrillic script inside, one gun, one weird gemlike thing implanted in my right wrist. Speed and strength enough to take on four men without breaking a sweat. Of course, there was the little matter of Martin Pores and his vanishing Mercury, but if I had just dug my way up out of a shallow grave maybe I'd hallucinated that bit and just wandered around dreaming of diner food.

I couldn't rule that out.

The only other thing was the tattoo. A black tribal-looking scorpion, high up on the inside of my right thigh. It itched and tingled, but maybe that was only because I'd scrubbed at it, thinking it was dirt.

My hands were capable and callused. My battered feet were healed, too. No sign of the bloody mess they'd been after walking miles of highway. Even if I'd just been wandering around in a hallucination, I'd been shoeless and bleeding. But now you couldn't tell.

For some reason, I turned my head and looked at the window. My hair felt weird. Like there should have been something in it. Lots of little somethings digging into the back of my head. Tiny gleams, little hard things.

For just a moment I had it, but it slipped away again. Frustration rose hard and hot in my throat, I swallowed it.

I knew my first name. I knew I didn't have a problem killing someone, but I preferred not to.

At least, not when they're human. When they're something else…

Something else?

"Maybe I'm insane." My own voice caught me off guard, hit the flimsy walls and bounced back to me. "That's an option, too. Consider all the alternatives, Kismet."

Kismet?

Another light turned on inside my head. Jill Kismet.

That's who I am. But who is she?

I waited, but nothing else came up. It was daylight. Sleepytime, because daylight was...safe.

I tested that thought. It felt right. "Daylight's for sleeping," I whispered. "Night is when I work."

Well, that was comforting to know. Or not.

I closed my eyes, told the gnawing in my belly to go away, and waited for dusk.

It was as good a plan as any.

5

I reached down with my left hand, slowly. Pushed my right sleeve up, heavy leather dried stiff with blood and other things. Unsnapped the buckle. Dropped the cuff on the floor, and turned my wrist so she could see.

The air left her all in a rush, as if she'd taken a good, hard sucker punch. "Jesus," she finally whispered, the sibilants lasting a long time. "Jill—"

"This stays between us." I was now back to sounding like myself, clear and brassy. All hail Jill Kismet, the great pretender. "I'm going to take care of it."

She didn't disbelieve me, not precisely. "How the hell are you going to do that?"

I shrugged.

She read it on my face, and another sharp exhale left her. "And if..."

I suppose I should have been grateful that she couldn't bring herself to ask the question. So I answered it anyway. "If it doesn't work, Anya, you will have to hunt me down. No pity, no mercy, no nothing. Kill me before I'm a danger to my city. *Kill Perry, too. Burn him, scatter the ashes as far as you can. Clear?*"

She grabbed the absinthe bottle. Tipped it up, took a good, long, healthy draft, her throat working. "Shit."

"*Promise me, Anya Devi. Give me your word.*" Now I just sounded weary. My cheek twitched, a muscle in it committing rebellion. The scar cringed under the assault of sunlight, I kept it out. The pain was a balm.

She lowered the bottle. Wiped the back of her mouth with one hand. "*You have my word.*" Quietly.

I dropped my right hand. With my left, I pulled the Talisman up. Freed the sharp links from my hair, gently. It was hard to do one-handed, but I managed. I took six steps, laid the Eye on the table. The sunsword quivered. "*For Gilberto. Will you...*"

"*You don't even have to ask. I'll train him.*"

Then she offered me the bottle.

Tears rose hot and prickling. I pushed them down. Took a swallow, the licorice tang turning my stomach over and my cracked lips stinging. When I handed it back to her, she didn't wipe the mouth of the bottle. Instead, her gaze holding mine, she lifted it to her lips, too.

I bit the inside of my cheek. Hard, so hard I tasted blood. The thought that it would be tinged with black made my stomach revolve again. There were so many things I wanted to say. Things like Thank you, or even, I love you.

Because I do. We are lonely creatures, we hunters. We have to love each other. We are the only ones who understand, the only ones who will ever understand.

Except I wasn't a hunter anymore, was I?

"*I need a car,*" I croaked. "*It won't be coming back.*"

* * *

When I woke, the dream faded. For a second I had everything, it trembled inside my head...then it was gone. And I needed to go, too. Dusk was rising, and something told me the hotel might not be...safe. The need to get out and move itched under my skin.

I found out something else, too: I liked heights. I especially liked gliding along rooftops like a ghost, peering into the streets below. Looking for something I couldn't define while dusk rose from every corner, cloaking the city in peculiar static heat, the rising wind bringing me an oddly familiar tang of river as everything exhaled.

Preparing for the plunge into darkness.

Everything about it was familiar. Even the shapes of the city streets, the arterial bloodflow of traffic, the quiet neighborhoods and the back alleys, the parts that lit up only when the light failed. And yet, everything was unfamiliar—the sneakers were too light, and I felt oddly naked. Like I should have more, a heavy weight on my shoulders and something flapping at my ankles, something on my face and those little weights tied into my hair. Not to mention the fact that my left hand kept dropping to my side like it expected to find another gun. Or something else.

The city revolved inside my head. I knew the street names, sometimes only after I dropped down to their level and looked around a bit. The town clung to the banks of the river, a big granite Jesus on top of a hospital downtown spread his arms in a menacing blessing, nightclubs pounded and weird things skittered in the shadows. Every building greeted me with a secret smile, little bits of the

geography whirling like snowflakes until they settled
against the rest of my mental map.

It was next to the granite Jesus, looking out over all
those tiny dots of light, that something else stirred inside
my aching head. I crouched in Christ's spreadeagle
shadow, watching the very last dregs of light swirl out of
the sky, and sniffed the wind. Even in summer, nights out
in the desert can get chilly. No trace of moisture in the
air, but a thin faint thread of something candyspiced and
wicked tickled my nose.

What the hell's that? Half-rising from the crouch, keeping to cover, I almost swayed because I didn't have a
counterweight hanging behind me to keep me steady. A
cloak of stillness folded over me, my pulse dropping, my
entire body chilling. Gooseflesh rose hard like little rubbery fists under my skin, I ignored it.

Follow that. It's not supposed to be here.

I was moving before I knew it, bolting across the
rooftop, the world around me blurring. Hit the edge going
full speed, a moment of weightlessness, and smacked the
pavement stories below with a crack like a shotgun and a
breathless feeling of *holy shit did I just do that?*

I would've been laughing with crazy joy, if not for the
gun unholstering itself and the sudden fierce buzzing in
my right arm, like a band of metallic flies was breaking for
the surface of an infection. Right at my wrist, too. It pulled
me along on a reel of silk, I flashed through a deserted alley and straight up a brick wall, barely touching the rough
surface, my left hand catching at the top and heaving me
over with little effort.

It was like flying. And I might've liked some time to
enjoy it before I collided with a long tall thin thing out of a

nightmare, its flesh glowing waxen-pale as it snarled, flying backward with its legs and arms drawn in, spiderlike. Its eyes glowed with a powdery sheen, and the thing it had been crouching over was a rag of bloody bone and meat that had once been a human being.

Trader. Put him down quick, Jill. But not so quick you can't question him.

Well, at least now I had a goal.

He smashed through two struts, snapping them like matchsticks, and the strength flooding my veins was definitely bolting up my right arm from the...thing, the gem, whatever it was. I was on him in a hot heartbeat, punching him twice and something cracking in his torso; we skidded and a lick of hot pain went up my arm. Skin erased by concrete, the smell of blood, and the Trader's chin jutted forward. His teeth were sharklike points, steaming saliva dripping and foaming, and we hit a retaining wall with a sound like a good hard break on a pool table. Something snapped in my side just like the struts, the pain was a spur. His teeth buried themselves in my shoulder, grating on bone, I screamed. Not with the pain.

No. I screamed in pure frustration. I knew what to do, but I didn't have the tools to do it. I didn't have my knives, or my coat, or—

The gun bucked in my hand, its roar oddly muffled. A hole opened in his back, the exit wound blossoming obscenely. The Trader howled through his mouthful of my flesh, blood squirting and whatever venom he had on those sharp triangular teeth burning as it sizzled, spattering my neck.

He didn't quit.

I shot him again, twisting, and the thought—*thank God*

for judo, Jillybean, get him good—seemed completely normal. Another hole opened in his back. Why was he *still* moving? Squeezed the trigger again, and his torso was mangled now. Another hole opened in his back, this one spattering and spraying wider than the first two. A mist of copper droplets hung in the air.

I got lucky.

The flat, shine-dusted eyes glazed. He twitched, teeth grinding in the ruin of my shoulder, and I let out a sound that probably would've haunted a nightmare or two if there was anyone around to hear. It took working the gun barrel into his mouth and cracking the jaw to get the teeth to loosen up as his body twitched and jerked. I jammed it further back—he was still twitching—and squeezed the trigger again, the roar way too close for comfort.

The back of its head evaporated.

Corruption raced through its tissues, little veins of dust spilling from a crackglaze like fine porcelain glued back together and unceremoniously busted again.

Would've been easier with my knives. Where are my fucking knives? It didn't matter. I scrambled out of his slackening embrace, my sneakers squishing and sliding in a tide of brackish fluid. It was blood. But the edges of the red fluid held a taint of black, hungrily threading through and turning it to dust as the body twitched and jerked, heels drumming in a weird dance against the rooftop, the mangled head spilling brainmeal as the neck twisted. My ribs flickered; heaving breaths shaking me like wet laundry. I hit one of the listing iron struts reaching up like fingers—it was bent crazily where he'd gone right through it.

Yes, I could see now it was a he. He'd been naked, and

his genitals were altered, too. Barbed and spiked, like... I don't even know what like.

They always go for body mods. Part of the personality of someone who'll trade their soul away. I know that. It was a relief to find something I did know for sure. Even if this was weird as fuck.

I was making a whistling sound. Hyperventilating. Something inside me clamped down, made my pulse and respiration calmer, my eyes locked on the twitching, disintegrating body.

You must watch death you make, a man whispered from my soupy, darkened memory. *Is only way,* milaya.

Mikhail. I remembered his name, now, with a lurching mental effort. Sweat stood out, cold and slick, all over me. The gun was steady, pointed at the swiftly rotting corpse as if it might take a mind to get up for round two.

You never know. You just never know.

My shoulder burned, but I ignored it. The gun didn't waver. So this was what I did. I leapt off multistory buildings like I was stepping off a patio. I found weird smells. I got into fights on rooftops.

I killed things that shouldn't exist.

The gem on my wrist glowed softly.

When you're ready.

Is that what he'd meant, my blue-eyed breakfast-buying hallucination? Was I having another hallucination now?

That's the trouble with waking up in your own grave. A whole lot of weird shit suddenly seems pretty reasonable.

Maybe that wasn't your *grave. Maybe your name isn't Jill. Maybe Mikhail is something else. Can't assume. That's what he said, all the time. "Do not ever assume. Is quickest way to get ass blown sideways."*

I stared at the bubbling mass until it was clear it wasn't going to get up and come after me again. The night air was full of traffic sounds, faraway sirens, whispered secrets. My shoulder had stopped bleeding. When I looked down, craning my neck, the bubbling pink froth squeezing out of the flesh as it knit itself back together sizzled a little, eating at the T-shirt. Bile whipped the back of my throat, I forced it down by swallowing. Bad idea, because then it hit my stomach and revolved. I was kind of glad I hadn't eaten anything, because I heaved once before I got myself back together and used the spar behind me to muscle my way back to standing. My knees definitely felt gooshy.

The next step was examining the victim and looking for evidence. Like a cop.

Not a cop. A hunter. You do what the cops can't.

My own voice, hard and clear, addressing a class of bright-faced boys and girls in blue dress uniforms.

I will be blunt, rookies. You'll all be required to memorize the number for my answering service, which will page me. Pray you never have to use that number. Three or four of you will have to. A few of you won't have time to, but you can rest assured that when you come up against the nightside and get slaughtered, I'll find your killer and serve justice on him, her, or it. And I will also lay your soul to rest if killing you is just the beginning.

"Holy fuck," I whispered. The city whispered and chuckled.

I shuffled like an old woman, back to the victim. There was a pile of clothing—workman's boots, overalls, a red plaid shirt, a billfold in one of the pockets. A nice wad of fifties and hundreds that I took without compunction, ID showing a sullen, lean face—it was dark up here, but I had no trouble picking out the features of the thing I'd just killed. Back when it had been human, its name had been Eric Allen Dodge, and he lived in the Cruzada district. Staring at the address gave me a map of the city, different routes I could take to get out to his house if I needed to give it a looksee. There was one more thing, and I held it while I crouched to look at the rag of meat and bone he'd been hunched over when I hit him.

The victim was female. There was enough of her left to tell, mostly because the breasts were chopped free and laid to one side and her plumbing was oddly untouched.

He must've been saving that for last. My gorge rose again. What did it say about me that I could guess?

Not enough blood on the roof, so he'd killed her elsewhere and brought the body here. Her heart, a fist-sized lump of flesh, was set neatly aside with her tatas. There were other bits, something that was probably her liver, long strings of guts. Her face had been savaged. About all I could tell was that she'd probably been dishwater blonde or light brunette; her shoulder-length hair was matted with clotted blood and filth. White slivers of teeth poked through the hamburger of what was left of her features.

Her left hand. A gleam of gold—wedding ring, on the third finger. Just where silver rested on my own left hand.

"*Do svidanye,*" I murmured, and looked at the only other thing that'd been in Dodge's wallet.

It was a plain, thick, dove-gray business card. MONDE NUIT, it said, and an address out near the meatpacking district. I knew exactly where the meatpacking district was, and the location seemed...familiar.

More than familiar.

Wasn't this just my lucky night.

6

The place looked foul. The atmosphere over it had thickened like a bruise, my left eye smarting and watering as it untangled layer after layer of rotting cheesecloth. *Etheric bruising,* my helpful unmemory piped up. *That means it's a haunt. You know what a haunt is, right? A place where wild animals go to feed. There's 'breed in there, and Traders. You need silver.*

Silver. My right hand flashed up, touched my hair. That's what should be there. Silver charms. Tied in with red thread. It was traditional.

Doesn't help me now, though.

I loitered at the edge of the parking lot, sunk in shadows. There was brush here, and I crouched easily, sometimes moving to keep muscles from stiffening, sometimes utterly still and watching. The place looked familiar—a long, low building, parking lot shading to gravel at the edges, a couple of gorillas at the door and a line waiting to go in. Faint thumping bass reached me as I studied the shapes of the people in line. They moved...oddly. Scary quicksilver grace or twitching almost-stasis, and even at this distance

I could see the twisting under the surface of their normal shapes. The twisting threatened to give me a headache until I figured out I could simply make a note of it and it would stop bothering me. I just had to acknowledge it.

Someone in there knows who I am.

But these were things like the thing I'd killed on the roof. *Wrong.* And very, very bad. I had no silver. Just the business card and—

A long black limousine took a right into the parking lot, crunching on gravel before bumping inelegantly up onto cracked pavement. The line twittered and whispered with excitement. The car glowed, wet light from the tangle of red neon over the building's front sliding over its sleek flanks. My focus narrowed and I leaned forward, coming up out of the crouch as if compelled. My body obeyed smoothly, but my right wrist twinged. I glanced down, but the gem set in the skin was the same, a colorless sparkle. The wind touched my hair, playing with the curls, cool with the flat metal tang of river water, the desert's sand-baked exhale picking up the water and vanishing.

The limo banked easily, like a small plane, and one of the bouncers stepped forward to open the door. I took another two steps, gravel oddly soundless underfoot. My right hand touched the gun butt, fingers running over it like they expected to read Braille.

A pale head. He rose out of the car on the other side, and a rippling sigh of excitement went through the line. I moved forward, impelled, cutting through a line of dusty parked cars. The limousine scorched, dirt-free, the only thing in the lot that didn't look tired or filthy. My hand curled around the gun, but I didn't draw it yet. The ring on my left hand ran with blue light, a seashine gleam.

They became aware of me in stages, as if I was a storm moving through from the mountains. First the eerie-graceful part of the line, with their seashell hips and liner-drenched eyes, stilled. Their heads came up, and sculpted nostrils flared. Cherry-glazed lips parted, and a collective exhale lifted from them along with a bath of nose-tingling corruption.

They were beautiful, but under that beauty lay the *twisting*.

The jerky, oddly-shaped ones were next. They hissed, lips lifting and sharp-filed teeth showing, some of them crouching. One of them, a broad wide manshape dressed in a caricature of a construction worker's plaid shirt and Carhartts, his work boots stained with something dark and fetid, actually growled. The sound rose in a rumble like boulders grinding together, and some sure instinct made me pause, staring at him. Yellow eyes, unholy foxfire in the irises and the pupils flaring and constricting like a cobra's head. He tensed as his knees slowly bent.

He's getting ready to spring.

Movement. The pale head of hair was approaching. They cringed and fell back from him, but I didn't look. I stared at the Trader, my fingers slowly tightening on the gun. If he jumped me I had some running room and cover in the parking lot. Maybe I could tangle them up and—

There was a blur of motion, cream-colored linen streaking. A pale clawed hand flashed out, and the construction worker fell sideways, arterial spray blooming high and red. The drops hung in a perfect arc, and I saw each one was tinged with that tracery of black, hungrily gobbling at the fluid as it splashed.

Holy shit. I stared.

He stepped out of the way, polished wingtips gleaming

just like the car, and my gaze snapped to him. The gun left its holster with a whisper, and my arm was straight and braced.

Pallid hair in a layered razor cut. Blue eyes, and the face wasn't beautiful. He looked normal—average lips, average cheekbones, an average all-American nose. The suit was linen, sharply-creased and expensive, and the eyes were bright blue. He regarded me with pleasant, cheerful interest, and I blinked before my left eye gave a twinge and I caught a glimpse of the *twisting* rippling under his flawless skin. A wine-red tie, he lifted his right hand and touched the half-Windsor knot, as if it had been knocked a millimeter out of place. Taller than me, his shoulders braced and his hips narrow, my mouth suddenly filling with copper adrenaline and my pulse dropping into a low steady rhythm.

Because this was a face I knew.

His left hand twitched. The fingers drew up like claws, and his paleness was a shade or two darker there. Something had happened to that hand, something my brain shied away from even as it threatened to plunge through the fog and *remember*. A spark popped from my ring's silver surface, photoflash blue.

"I know you." My lips were numb, but I simply sounded wondering. "From…" Words failed me, balked and twisted away. "From somewhere. I *know* you."

He studied me for another long moment. His smile widened.

He actually *grinned*. Pearly teeth, very sharp but very normal as well. It was a television newscaster's beaming, wide and practiced. Those blue eyes lit up, and another ripple went through the crowd.

"Of course you know me." Even his voice was reassuringly normal. Bland as the rest of him. "Our darling little Kismet, returned. How lovely." He stepped forward off the curb, but the bruisers looming behind him—one with a submachine gun, the other just a pile of over-yeasted muscle—didn't move. I almost twitched, but *he* made a soothing noise. A low exhale, his tongue clicking as if I was an animal to be gentled. "You look beautiful."

7

I twitched outright this time, nervously, the gun tracking him. He paid no attention, heel-and-toeing it across the concrete as if we were on a dance floor. He only stopped when I took a restless step sideways, and that brought him up short. But he leaned forward, balanced on his toes, his entire body focusing on me.

"My lovely," he whispered. "My own. Of *course* I know you. What have they done to you?"

They? Whoever it was left me in the desert. In a grave. I rotted, but I came back.

No. That wasn't quite right. I hadn't come back. I'd been *sent*.

"They sent me back. To…I don't know." It was work to whisper. My throat was suddenly dry. Queasy heat boiled through my stomach, and I was suddenly aware the entire crowd of them was too still to be human.

If they jump you now, a clear cold voice warned me, *you're not going to have an easy time of it. You're not even really armed. Just this gun with useless ammunition. You need silver. And lots of it.*

Well, it was a fine time to remember that. And what did this have to do with the thing on the rooftop and the flayed, opened-up body, its organs set neatly aside?

I backed up, even more nervously. One step, two. He kept leaning forward.

"Don't." His unwounded hand came forward. The body of the Trader behind him slumped, twitching and jerking as corruption raced through its tissues. "Don't leave, dear one. Come inside. You look hungry."

What a coincidence. I was suddenly *starving*, an empty blowtorch-hole in my guts. I examined his face. Whatever lived underneath that skin rippled.

It didn't look good, and the business card in the wallet of a murderous *thing* was not an endorsement. But...he was familiar. Whoever he was, I *knew* him.

That doesn't mean he's any good.

Did I have any other option?

My gun lowered slightly. The night exhaled around me, dangerous sharp edges and the neon glaring, the hunger suddenly all through me. My right wrist twitched, a fish-hook under the skin yanking restlessly.

"That's it," he crooned. "Come inside. There's a bed, and sharp shiny things to make you feel safer. You want knives, don't you."

A guilty start almost made it to the surface. I stared at him.

His smile widened just a notch. "And a gun or two. And a long, long black coat. And shining chiming things to tie in your lovely hair." His tongue flicked out and touched his bloodless lower lip. In the uncertain ruddy light it was a startling wet cherry-red, rasping against the skin. That quick little flicker made me nervous again, and I sidled another step. That brought him forward in a rush, fluidly, his bones moving in ways a human's shouldn't.

Even that was familiar. Half-disgust boiled under my breastbone. The other half was something I couldn't name. "Perry." I found his name. But nothing else. It was like thinking through mud. "You're Perry."

His irises glowed, sterile, cold blue. Thin threads of indigo slid through the whites of his eyes, a vein-map. His pupils dilated a little. "At your service. In every conceivable way, Kiss. That's what I call you. A pretty name for a pretty girl. Come. There's food. And drink. And a place to rest." His head cocked slightly. "And answers. You would like answers, wouldn't you? Your perennial plaint: *Tell me why.*" A short, beckoning motion, his long, expressive fingers flicking. "You'll be under my protection, darling one. Nothing to fear. Just come, and let me soothe you."

It sounded good. Better than good. For a moment something else trembled under the surface of my memory, but it retreated again. Maddening, the feeling that I should know. That I should *understand*, instead of pushing myself blindly forward from place to place. The ring was warm, a forgiving touch against my flesh.

The gun twitched. My finger eased off the trigger. It lowered slightly. "First tell me something."

"Oh, anything." He eased toward me again, supple and weightless as if he was simply painted on the air. "Anything you like."

I searched through every question I had. There were too many of them crowding me. His pupils swelled, and the roaring sound filtered into my head again. The wasps, eating and buzzing, little tiny insect feet prodding as they crawled over me again. A galvanic shudder racked me. The gun dropped even further.

"Who am I?" I whispered. "What the hell *are* you?"

The laugh was another rumble, as if a freight train was passing me by again. It came from him, a subvocal roar, plucking at the strings under the surface of the world, and his fingers closed around my arm. Everything in me cringed away from that touch, but his fingers were warm and exquisitely gentle.

"You are my Kiss." Very gently, experimentally, he pulled on my arm. The ring sparked again, but it was unimportant. I followed, numb, the wasp-roar filling my skull like the cotton wool of illness. "And I, my darling? I am Legion. I am unconquerable fire." His grin was absolutely cheerful, and oddly terrifying, but all the soothing in the world was in that voice. "But don't worry. I am also your humble host this momentous evening. You've arrived just in time."

He led me past the bouncers, the submachine gun dangling as they watched, slack faced. The crowd muttered, hissing, but he paid them no notice. The doors were open, a red velvet curtain hanging in tattered folds, and he drew me through it and into the pounding music. I could barely gasp in a breath before the noise folded over my head like wings, and his grip on my arm never faltered.

* * *

I had a confused impression of swirling bodies on a dance floor lit with migraine stabs of brittle light, a monstrosity of a bar with two slim male shapes handing out what could have been drinks in twisted sparkling glasses, the press of the crowd alternately feverish and cold. The whirling crowd snarled, pressing back against each other as stipples of light flashed around me. Those little sparkles weren't from the disco ball—and who the hell has a disco ball nowadays? It was a slowly spinning planet, ponderous, a great silver fruit that pulsed with malevolence.

No, those little sparkles were half-unseen spikes surrounding me, their tips fluorescing up into the visible. An aura.

An exorcist's aura. Be careful, Jill.

I wished that voice had spoken up before. I'd killed a thing on the rooftop, a thing like these *things*. Now here I was in the middle of them, nowhere near as terrified as I should be.

This was *normal*. And what did that say about me?

It had something to do with him. With his hand on my arm and the thrumming growl coming through him, the noise that carried us both through the press of the crowd.

There was an iron door behind a frayed red velvet rope, and as soon as he pulled me through and the door shut with a clang I found myself on a staircase, going up.

So far so good. I'd been here before, several times. The gun dangled in my nerveless hand. He drew me up the stairs, and under the bass-throb attack of the music played at jet-takeoff levels I swear I heard him humming. A happy little tune, wandering along like a drunken sailor past alleys full of cold, dark eyes.

Another door crouched at the top, and he pushed it open. White light flooded the stairwell, and I blinked.

The room was white, too. An expanse of white carpet, a mirrored bar to one side, a huge swan bed swathed in bleached mosquito netting, a bank of television screens flickering at odd intervals. Some of them were dark, some fuzzed with static; others showed the club's interior and exterior, flicking rapidly through surveillance angles. Still more held news feeds, footage of explosions and disasters shuddered soundlessly. Once the door slid shut it was eerily quiet, a faint thumping through the floor all that remained of the noise below, a dozing animal's heartbeat.

He led me across the room, pushed me down on the bed. I sat without demur, my feet placed side by side like good little soldiers. He finally let go of my arm, stepped back, and brushed at stray strands of my hair that had come loose.

I didn't flinch. I just waited for clues, my eyes fixed on the blue gleam running under the ring's surface.

"There." The smile was still wide, but he looked pained. "That is…perfect. Just *perfect*. I've often thought that if I could have you sit just there, just so, all the problems would fade into insignificance."

"Problems?" I cradled the gun in my lap. The buzzing wouldn't go away. Rattling, chrome wasps in a bottle.

The thought that some of the carnivorous insects might have been left inside, maybe in my sinus cavities, nibbling at my brain, sent a rippling jolt through me. The bed made a soft shushing sound, silk sliding and netting twitching. The bottles racked above the mirrored bar were all clear glass. Some held gray smoke, shifting in screaming-face shapes. Others held jewel-glowing liquids, and the harsh white light stroked them.

"I have no problems, darling. Now that you're in my sight. Apple of my eye, flesh of my flesh." He stalked to the bar, his wingtips crushing the pristine carpet. "And you must be hungry. One moment."

My breathing had turned shallow. The horrific buzzing rattled my skull, I hunched my shoulders and went still. The air was curiously flat in here. The bed smelled faintly of fabric softener, but that was it. There was nothing else. It was the equivalent of a blank page.

There's something you're not seeing. Look deeper. Look again.

If I could get the meat inside my head to stop sounding like an overworked lawnmower on crack, I would. The sound crested, filling my bones, shaking me like a terrier with a toy in its sharp white needle-teeth. My ribs heaved, lungs burning, as if I was chasing something across rooftops.

The business card was crumpled, but I lifted it anyway. It still said the same thing.

Think. A card in a wallet. Doesn't mean much. Or it could mean everything. Which one are you betting on?

"*Et voila,*" he murmured. A flicker of motion jerked my head up, and I stared.

In the middle of the arctic expanse of carpet, a table had bloomed. Covered by a fall of snowy linen, a bloody half-closed rose in a vase like fluted ice, two places set with exquisitely simple porcelain. Forks and knives and spoons of heavy, pale golden metal. A bleached, brassy candle-holder like a twisted tree held thin white tapers. Their flames were colorless, standing straight up.

"Now." He indicated the chair with its back to the bed, a high-backed, spine-shouldered piece of pallid metal with a cushion of faded-red velvet. "I have no violinist, and no apples. But I think we shall do very well. Come, sit."

The buzzing receded like a sand-gurgling wave. I crushed the business card in my fist, suddenly very sure I didn't want the twisting under his skin to see it.

"I." My throat closed up. I cleared it, a harsh sound rustling the mosquito netting. "I, ah, have questions."

"Of course you do." He set down two water-clear champagne flutes. "And I'm in a position to give you answers. Plenty of them, too."

"Then start." My voice didn't belong to me. There was some other woman using it, her mouth twisted half up into a pained, professional smile and her hand ready on the gun in my lap. She peered out through my eyes, taking note of everything in the room and chalking it all up on mental lists—how easy it would be to get her hands on it, how much damage it would do, what her chances were. Percentages and likelihoods, all whirring inside our shared brain like clockwork gears. "Who buried me in the desert?"

"Well." A dusty bottle appeared out of nowhere. Its cork popped deftly free with a wrenching, violated sound, and the fizzing, pale-amber fluid poured in a couth stream into the flutes. "Hardly dinner conversation, Kiss. But I suppose you have a right to know." He set the bottle down with a click and picked up both glasses, cocking his head as he stared at me. His tongue flicked again, a blot of cherry-red, shocking against the paleness. "When I saw you last, you were dead."

"When was that?" She shifted slightly, the woman suddenly using my body, and cursed us both for putting us right in the most vulnerable location in the whole damn room.

"Oh, about two months ago." His teeth flashed, lips parting. "What would you like for dinner, my dear?"

I shifted again, uneasily. I was *starving*, but that other woman was warning me not to take a single sip or bite of anything he'd give me.

Where had she been when Martin Pores was feeding me?

"Knives." I swallowed hard. "You said knives. And...a coat."

"Don't be uncivilized. Sit over here." Faintly annoyed now, a shadow between those feathered eyebrows. The rippling under his skin had quieted, but the indigo threading through the whites of his eyes warned me.

My legs tensed. They carried me upright, and the gun dropped to my side. His teeth looked a lot sharper now.

So did the rest of him. A shadow of bladed handsomeness passed over his face, his eyes burning.

One step, two, my sneakers making little dry sounds against the carpet. Everything up here was new, freshly unwrapped. Like the whole stage had just been waiting for me to step onto it, under a brilliant skull-white spotlight.

"Right here." He indicated the chair. "That's a good girl. We'll have a nice, happy dinner. The first of many."

Does that mean I've never eaten here before? I think that's a fair guess. And I'll bet I had my reasons. The time for me to make any move was narrowing, ticking away in microseconds. The gun twitched, my pulse thudding along even and sonorous like a deep underground river, my right wrist suddenly burning. The buzzing had moved out into my fingertips, and it fought to bring the gun up, squeeze off a shot and let—

Footsteps. High and hard. The door burst open, and I whirled, gun trained on the new arrival.

8

*P*erry was suddenly *there*, slim pale fingers tensing and crackling at the man's throat. Man, or boy, he was so slight I couldn't tell. His ears came up to high points and his teeth were only bluntly human, but dapples of shadow-bruising ran over his skin, and his hair writhed in fat brown dreadlocks like it had a mind of its own.

He choked, and Perry hissed. The sound was freight trains rubbing together at midnight in a cold deserted yard, overstressed metal squealing in pain.

Helletöng, I realized. The language of the damned.

Which gave me all sorts of interesting ideas about the position I was in. The hiss-roar died away, and the Trader's face turned an unpleasant purplish.

"I thought I said I wasn't to be disturbed." Perry cocked his head, each word quiet and level. "This had better be—"

"—*caught*—" The Trader choked again, and Perry eased up.

"What?" More 'töng, plucking at the strings below the surface of the world. I could glimpse the spreading stain, corruption welling up and torquing reality one way or another, my blue eye suddenly hot and dry. "Speak *up*," Perry snarled.

He probably could, if you weren't holding him a foot off the floor and cutting off his air. But I kept that thought to myself. It would probably be unhelpful in this situation.

It was looking like I was going to need all the help I could get. Lights were turning on inside my head, flickering in rapid fire, and the things they showed weren't very nice at all.

"Caught one," the Trader wheezed as the fingers in his throat loosened slightly. "We caught one. Watching us."

"Indeed." Perry went still for a few seconds. A hot, dry draft reeking of spoiled honey brushed the room. Even immobile, you could see his molecules trying to escape, jittering away. Under his suit coat his back shifted, something straining inside the shape he wore. Horror crawled up into my throat, my brain shivering away from the suggestion underneath. Like a twisted alien body under a blanket, so horribly *wrong* a chill walks up your spine with ice-glass feet.

I've seen that before, though. I survived seeing it. I know I did.

Perry glanced to the side, his profile severe and handsome, a classical statue's long nose and relaxed mouth. His eyes scorched, and he made a sudden swift movement. A greenstick *crack* echoed, the Trader's feet flailed, and the hellbreed dropped him like a dirty rag.

Bile whipped the back of my throat. My face stayed frozen, numb. *Keep your pulse down.* Training clamped down on my hindbrain; I could actually *feel* the pressure sinking in, hormonal balance mercilessly controlled, heartbeat and respiration struggling to escape those iron fingers.

Mikhail was always on me to keep my pulse down. I stared at the body as it slumped to the side, twitching and juddering, dusky corruption racing through its tissues. The naked, hairless chest, the ribs flared oddly to support different musculature, legs in a pair of fluttering black pants caked with something filthy and iron-smelling at the bottom. The stink of death-loosened sphincters ballooned out, exploding across the sterile unsmell, and I shivered.

Then I stilled, hoping that hadn't been a mistake.

"There's no need to fear." Was he trying to sound *soothing*? Perry rolled his shoulders back in their sockets, cartilage crunching. "This will only take a moment, darling mine. You can even watch."

He stood there, staring to the side, the indigo threads in the whites of his eyes swelling and retreating obscenely. As if expecting a reply.

I searched for something to say. Finally, I cleared my throat again. "Is that what's called killing the messenger?"

He actually *laughed*, and the horrible thing wasn't how loud it was. No, it was the sheer gleeful hatred, his lips smacking like I'd just told the world's funniest joke. The laugh cut off in midstream as more swelling crackles slid around under his pale, perfect skin.

"You could say that." He stepped daintily aside as the corpse's legs jerked. "But it's also a lesson. They shouldn't interrupt me, not while I'm with *you*." A sidelong glance, sipping at my face. "Come along. This should be...*instructive*."

What else could I do? I followed.

* * *

Down on the ground floor, twenty seconds spent passing from one iron door to another along the edge of the vast belly of the Monde. The damned paid no attention, writhing against each other while the disco ball spun slightly faster and the music took on a screaming, spiked edge. I glanced out over their sea of chains and leather and slim legs, sweet curves and the bloom of powdery rot on each of them, and something else lit up inside my head.

Hunter, Jill. You're a hunter. And these are what you kill.

Which opened up huge new vistas of contemplation I had no luxury to indulge in, because this second door gave onto a hall lit by low bloody neon tangles, crawling like worms against the wood-paneled walls, and my fingers tightened on the gun again. More doors marched down the hallway on either side, and again recognition rose to choke me. Little half-remembered scenes played out inside my skull, the woman who shared my body unlocking mental doors and throwing them open—just like Perry, his hair and clothes now dyed scarlet, chose a door on the left and flung it wide.

"Well, well, well," he chanted, mincing into the room beyond. "What have we here? Oh, look. A stray cat."

A cold spear went through me. *Cat?*

The last time I'd been here, these doors had all been standing open, torn-out teeth in a dead smile. Behind the one at the far end of the hall had been a table shattered to matchsticks, an iron throne demolished, and something hanging in silvery chains. Something horribly battered, and as I'd walked in the chains had rasped against each other, fat, dry-sliding tongues.

I stared down the hall. If I walked to the end, would I find a room where the table was put back together as if it had never been broken, mirror-polished and solid? And the throne at the end...would its metal spikes be repaired? Or would a new one have been brought in?

A low, terrible growl cut across the hallway. It was a cleaner sound than 'töng, and it turned another key inside the broken lock my head had become.

—pair of dark eyes, tawny sides moving, the sun picking out gold along a cat's sleek lines, and he nuzzled my throat, kissing while I shook. The crisis tore through me again, and the kiss turned to a bite, pressure applied with infinite care, the skin bruising as he sucked. The neck's erogenous in the extreme for a cat Were, and Saul—

Saul? I jolted back into myself. My lips shaped the word, but I said nothing.

He was *important.* My pulse sped a fraction, control clamped down, and I began to get a very bad feeling about all this.

"Hold it down. She'll want to see this." A low, delighted laugh, and the wasp-buzz was a dark curtain inside my head, bulging over some horrible, unknowable shape. "Oh, this couldn't have been better if we'd *planned* it. Kiss?" Calling me, like a dog. "Kiss, my darling, come inside."

I hated him calling me that. Another key, another broken lock, muscles hardening as I *twisted* it. The effort was both physical and mental, the gem on my wrist scorching, threads of silvery pain sliding up the nerve channels all the way to my elbow.

This time, the buzzing was a curtain of shining metallic insect bodies, and the gem on my wrist vibrated as the curtain pulled aside. Dawn rose inside my head, but it was the sterile white light of a nuclear sunrise, everything inside me turning over and shattering as consciousness flooded me.

Jill. Jill Kismet. Hunter.

The memories slammed through me all at once, my entire body locking down, muscles spasming and ruthlessly controlled. Fighting in the dark, night after night spent cleansing the city streets of things like the dancing mob in the belly of this building—and Perry, pulling the strings, our bargain sealed by a scarred lip-print on my right wrist.

I hated everything about him. Everything. But that wasn't important right now. Training jacked my hormone balance, adrenaline a bright copper flood across my tongue, the bloody neon light flashing as my eyelashes fluttered. The ring was a scorch on my left hand, silver reacting to the etheric contamination filling this bruised, hollow place. I dropped back into myself with a thud, and heard Perry laugh again. A low, very satisfied chuckle, a razor against numb flesh. There was a wet sound, and the growl cut short as if a door had slammed in the middle of it.

I knew that sound. It was a Were. Probably a cat Were, too. He'd just been punched in the gut.

If there was a Were here at the Monde, he was looking at a whole lot of hurt. And if it was who I thought it was...

...I couldn't let that happen.

9

*I*mmobility shattered. My eyes flicked open. I drew in a deep breath spiced with hellbreed corruption, the copper stink of blood, and a sudden colorless fume of rage.

I *moved*.

The door slammed open, hitting a wide-load Trader—chunky-thick, plaid shirt, bare feet misshapen and horned with calluses—with a sound like an axe sinking into good, dry cordwood. I twisted in midair, gun roaring, and the second Trader—slim, dark, head exploding in a mess of bone and brain—folded down. A head shot, and a good one, but how I was going to deal with Perry was a whole 'nother ball of wax. I landed, whirling as Perry made a sound like a frozen mountainside calving, chunks of over-stressed icy stone groaning and tearing free.

The room was small, a brass drain hole glinting in the middle of the shallow-sloped concrete floor. Soaked in the neon glow, my foot flicked out, catching the third Trader—blonde, female, modded out with claws and blood-glowing compound eyes—just under the chin with a jolt and a sound of bone breaking, like glass hammers shattering in a burlap bag. *Should really have boots for this sort of work.* The thought was there and gone in a flash, because I dropped, instinct taking over as a pale smear bulleted past me. It was Perry, snarling, his hands outstretched, and if I hadn't shed momentum and hit the ground he would've crashed right into me. As it was, he hit the wall with a *crack* that might've been funny if he hadn't still been making that huge rock-crushing noise.

The man they'd been holding up slumped, his body heading shapelessly for the floor. I grabbed him and flung us both backward toward the door as Perry slid down the wall. Spiderweb cracks radiated out from the crater he'd put in the dark-smeared wood paneling, and a pair of chains hanging on the opposite wall jangled musically, little spots of white gleaming on their thin surfaces.

Orichalc-tainted titanium chains. I had no time to think about what they would do to whatever they would chain down in here.

Time to go to work, Jillybean.

The glass tangles lighting the room swayed, shadows dipping crazily. My sneakers slipped, and I felt, of all things, a brief burst of silver-sharp irritation. *Would never happen in boots, why couldn't they bury me with my boots on?* The gem on my right wrist turned scorching, a tide of wine-red strength flooding up the bones and veins, jolting in my shoulder and roaring through the rest of me.

I was hoping it wasn't Perry's force I was drawing off. Whose else could it be? It didn't matter. Deal with the devil and dance another day.

Nice to know some things hadn't changed.

Neon tubing smashed with a tinkle as I ran right into the wall across the hall, the man's bulk surprisingly heavy.

I had one hand wrapped in his skein of dark hair, the other tangled in the shredded remains of his T-shirt, and he was bleeding. The blood was red, no trace of black at its fringes, and I hauled him up. My back burned, glass slivers digging in, and warmth trickled down from broken skin.

His head tipped back, a lean dark face horribly bruised and swelling, and a heatless shock of recognition went through me.

Wait. Not Saul. "Theron!" I yelled, and pitched aside. We went down in a heap, rolling, and another part of my aching head lit up under klieg-light memory. *Theron. Werepanther. Works at Mickey's out on Mayfair. Good backup.* "Get *up*! Let's *move*!"

Which brought up a problem: I had no weapons except the gun, not even any silver-coated ammo, and another consideration surfaced, one I had no time to indulge because a massive sound rose from the room we'd just vacated.

Perry was not going to be happy. Just guess how I knew *that*.

What would've happened if I'd eaten something? A chill walked down my bloody back, but Theron was up. He shook his head, stared up at me like he didn't quite credit what he was seeing.

"*Move!*" I yelled, and shoved him toward the end of the hall that gave out into the Monde's interior. No exit the other way, and legions of the damned between us and the outside.

Fun times, Jill! Never a boring moment! Get your ass moving!

Theron took off, a graceful unerring lope much faster than I thought he'd be able to move. I skip-shuffled back just as the Trader I'd hit with the door was propelled out into the hall, wide shoulders slumped and his face a mask of black-tinged blood from his mashed nose. Somehow it had splattered *everywhere*, and a fresh gout stained his flapping Hawaiian shirt as he saw me and snarled, hunching like a demonic football player. His modified feet twisted so the toes splayed and great horny toenail-claws dug into the flooring.

Don't worry about him. Worry about Perry, who's due out any sec—

The doorway evaporated. A wash of crackling-blue hellfire burst out, unholy flames blooming with a hiss I could hear even over the pounding throb of music through the walls. The glare swallowed the crouching Trader whole, and he went up like a fatty candle.

I drove backward, legs pumping, hoping I wouldn't tangle with the Were as we both flung ourselves for the door that would lead out into the Monde. Trigger-finger cramping, lungs burning, had to remember to breathe, steps jolting up through my hips and shoulders as my sneaker-clad feet stamped hard, I threw myself back just as Perry rounded the corner, wreathed in pale-blue livid hellfire and his bland face suddenly sharply starving-handsome again.

I didn't hit the door because Theron had, busting it clear off its hinges with a short bark of effort, a cat's coughing cry. So I sailed back, crashing into a knot of dance-writhing Traders, scrabbling to get *up get up get UP* just as the flames belled out again, little tiny fingers sinking into the wall on either side of the hole. Perry was suddenly *there*, filling up the space.

And he looked *pissed*.

10

I was up again in a hot second, my heel grinding into something soft and my elbow whapping a female Trader a good one in the face. The music was still going, and I hoped like hell Theron had already made it past the bar. He'd have only the Traders at the door to worry about then, and he could be out in the night in a moment, vanished with a Were's speed and agility.

What was he doing here in the first place? What's going on?

That wasn't my problem right now. My problem was the hellbreed who stepped mincingly out of the blurring, grasping fingers of blue flame and twitched his shoulders, the air peaking in high points of disturbance behind and above him. His eyes were the same color as the hellfire, indigo spreading around the edges of the burning irises and threading down over his cheeks in a veinmap tattoo. Everything turned over inside me. I remembered something else—*yellow flame dripping from my hand as I pulled on the mark on my right wrist, etheric force jolting up my shoulder, sick fury and rage twining together to fuel the fire as I burned the whole hellish mess to the ground—*

I gained my balance with a huge lunging effort, raising the gun. *Keep moving.* More skip-shuffling back, covering ground as fast as physics would let me, the noise was massive and confusion just starting to spread out in ripples.

Two shots popped off, both of them good solid hits. Perry's head snapped back, a gush of thin black ichor hanging in the air as time slowed down and details stood out sharp and clear. Still moving back, flicker of motion in the corner of my eye, I threw myself aside as a stick-thin male Trader in a black T-shirt and jeans leapt for me.

A dark blur hit the Trader from the side, a coughing roar cutting the sonic wall of music. Spatters of leprous light flicked as the ball overhead swung, and the mood of the crowd tipped crazily.

Theron had the Trader down, blurring through panther form into humanoid, claws tearing. The shape-between isn't anyplace Weres linger, but even there they are beautiful, and he'd just saved my bacon.

Except I'd been planning for that hit, and now I was scrambling to recover as Perry's head tipped back down, the ichor closing over the hurt and sealing it away. Without silver, bullets would barely slow him down.

Great.

Perry twitched his shoulders again, grinned murderously, and launched himself for me with the eerie stuttering speed of hellbreed. The crowd exploded away, the grace of confusion vanishing as awareness of the fight raced through them like ink dropped in water.

"*Jill!*" Theron yelled, and I had at least the satisfaction of him knowing who I was. If we got out of here, I could ask *him* some questions, too.

Like how I'd ended up dead. Who had buried me. And what the bloody blue *fuck* was going on.

"*Get out!*" I screamed. "*Theron! Get the fuck ou—*"

Perry *arrived*, blinking through space, and my right wrist sent a spike of clear, hot pain all the way up my arm, detonating in my shoulder, tearing across my ribs, and jerking down my legs in one swift lunge. I spun, hip twitching out to provide momentum, my foot coming up as the gem in my flesh let out a high, crystal-stroked sound. My sneaker crashed into Perry's jaw, force transferred and the jolt snapping something low in my right leg; red pain bolting up to my hip. Knees pulled in, the world turning over as I pushed off, deflecting him by critical degrees, and at least I was light without weapons or anything else hanging on me.

I *flew*.

Landed hard, breath driven out of me in a howl as my abused right leg gave way, and Theron was suddenly *there*. Skidding to a stop, fingers tented on the floor, bruised face a mask of effort as he snarled. I almost overbalanced, but he uncoiled with sweet grace, legs driving him up as his hand closed around my left arm and Perry tumbled through the crowd, knocking over Traders and other 'breed like ninepins. He hit them hard, too, the crunching of bones breaking and screams of the wounded drowned out the feedback squealing of the music.

Theron left the ground in a leap of such effortless natural authority I half-expected it to be easy for me too. I pushed gracelessly with both legs, trying to help, ignoring the bones grinding together in my right shin, a red firework of agony.

His grip popped my shoulder out of its socket with a high, hard burst of pain, my head snapping aside and tendons screaming, the rest of me a boneless flag flopping in the wind. We tore through the moth-eaten red velvet curtain and burst out into the cool darkness outside just as the music juddered to a halt behind us and Perry's cheated howl shattered several chickenwire-laced, painted-black windows.

The parking lot reeled drunkenly as Theron yanked me again. A submachine gun opened up in a burst of deafening chatter, glass shattering and metal pop-pinging as bullets dug a sewing-machine trail behind us. My stretched shoulder gave another flare of deep-purple pain, a symphony of damage playing colors behind my eyelids as I tried to return fire.

This ammo won't do any good. Been lucky so far, but luck won't hold. Goddammit.

We hit yet again, Theron compressing like a spring, and plunged into the scrub brush at the edges of the lot. He cursed, the whisper-screaming of obscenities over a deep rumbling groan. Nobody knows where a feline Were's purr comes from, but this was a warning growl, shaking my bones and sending a deep pulse of heat through torn muscle and abused flesh.

Behind us, screams and cries lifted into the chill night air.

Now they were hunting us.

* * *

Being carried along by a cat Were is an exotic experience, even if you can understand what's happening to you. Being dragged by a cursing, slowly healing, very angry Werepanther was a new one even for me.

Or at least, it felt new. I hoped it was.

He skidded aside, and the dark of an alley swallowed us. I hung, almost limp, in his grasp. My entire body twitched, the meat senselessly protesting a brush with its own mortality. Stupid body, getting all worked up because I could have died.

I guess even if you've done it once, it's not something you want to do again.

"Jesus," he kept saying. "It's you. It's *you.*" Like he couldn't believe it. Like he was relieved.

I seconded that emotion. Except I was tired, and hungry, and nothing about tonight was going in a way that could remotely be considered well.

But I knew who I was. I knew who he was, I knew what we both were, and I knew enough about Perry to guess we should keep running.

I just couldn't figure out how I'd ended up dead.

Theron propped me against the alley wall, long sensitive fingers feeling for my shoulder. "This is gonna hurt," he announced, and I nodded.

"Do i—" I began, but he popped the balltop of the humerus back into the socket before I could finish. I swallowed a half-scream, my teeth driving hard into my lower lip and bursts of color exploding behind my closed eyelids again.

"Sorry." He sounded genuinely sorry, too. His breath touched my cheek, I found out my head was lolling. "Jesus Christ, Jill. It's *you.*"

"So they tell me." I tilted my head, straining my ears. *They're going to be after us.* Everything on me hurt savagely, muscles twitch-screaming and bruises rising for the surface of my skin. My right wrist burned, a live coal

pressed into the flesh—but the heat was strangely soothing. It didn't feel normal. *Yeah. Normal. We've missed* that
train by a mile. "We can't stay here."

"Where have you been?" He still had my arm, as if I
might disappear if he let go. "You tell me that. Where have
you *been*? Saul..."

I perked up at the sound of that name. "Saul? Is he all
right?"

His eyes flashed gold-green for a moment, rods and
cones reacting differently than a human's at night. Then
a brief sheen of orange—when Weres and 'breed get excited, the eyes get all glowy. The knowledge slid into place
like I'd always known. Maybe I had.

It didn't disturb me. Weres were safe.

I was sure of that much, at least.

"He's..." He stared at me for a long moment, his jaw
working and the bruises crawling up his face livid even in
the gloom. "You...don't remember?"

"I woke up last night in my own grave, Theron. I'm
not sure what I remember. Or who." My knees felt suspiciously weak, I leaned back into the wall. Whatever was
dumped in the trash piles here reeked to high heaven, but
at least it might cover up *our* smell. Neither of us were too
fresh right now. I reeked of gunfire, rotting Trader blood,
and effort, Theron of musky, unhappy cat Were and fresh
blood. We both carried the sweet whiff of hellbreed corruption.

It was a heady mix, but not a particularly nice one. My
shoulder throbbed, but I took stock and discovered I could
fight. If I had to. And he was moving okay for a Were
who'd been taken in by hellbreed.

Lucky. We were both goddamn lucky. I holstered the

gun. It was next to useless against 'breed without silver-coated ammo.

But I'd find a way to make it work.

I searched for a way to explain where I'd been. I didn't even know how to explain it to *myself*. "I remember some things. Others, not so much, and some things I only remember too late." *Like hating Perry. He seemed so familiar.* I was too tired to even shudder. "Glad I found you."

"Me too. They were about to…look, you don't know *anything*? Where have you been?"

My pulse dropped, breathing evening out. It wasn't relaxation—my jacked-up hearing caught the pitter-patter of hellbreed feet, too light or too heavy to be human, too fast or way too slow. Probably some Traders, too, and drawing close. "Dead, Theron. Weren't you listening? We've got to get out of here, they're looking for us."

"You even *smell* different," he muttered, but he grabbed my arm again. "I can run. You just hold on."

"I can run—" I began to protest, but he simply yanked at me while he turned, a graceful, complex movement ending up with my arms around his throat. He straightened, and my legs came up instinctively around his middle. Just like an uncle taking a kid piggyback riding, and I was breathing in his hair.

"We're running for the barrio," he said over his shoulder. "Relatively safe there, even with the war."

"War?" I took a deep breath. Cat Were, musk and wildness—familiar, but it wasn't him I was thinking of.

Saul. Where are you, catkin?

The last thing I remembered was Galina's face when she told me he'd been taken. By hellbreed. But there was a maddening blank spot after that, bruise-colored, aching, and blank as a dead TV monitor. I had no time to settle down and *think* and try to figure out what to do about it.

"War on Weres, Jill. You've been out a while. Things are...complex." He tilted his head and tensed.

The skittering footsteps drew closer. The night pulled itself taut, a drumskin over vibrating hatred. "I can fight." But I held on.

He burst into motion, bolting for the blind end of the alley. Up the wall in a breathless rush, and the city yawed underneath. Fur scraped my arms, he dropped halfway into catform, and I hugged him as tight as I could, my right wrist coming alive with sweet piercing pain. I hoped I wasn't throttling him—and I hoped he could run fast enough.

Because a choked cry rent the darkness behind us, and I knew they'd found our trail.

11

We almost made it. The edge of the barrio was temptingly close, but there were just too many of them. They were between us and safety, and we crouched on a rooftop in the lee of a billboard for car insurance. Traffic crawled along Lluvia Avenue below, rubies one way and diamonds the other, civilians with no idea a running battle was going on above their heads.

I slid from Theron's back as he gasped, his sides heaving. Hauling my ass around probably hadn't done him any good.

"Catch your breath," I told him, and slid the gun free. Even if the ammo was no good, it would at least slow the Traders down, and if I could bleed them out badly enough the corruption of their bargains would finish them off.

Hellbreed were a different proposition. But I'd think of something. "Run for the barrio. I'll draw them off."

"You...and your...Lone Ranger...shit." He didn't look good—cheesy-pale, those bruises, and if my eyes weren't fooling me, thinner than when we'd started this whole barrel of fun. His metabolism was at scorch level to heal him and provide the speed he'd just used to cart me halfway across the city. "Never...ends...well."

Now that sounds familiar, too. I cast an eye out over the rooftop. "Quit talking. It's wasting breath, and I need you ready to run when I make a diversion."

He gulped, his sides heaving, and shuddered. His breathing evened out, and he closed his eyes. "You have...*no* weapons. How...are—"

"I've got *a* weapon, I'll think of something." I checked the gun, my fingers moving with ease. The ammo clipped to my new belt, worse than useless, was still comforting. "More than one way to skin a hellbreed, Theron."

"What do you remember?" He was perking up. This was a good hiding place. I almost didn't want to leave it, but sooner or later they *would* find us. When they did, it would be ugly. He needed food, and rest, and the cold machine of calculation inside my head piped up with the thought that maybe he could tell someone who would care that I was walking around...alive? Kind of alive? Undead? Not-dead-anymore?

Did I have any friends?

"I sort of remember Galina telling me hellbreed took Saul. Not much after that. Or before, for that matter." I sounded flip and casual, unconcerned. *Don't let him know you're worried, too.* Scanned the rooftop, crouched in a well of shadow, my ears perked for any faint hint of the things I'd spent the years since Mikhail's death hunting. I remembered now, murderous nights and adrenaline-soaked cases, the world skating close to the edge of apocalypse with distressing regularity, and the Traders and 'breed working, busy as beavers, to send it careening over that edge.

I couldn't kill them all. For one thing, more would replace the ones I put down, just like pimps and dealers moving into suddenly vacated territory. Always more where those come from, and hungry, too.

But I managed to kill enough to keep them slinking in the shadows, instead of swaggering. No wonder they'd all snarled at me.

And Perry, what had he been planning to do with me?

Don't worry about that right now. Keep your attention on the roof.

To give the Were credit, he didn't look very surprised. "Saul's...alive. Last I saw."

Relief exploded inside my chest, so hard I almost sagged. "Oh. Okay. Good." But something bothered me. "Last you saw?"

"He's in the barrio."

Well, that wasn't bad. Weres ran herd on the barrio's seethe, since a girl with my skin tone could catch too much flak there. "And?"

"It's complex, hunter. Listen—"

"Hold that thought." I tensed, prickling silence closing over me. *The first thing any apprentice learns,* I heard Mikhail murmur, way back in the soup my head was threatening to become. *To be quiet little snake under rock.*

Apprentice. Gilberto. Lank hair, acne-pitted skin, dead eyes. *My* apprentice. The chain of memory pulled taut, the curtain in my head rippling, but I had no time to follow that chain into the cold deep and see what it dredged up.

Because there, at the edge of the rooftop, a shadow slunk. Lifted its wax-bald head, sweat gleaming over its naked hairless chest.

It crouched. The snuffling sounds carried clearly, and

Theron had become a statue next to me, the way a cat will pause with a paw in the air when something catches its attention.

Are there more? My eyes moved, silently, the blue one hot and dry as it looked *beneath* the visible. The strings under the surface of the world resonated, each quivering individually as the tension in its neighbors communicated itself. *Can't see them. Doesn't mean they're not there.*

The Trader hunched, and sniffed again. It was on all fours, its haunches higher than its head and encased in a ripped pair of faded jeans. Its face was damn near buried in the floor of the roof, and those snuffling sounds were wetly suggestive.

I couldn't even tell if it had originally been male or female, and at this distance only a suggestion of the body modifications it had Traded for could be picked out, even with my vision on overdrive and my left eye suddenly feeding way more information than I needed directly into my brain.

"Theron," I whispered, barely mouthing the words. "When I move, run for the barrio. Don't argue."

He said nothing. My right wrist hummed, a subaudible warning.

The thing snaked its head, muscle rippling oddly up its bare back. A flat shine reflected from its eyeballs, like a drift of pollen on stagnant water under a strong light. *Dusted. Trader, not 'breed.*

Hellbreed eyes actually *glow*. If you can call that diseased shine a form of "light." There aren't proper words for it.

Thank God.

I was barely aware of moving, streaking across the

rooftop, sneakered feet slapping. The Trader's malformed
head flung up, and I saw the dustshine runneling over eyeballs dried and useless as raisins. The nose was a ruined
cavity, double sinus-dishes like sinkholes, the mouth wet
and open to take in more air. That mouth was slit on either
side, cheeks gashed so it could open even wider. A spiked
collar strapped around its skinny throat, leather and brassy
metal both glowing with unholy foxfire.

That's so it doesn't swallow the prey, like a cormorant.
I had enough time to think that before I hit with a crunch,
tumbling it off the roof. It shrieked, a high panicked cry,
and I shot it four times while we were still in midair. *Bleed
it out, rip its throat out if you can, brace yourself, Jillybean, this is gonna hurt.*

I hoped Theron was running.

* * *

Hit *hard*, spilling to the side in a tangling roll to shed
momentum, bones snapping, and the Trader's cry cut off
midway. *Made enough noise.* My right leg crunched with
agony, my tender shoulder gave a high, sustained so-
prano note of overstress, my head hit concrete with a
stunning crack, and I *yanked* on all the etheric force I
could reach.

It jolted up my arm, hot and pure, a completely different
sensation from the hot twisted flood of Perry's mark. Add
that to the list of things I didn't have any goddamn time to
figure out—I jackrabbited to my feet, the shattered edges
of my right femur grating together, and the pain was a
spur as the gem on my wrist lit up like a Christmas or-
nament and etheric force tied the bone back together. The

sea-urchin spines of my aura, hardened by countless exorcisms, lit up, too. The points of light swirled around me in a perfect sphere, and brakes squealed. Tires shredded as the 'breed closed in, traffic snarling around me.

I'd landed right in the middle of the goddamn road. An ungodly screech, and the first hellbreed jagged toward me from the right, leaving the ground in a leap that violated physics and sanity all at once. It was a female, long golden hair in dreadlock snarls and her too-white teeth bared as they lengthened, her eyes full of low red hellfire dripping, riding the updraft of her rage and crackling out of existence. She wore fluttering orange silk, a loose shirt and pajama pants. Her claws were bony scythes.

Think fast, Jill. I threw myself aside, a nail of red pain in my thigh, my feet thudding onto the hood of a big red SUV oddly slewed in the road. A teenage boy in the driver's seat gawped at me, and I leapt again, straining, the gem on my wrist feeding a burst of controlled fire through me. Blue light flashed—another spark from the ring—and I was still gawdawful *fast*, almost hellbreed-fast, especially when I wasn't weighed down by weapons and a long black coat.

Though I'd like my coat now. And some ammo. And for my birthday I'd really like a pony. Ignored the thought, my foot flicked out, and I kicked the dreadlocked 'breed in the face. The impact jolted up to my hip, taking a break in my still-healing femur, and I screamed as she did, two cries of female effort.

No, three. I couldn't worry about the third one. I dropped back down onto the SUV's roof, and the 'breed twisted. For one eternal moment she hung in the air over me, time slowing down and I braced myself because her claws were still out and this was going to hurt when she landed. I had nothing but the gun and it was rising but the ammo wouldn't help.

The third voice was a stream of obscenities cutting across the 'breed's desperate howl and my own. Gunfire crackled and the dreadlocked 'breed tumbled aside, half her head evaporating in a mess of black ichor and zombie oatmeal.

What the fuck? That wasn't me!

The newcomer uncoiled over me with a bound that was pure poetry, long leather duster flapping once like wet laundry shaken with an authoritative *crack!* Silver sparked and popped in her hair, beads tied to tiny braids in the straight shoulder-length mass, and her blue eyes were alight with hard joy. The ruby above and between her eyebrows was a point of living flame, and she turned in midair, firing at another hellbreed streaking out of the shadows.

Holy shit, I know her!

But I could not for the life of me come up with her name. An angry swarm of buzzing scraped the inside of my temples as I strained, frozen for a few critical moments.

The Trader who landed on the hood of a small black sports car, legs swelling with muscle and his entire body lengthening as he exploded out of the crouch and for her back probably didn't know her name either. He'd never learn it, either, because I shot him four times in midflight, the recoil jolting up my arm controlled almost as an afterthought. The hollow points tore up his head and chest bad enough to put him down on the road with a thud.

Hopefully the bleeding out would do the rest, but if it didn't I'd figure something else out.

Horns screeched. A rending crash, a blue minivan rear-ending another SUV down the line. Someone was screaming from the sidewalk, I hoped it wasn't collateral damage. *Fucking civilians, we're doing this out in the middle of the road, what the fuck?*

The woman landed, her right-hand gun blurring into its holster and her fingers jerking at something attached to her belt. "*Status!*" she yelled, and wonder of wonders, I understood exactly what she meant.

She was asking if I could fight. I could, I'd be more than happy to, it would make me ecstatic, I just needed some goddamn ammo that would put these fuckers *down.*

"No ammo!" I rolled off the SUV's roof and landed with a jolt on the road. My legs burned, bone messily healing, crackling as etheric force jerked at them to set the breaks correctly. It was the gem on my wrist doing it, and I didn't care. Traffic was at a complete standstill. "Civilians all over! Werepanther up on the rooftop, hope he's headed for the barrio! Fucking hellbreed chasing us! *Perry!*"

"Figures." She half-turned, eyes roving. Every piece of silver on her ran with blue sparks under the surface, and the ring on my third left finger responded with crackling of its own. "What you packing?"

".45. One. Nothing else. Regular ammo." Frustration turned the words into hard little bullets, but I sounded tight-mouth amused.

There was another impact. We both turned, guns coming up, and the thing in her right hand was a bullwhip, sharpsilver spines jingling at its end. She twitched it a little, assuring free play, and my fingers suddenly itched. I wanted one, too, in the worst way.

Theron rose from a crouch. "Devi." He tipped his head. "Look who's back."

Her name lit up inside my head, another klieg light of memory and meaning. *Devi. Anya Devi.* I let out a sigh of relief. If she was here, things had just gotten exponentially better.

So why did my heart suddenly pound in my wrists and throat for a moment, before training clamped down again? Why did I feel suddenly guilty?

Her face twisted a little, smoothed out. "Barrio?"

He shrugged, eyes lambent. "Was trying."

"Galina's." She glanced at me like I would protest, but I didn't have a damn thing to say. I scanned the perimeter, kept my fool mouth shut.

Theron looked relieved and stubborn all at once. "Can't make it. Too many of them, wait for daylight."

I lowered my gun, did another half turn. Traffic was hell-to-breakfast higgledy-piggledy, and people were actually starting to get out of their cars to get a closer gander at the trouble. Idiot lookie-lous.

But then, they didn't know hellbreed were on the loose. We kept it a secret, we hunters.

Monty's going to have kittens over this. Was I in the middle of a case? Were the cops betting on when I'd show up again, was Vice running the pool on sightings of me, nervous because I'd been out of action for a little bit?

We had to vanish soon, or the crowd would get hurt. As it was, the cops were going to have trouble with this one.

The woman sighed. "Goddamn stubborn Weres. Jill? You with me?"

Do you even need to ask, Devi? But I probably would've asked me, too. "Yeah."

"Are you safe?"

I looked over my shoulder, shaking aside my tangled hair. The scar down her right cheek was flushed, and she didn't look happy. Her gaze was disconcertingly direct, and for a moment I thought I could see all the way into the back of her brain. I didn't look away. "Safe?" I sounded honestly puzzled. I was a *hunter*. What was she really asking?

"Never mind. Here." Her left hand flicked, tossing something; I plucked it out of the air.

It was an extended clip, and I caught a glint of silver from the top bullet peeking out. Silverjacket rounds, just the thing to pierce a 'breed's tough shell and poison them, weaken them enough so you could tear them to itty-bitty pieces and make the night a fractionally safer place.

For the umpteenth time that long, long night, relief swamped me. The waves of feeling under my skin were like caffeine jolts, or like some drug that hadn't been invented yet.

Thank you, God. My fingers flew, drawing the old clip out, clearing the chamber, racking the new clip, chambering a round. The relief turned into a calm steadiness.

Now we can do some shit. Oh yeah.

She drew her left-hand gun again. A howl rose on the exhaust-laden wind, and sirens began baying in the distance. The ruby at her forehead gave a sharp glitter, and I saw old yellow-green bruising on the side of her neck. "Stay low. You hear me, Kismet? No heroics. Stay low, follow Theron, and I'll do the rest. And Jill?"

"Yeah?" My throat was full. The buzz inside my head crested, threatening to shake me. Her territory was over the mountains, why was she here?

I said goodbye to her once. And she promised to do...something. What? What was it?

"If you become a liability, I'll put you down myself." She was braced for action, I realized. As if I was the enemy.

Or as if I was a question mark.

That was new, and unwelcome. We were hunters, she and I. It's a bond deeper than blood, and there are no lies told or implied, no quarter asked or given. Why would she even *say* that?

My right wrist ached, and I had a sudden, very bad feeling about all this. But the first wave of hellbreed had massed and moved out into the streetlamp glow, civilians were screaming, and Theron arrived right next to me, his hand curling around my left arm again. Devi let out a short sharp breath, and every inch of silver on her ran with blue light.

"Time to go," Theron said, and the race was on.

II: Kyrie Eleison

Lord, have Mercy

12

Ramshackle frame houses slumped in a jam-packed neighborhood deep in the barrio's seethe. The street here was maybe paved once, but patches of dirt rose up through the ancient concrete-like mange. Chain-link fences enclosed haphazard, yellow-grassed, postage-stamp yards, and patches of sidewalk here and there were linked together with dusty boardwalks that looked ancient as the *Mayflower*. Everything looked deserted, but I would have bet my roll of stolen cash *and* my gun that there were eyes on us.

I leaned against Theron, my stomach empty and a hot weight of bile rising in my throat. "Fuuuuck," I whispered, drawing the single syllable out, and Anya Devi laughed, a sarcastic bark. Her coat was flayed by hellbreed claws, her hair was scorched, and her eyes were alight. Dried blood crusted her hair and her cheek, and thin blue lines of healing sorcery sank into her skin, pulsing through her aura.

I'd wanted to help apply the sorcery, since God knew I had enough etheric force humming through my right hand. But she'd shied away. Just like I'd twitched away from Perry.

I didn't know if I liked that.

She was braced against a graffiti-scarred storefront, leaning forward, elbows on her bent knees while her sides heaved. Her breathing evened out, and she shook her head, silver chiming. "They want you *bad*, sweetheart. That's a good sign." She checked the street. "We're clear. Theron?"

He ran his free hand back through wildly mussed dark hair. The bruises were getting better, but the circles under his eyes were so dark they looked painted on. His shirt flapped low on his right side, crusted with blood, but he was moving all right. "I could use a burrito. And a good stiff drink wouldn't go amiss either."

"In a few minutes. Jill?"

I wiggled my left toes. I'd somehow lost a sneaker, and my sock was torn up and filthy. I wasn't bleeding very badly. Everything on me ached, but the wounds just closed up on their own each time the gem sent another hard, high burst of singing rattles through me. It felt like a jet plane just before takeoff. "Food sounds good." *Booze sounds better. And a chance to sit down and think about some shit wouldn't be bad either.*

"Good fucking deal." Devi hauled herself up. "Wait a second, though."

Her hand came down and gripped my right wrist. I almost flinched, the motion controlling itself as she turned my hand palm up, the gun pointed off to the side. Theron had my other arm, and I was effectively trapped.

But I suffered it. For a bare half second I wanted to twitch away, but my control reasserted itself. She was a *hunter*.

I could trust her.

She studied the gem in the streetlamp glow, blue eyes unblinking. "Huh. Where'd you get that?"

"It was on me when I woke up." I weighed it as she glanced up at me, decided to drop the other shoe. "In...in a grave."

"Yeah?"

"Shallow. Out in the desert. Just off a railroad line. I caught a ride into town last night." I shuddered. *There was a diner, and a blue-eyed man who gave me my gun back. And Martin Pores, nice guy who pulled a vanishing act.* "Almost got mugged. Then I went to Walmart."

Theron made a small sound. We both looked at him. His mouth was twitching. Another snorting half laugh escaped him, and one corner of Anya's mouth twisted up.

She sobered almost immediately. She eyed the trickle of hot blood easing down from my scalp. Head wounds are messy; this one had been caused by a bit of shrapnel, and it was still weeping a little. I'd probably have lost most of the pints I was carrying if not for the healing.

Superhuman healing. As if I was still hellbreed-tainted. But the gem didn't *feel* like Perry's mark on me—the scarred lip-print, a hard little nugget of corruption working in toward the bone.

This was something different. And I didn't like the idea that she might be checking me for...what?

Which just brought up the question of what the hell had happened, what had ended up with me in a shallow grave and a hole in my memory the size of the breathing city itself.

Her free hand came up, and she smeared a little of the blood on my forehead. Rubbed it between her fingers, considering, and actually sniffed it. Examined her fingers in the warm electric glow from the bodega's porch light. Racks of novenas in the window behind her rippled, and I blinked, swaying.

"Devi?" Theron, carefully.

"She's clear. I don't know how or why, but she's clean." Anya blew out between her lips, her *bindi* winking at me. This close, I could see that it was, indeed, a sub-dermal piercing. You'd think the prospect of getting hit in the face would've made her refrain, but I *so* wasn't one to throw sartorial stones. "I suppose if you knew what'd happened to you, Kismet, you'd let me in on it?"

"I have some memories," I repeated. My eyebrows drew together as the hornet buzz returned, threading under the surface of my brain. "Fragments. I remember...I was on my way to the Monde to question Perry. Because...Saul. They had Saul." And now I had a question of my own. "What are you checking me for, Devi?"

"Great." She said it like a curse, and let go of my wrist, wiping her bloody fingers on her leather pants.

I seriously wanted a pair myself. My jeans were torn and flapping. Some of the pints I'd lost were a result of roadrash—you get to going faster than the average human, and you can erase a metric *fuckton* of skin.

"Devi?" Very carefully, each word calm and neutral. "What are you checking me for?"

She shook her head, silver beads chiming. "Later. All right, Theron. You're right. Let's go. But then I'm taking her to Galina's."

He nodded. "Come on, Jill. Someone wants to see you."

I took hold of my fraying temper. If Devi wanted to clue me in later, fine. I could trust her that far. "Great." I didn't have to work to sound sarcastic. "Is it someone else who wants to kill me?"

"Oh, no." He paused. "At least, I'm almost sure he doesn't." He seemed to find this hilarious, and snickered at his own joke as he drew me away from the bodega and out into the street. Anya drifted behind us, rearguarding. Dust rose on the faint night breeze, Santa Luz taking a deep breath in the long dark shoal before dawn.

"Wonderful." I let out a short, choppy, frustrated sigh. "But I would like to know what the fuck *happened* to me." *Boy, would I ever. And I want weapons. And some more silver.*

And while I'm dreaming, I'd like a pony, too.

"Later, Jill." My fellow hunter didn't sound happy. "When we get to Sanctuary, I'll tell you everything I know. We've pieced together some of it. But the only person who knows everything is you." She paused. "*Was* you."

Fantastic. That's just great. This is getting better and better.

Still, things were looking up.

13

The house looked like a ruin, its porch sagging and groaning under our weight. But when Theron opened the unlocked door, a heavenly smell of bacon and eggs came drifting out, and the entry hall was brightly lit and tile-floored. Stairs went up to the second level, a wrought-iron banister rising in a sweet curve, and it was obvious someone had spent serious time making the inside as beautiful as the outside was decrepit.

I stood there, my sock foot smearing blood and dirt on the tiles, and blinked. Down the hall was even more bright light, and someone was humming tunelessly as a hiss of something cooking in a pan reached us. Devi crowded in behind me, sweeping the door shut and locking it. "Jesus." She blew out between her teeth, and you could hear her eyes roll as if she was a teenager. "I mean, *really*."

"Who would try to break in or steal from us *here*?" Theron swept his hair back. He was perking up big time. "Hello the house! Break out the *cervezas* and bring me a burrito! Look what I've got!"

The arch off to our left was suddenly full of motion.

Two women, their long, tawny hair hanging loose except for twin braids holding it back from their faces, appeared. *Weres,* I realized, seeing their fluid economy of motion, their wide, high-cheekboned faces. Their arms were bare and rippling with clean muscle, both of them in flannel button-downs with the sleeves ripped off. Barefoot and dark-eyed, they were both utterly beautiful.

Something hot rose in my throat. I blinked.

"Jesus fucking Christ," the one on the right said, staring at me. "It's...is it? It *is!*"

I realized I knew her face just as Theron laughed again.

"Amalia." I studied her. And the other female. *Lioness, both of them. From the Norte Luz pride.* The sensation of puzzle pieces sliding together, dropping with a click, was beginning to be disconcertingly constant. "Rahel."

They stared. Their jaws dropped, but Amalia pulled herself together first. "He's upstairs." The hall was suddenly crowded as she pushed past Theron, stepping close to me and brushing his hand away. "It's...brace yourself." A glance at the Werepanther. "Have you told her?"

He spread his hands helplessly. "Look at us. There hasn't been *time.* I was over by the Monde, just poking around—"

"Ah, yes," Anya Devi piped up. "*This* was the story I wanted to hear. Come on, I need food. And absinthe. Please tell me you have some."

Amalia's grip on my arm was just short of bruising. "He hasn't told you *anything?*" She pulled me up the staircase, each hardwood step sanded and glowing mellow gold. The good smell of healthy Were and cooking mixed together, and I began to feel like I might have survived the last few hours. "You look awful, by the way."

"Thanks." The word was turned into sandpaper by the rock in my throat. "There wasn't time to say anything. We've been on the run. Look—"

"He's fading. But you'll fix that *right* up." She virtually hauled me upstairs, and the balustrade turned out to run all the way along the open hall. Bedroom doors opened up off to the right, and at the end of the hall an antique iron mission cross hung on the bathroom door. I knew it was the bathroom because the door was half open, and I saw a slice of white tile and scrubbed-gleaming chrome, the edge of a claw-footed tub. "I'll bring you something to eat. Maybe you can persuade him to eat too, he needs it. He's going to be so…" She stopped dead, took a deep breath. "Listen to me babbling on. How are you? Are you all right?"

It was too much concern all at once. "Fine," I mumbled. My fingers dropped to the gun butt, smoothed the warm, comforting metal. A very nasty supposition was rising in my head, like bad gas in a mine shaft. *Fading? I don't like the sound of that.* "Um. Amalia—"

She didn't listen, just set off again. Paused for half a second by the second door on the right. "Brace yourself. Really. It's…my God. Come on." She twisted the balky old glass-crystal knob—everything in the house looked like it had been restored from one hell of an estate sale. "Saul?" Her voice dropped, became soft, questioning. "Saul, I've brought someone to see you."

My heart leapt into my throat. It hit the rock that had been sitting there for a good half hour, mixed with the bile coating my windpipe, and twisted so hard I almost choked.

Saul? The room was dark. Amalia drew me in, and the sudden gloom confused me. My one sneaker squeaked on the hardwood floor, and an overstressed tremor went through me, my skeleton deciding it could shiver itself to pieces now that the fun and games was over.

The room was very plain. White cotton drapes over a small window, a white iron bed, a long human shape on it. He was curled up, sparks of silver in his dark hair, and my skin tightened all over me.

Was I afraid? Yes. Or no, I wasn't afraid.

I was outright *terrified*.

"Saul?" It was a harsh croak. I tore my arm out of Amalia's grasp, and she let me. There was a cherrywood washstand by the door, my hip bumped it as I took two unsteady steps.

The shape on the bed didn't stir. A rattling sound rose from it—a long, shallow, tortured breath. The silver in his hair was charms, ones I knew.

Because I'd given him every one of them. Tied most of them in with red thread, too, while sunlight fell over us and a cat Were's purr made the air sleepy and golden. Sometimes he would drum his long coppery fingers on my bare knee, and I would laugh.

I was halfway to the bed before I stopped, remembering how filthy I was.

That never mattered to him. I inhaled sharply.

It smelled *sick* in here. Dry and terrible, a rasping against my sensitive nose. Like a hole an animal had crawled into to die. It was clean, certainly, every corner scrubbed and the bedcovers and drapes bleached and starched. Still, the reek of illness brushed the walls with shrunken centipede fingers.

Oh, God. "What's wrong with him?" I whispered. It was a useless question. I could guess.

"Matesickness." Amalia's own whisper made the air

move uneasily around me, little bits of fur and feathers brushing my drying sweat. "The closer you can get to him, the better. Lie down next to him. He needs to know you're alive." She backed up, reaching for the doorknob. "We thought you were dead. Weres don't survive without their mates. You know that."

"I was—" I began, but she swept the door closed, leaving me alone in the dark. I swallowed, hard. *I was dead.* The sudden certainty shook me all the way down to my filthy, aching toes.

I was dead, and Perry had something to do with it. Maybe even a lot to do with it. And now...Saul. My pulse picked up, a thin high hard beat in my wrists and throat and ankles, behind my knees, my chest a hollow cave.

The shape on the bed stirred. Just a little. I saw a gleam of dark eyes under silver-starred hair. Only it wasn't just the silver. There were pale streaks, gray or white, and that was new.

I took a single step. "Saul?" High and breathy, like a little girl.

He twitched. The rattling in-breath intensified. The gem on my wrist gave out a thin sound, like crystal stroked by a wet fingertip.

When you're ready.

I was beginning to think I wasn't ready for anything about this. But it was too late. I'd already clawed my way up out of my own grave, hadn't I?

You can't do that and not accept the consequences.

14

$\mathcal{M}$y knees hit the side of the bed. I stared down at him. His back was to me, and even in the dimness I could see he was skeletal. The sharp boniness of a hip under his boxers, ribs standing out in stark relief, shoulder blades like fragile wings. His head was too big for his neck, and he tipped it back. The silver moved in his hair, chiming sweetly, and a gout of something hot boiled up inside me. There was nothing in my stomach to throw up, but the shaking all through me demanded I *do* something. Kill whatever was hurting him, hold it down and put a bullet or twenty through its head—

"Jill?" A faint whisper. He inhaled, another long rasping rattle.

As if he could smell me, as filthy as I was. Shame boiled through me. God, couldn't I *ever* be clean?

No. You've never been clean, and he always was. Always.

The wetness on my cheeks was either tears or blood. "God," I whispered back. "*God.*"

That managed to make him move. Slowly, painfully,

hitching one hip up, rolling. My hands were fists. One of his scarecrow hands lifted, dropped back down on the white lace coverlet. He tried again, reaching up, and I grabbed that hand with both of mine.

He jerked in surprise. For a mad moment I was sure I'd hurt him, tried to ease up, but his fingers bore down with surprising hysterical strength. He pulled, and I went down onto the bed, trying not to land on him.

His stick-thin arms closed around me. The shudders came in waves, I wasn't sure if he was shaking, or me, or both of us, because he was saying my name. Over and over again, in that dry cricket-whisper that hurt my own throat, and I sobbed without restraint. He was *kissing* me, I realized, his thin lips landing on my bloody forehead, his leg snaking up and over me, body curled around mine as if he could hold us both down while a storm passed overhead.

Only the storm was inside my buzzing, aching head. Memory exploded, shrapnel tearing through my brain.

"I just want you to do one thing," he said into my filthy hair. *I almost cringed.*

Anything. Just stay with me. *I stilled, waited.*

"Just nod or shake your head. That's all. Now listen, Jill. Do you still need me? Do you want me around?"

"I—" How could he even ask me that? Didn't he know? Or was he saying that he felt obligated?

"Just nod or shake your head. I just want to know if you need me."

It took all I had to let my chin dip, come back up in the approximation of a nod.

"Do you still want me?" God help me, did Saul sound tentative?

It was too much. "Jesus Christ." The words exploded out of me. "Yes, Saul. Yes. Do you want me to beg? I will, if you—"

"Jill." He interrupted me, something he barely ever did. "I want you to shut up."

I shut up. For a few moments he just simply held me, and the clean male smell of him was enough to break down every last barrier. I tried to keep the sobs quiet, but they shook me too hard. The breeze off the desert rattled my garage door, and the last fading roll of thunder retreated.

He stroked my hair, held me, traced little patterns on my back. Cupped my nape, and purred his rumbling purr. When the sobs retreated a little, he tugged on me, and we made it to the door to the hall, moving in a weird double-stepping dance. He was so graceful, and I was too clumsy.

He lifted me up the step, got me into the hall, heeled the door closed. My coat flapped. My boots were heavy, click-ing against concrete. I probably needed to be hosed off.

I had to know. I dug in, brought him to a halt, but couldn't raise my eyes from his chest. "A-are you s-s-still—" I couldn't get the words out. I was shaking too hard.

"You're a fucking idiot," he informed me. "I'm staying, Jill. As long as you'll have me. I can't believe you think I'd leave you."

I cried for a long time, there in the dark. He held me, stick arms strong for a Were who was wasting away, and he kept repeating my name.

How could I possibly have forgotten *him*? Even if I for-got myself, I would remember him. If I was blind I would know him. I hadn't even known what I was missing, but it had been him.

I should have been looking for him as soon as I clawed up into the night and screamed.

I was. I didn't know it, but I was. And I couldn't even tell if that was a lie I was telling myself or the bare honest truth, because the sobs were coming so hard and fast they shook both of us.

We curled around each other like morning glory vines, and for that short while everything else faded away. He didn't say anything else, and neither did I.

There was no need.

* * *

It was the first good sleep I'd had since I'd come up out of the grave, and it wasn't nearly long enough.

The gun was up, pressure on the trigger and my arm straight and braced. I blinked, and Anya Devi, her blue eyes narrowed, held both hands up, one of them freighted with a glowing-green glass bottle. "Easy there, killer." She even sounded amused, the tiny silver hoops in her ears glinting. Her coat brushed her ankles, and I realized she was tense and ready. I wouldn't put it past her to dodge a bullet.

But she wasn't my enemy.

I lowered the gun, pushed myself up on one elbow.

The room was empty. Westering sunlight poured past the sheer white drapes, and crusty, dried crap crackled on my skin. I hadn't even washed my face. I felt cotton-stuffed, the way you do if you've ever fallen asleep after a long wracking bout of sobbing. Like I'd been cleaned out and Novocained. My mouth tasted fucking awful, too. My foot had swollen inside the one sneaker I still had on, and I wanted a hot shower, a gallon of coffee, and some weapons.

Not necessarily in that order.

Devi answered my first question before I could ask. "He's downstairs, eating. Has a lot of body mass to put back on." She offered me the venom-green bottle as I sat up, sheepishly lowering the gun the rest of the way. I sniffed cautiously and smelled licorice and alcohol.

Absinthe. Devi believes in the stuff the way other people believe in football, God, or sex. Mikhail'd felt that way about vodka. Me, I can take it or leave it—I save all my love for the tools to get the job done.

No. I don't. I save most of it for him. The rock in my throat eased, miraculously. "Sorry." Liquid sloshed in the bottle, I made a face. "What the fuck?"

"Good for you, cures everything. Go on, take a hit." One corner of her mouth quirked slightly. "Or do you remember hating it?"

I lifted it to my mouth. Took a swallow. It burned all the way down, and it was unspeakably foul. "Gah." My face squinched up, it coated the back of my throat and went off in my stomach like a bomb. But I took another long swallow. That was as brave as I could get.

It was booze, after all. And a belt was just the thing to bolster me.

She accepted the bottle back, took a long hit, her throat working. Then she lowered herself cautiously into a high-backed mission-style chair by the bed, the one thing I'd missed last night. Leather creaked as she sank down with a sigh.

"So." She studied the bottle. "You bleed clean. That's not a 'breed mark on your arm anymore. Couple months ago you disappeared. Found my car torched out in the desert, plus one very large crater that reeked of angry hellbreed out where those goddamn stones are. Or where they *were*, I should say, because whatever it was shattered them and fucked up the ley lines but good. We're in the middle of a war here, and all of a sudden you show up at the Monde, bust Theron out just in time, and..." Her straight eyebrows went up, the scar down her right cheek—the claw had dug in right at the outside of her eye, like a tear—crinkling a little as her mouth twisted. The *bindi* gleamed, a sharp dart of light. I studied it while I waited for her to finish the thought.

While she decided what to do with me, was more like it. I had no illusion that anything else was going on. She was up on everything happening in my town, and I was...what?

Confused, still not thinking straight, and still exhausted.

"I bled clean before," I managed, through the pinhole my throat had become. "Even though I had the mark."

She said nothing. Examining me like a gunfighter, the silver in her hair glowing, her gaze disconcertingly direct, like every hunter's. Crow's-feet touched the outer edges of her eyes, and the lines as her mouth pulled tight against itself would only keep carving themselves deeper from now on.

It is our job to keep gazing, unflinching, on the worst Hell has to throw at us. It is our job to never look away.

When she said nothing else, the silence stretched uncomfortably. I stood it as long as I could. I itched all over, and the need to find more weapons itched as well, right under my skin where nothing but metal and ammo would scratch. "I barely even remembered my own name. I killed a Trader on a rooftop. He had a card for the Monde. I went there. Perry seemed...glad to see me."

She let out a short, plosive breath and settled into immobility. The quality of a hunter's concentration can spook civilians; something about our trained stillness just makes them uncomfortable. "Right into the lion's den. Well, at least *that* hasn't changed."

I searched for words to boil the whole complex tangle down to its essentials. "He was...I heard Theron. I thought it was Saul. Everything came back. At least, everything up until a certain point. So I got him the hell out of there."

"Good. He shouldn't have been there." She let out a sigh, her shoulders sagging for a moment. "So here's the million-dollar question, Kismet." She took another hit off the bottle, venom-green liquid sloshing. "You still a hunter?"

Why the hell would you ask me that? "It's not like I have a choice of career options."

As soon as I said it, I knew it wasn't strictly true. You could lay it down and walk away at any moment. Nobody would say a word, or judge you.

Idiots, Mikhail used to snarl sometimes. *They think we do this for them. Is only one reason to do,* milaya, *and that is for to quiet screaming in our own heads.*

I found out I'd laid the gun in my lap, and I was twisting the ring around my finger. *Do svidanye.*

Honest silver, on vein to heart. Now it begins. Bile crept up into my mouth. It took a few hard swallows before I could speak, the silvery insectile curtain inside my head shifting a little as...something...peeked out.

"Mikhail," I whispered. "I found out...something. About him."

She nodded. "You did. Here's another million-dollar question, Kismet. Do you want the last two and a half months back? Or d'you want to head out onto the Rez with that Were of yours? There's no..." She paused, swallowed hard. Her eyes had darkened. "There's no obligation, Jill. You did what you had to do."

"What did I do?" I was honestly puzzled, and the hornet buzz inside my head threatened to rise again, swallowing thought whole and triggering reaction. I shoved it away, my shoulders tensing as if I'd been hit. "That's the one thing I can't remember. I woke up in my own *grave*, Devi. I'm as confused as it's possible to get. I'm digging myself up, then this guy drops me off in an alley, and all I can think of is getting some ammo. But I didn't remember the silver, or...*Jesus* fuck-me *Christ*. Of *course* I want my goddamn memory back. What are you thinking?"

"I have...an idea." The admission, pulled out of her. "But have you considered that you might not want your memory? That there might be things you'd prefer to forget? This isn't the type of job that gives you happy dreams. Saul loves you, you've got a chance to—"

I slid off the bed. I had to get that goddamn sneaker off before it turned my foot gangrenous. "There's a war on? Against Weres?" *And you expect me to sneak off into the sunset. Great. Well, now I know what you really think of me, right? Great.*

She let out a longer sigh, one she probably practiced on her apprentices. "They're driven into the barrio. Galina's doing what she can, but—you remember Galina, right?"

"Of course." I limped for the door. "I remember almost

everything, up to the moment I pulled up in front of the Monde. I was working on a case, which I'm guessing is wrapped up now. Can you find me some clean clothes? And more weapons?"

"I can, but Jill—"

"I've got to pee." And with that, I made an inglorious retreat out into the hall. I wasn't lying—I really did have to piss like a racehorse.

But I was afraid that if I stayed in there any longer I'd lose my temper. Or, even worse, I would look down at the space on the bed next to me, the pillow still dented from Saul's beautiful, wasted head, and entertain ideas of riding off into the sunset after all.

15

I was taller than Anya, and broader in the hips. But the leather pants fit me just fine, and the black Angelcake Devilshake T-shirt too. I knew that wasn't mine—I'd started buying my tees plain and in job lots, because they ended up shot and blood-drenched, not to mention sliced, diced, and dipped in unspeakable foulness so much. Just like the rest of me.

Even the sports bra and unmentionables fit just fine. There was a pair of scarred leather boots that looked damn familiar, and hugged my feet as if they'd been broken in but good.

But it was the weapons that did it.

Another modified .45, this one shiny instead of dull black. Holsters for both the old gun and the new. A complicated array of leather straps that came alive in my hands, buckling itself on like an octopus hugging me, holding weapons. Knives with silver loaded along the flats, from the big main-gauche to a slim stiletto almost lost in its sheath. Cartridges of silverjacket ammo, and the crackling-new bullwhip with wicked-sharp sweetsilver jingles at its tip, secured in its own little loop.

The coat was a little too long, a black leather trench instead of a duster like Devi's, and it smelled like comfort. Copious pockets and more loops sewn in for the pile of ammo Devi had brought up in two paper grocery bags. The more I slipped into the loops, the better I felt.

"Thou Who," I whispered, and shut my mouth. The prayer had no place here, but it kept going under the surface of my conscious thought. When I repeated it, the wasp-noise retreated, left me alone.

Thou Who hast given me to fight evil, protect me; keep me from harm.

Except it was useless. I'd ended up dead. There were Weres hiding in the barrio. And Anya was still here, instead of back over the mountains in her own territory, keeping the scurf down and the Traders under wraps.

The bathroom was white tile, clean as a whistle, and my dirty clothing had been whisked away by a tight-lipped Amalia. The shower was ancient, the kind with the curtain attached to a hoop bolted to the wall, and the mirror showed a gaunt woman with mismatched, exhaustion-ringed eyes and a habit of not meeting her own gaze. I was milk-pale, but the shaking in my hands went down with every weapon I strapped on.

Oh, yes. This was what I'd been missing.

The knock startled me, and I thought it was Anya. But when I swept the door open, it was him.

He was still too thin, leaning against the wall. The plaid flannel shirt and jeans hung scarecrow on him, and his hair fell in his dark eyes, scarred with small silver charms. His cheekbones stood out sharply, his proud

nose a blade of bone and skin, and his mouth turned
down at both corners.

My jaw dropped. I stared.

Weres are beautiful. There is no corruption in them,
nothing like a hellbreed or Trader. Hunters can track
'breed; humans have an advantage in hunting what we're
akin to. But in Weres, everything is burnished. It's human-
ity, yes...but with so much of the crap burned away.

He was holding something up, his expressive fingers
just knobs of bone and skin. "I thought..." His voice was
a rasp, he coughed and the words came a little easier.
"Thought you'd want this."

It was a stick of kohl eyeliner. I grabbed for it. "My
God. Thank you. I didn't even know I was missing—"

"Are you all right?" The words cut across mine, and all
of a sudden the leather on my back didn't feel very much
like armor anymore. "What *happened* to you? I couldn't
find you anywhere, Jill. Not even the wind carried a hint.
You were *gone*."

*Everyone keeps asking where I was. You'd think I'd
know.* "I woke up in my own grave." The words were beginning to sound routine.

Not really.

He stared at me. Not disbelievingly. Apparently the idea
that I could wake up in my own grave wasn't very outlan-
dish to him.

Of course not. He knew me better than anyone.

I searched for something else to say. "I'm here now."
I clutched the eyeliner like it was going to try to escape.
"The last thing I remember is screeching up to the Monde,
because they'd taken you. Right outside Galina's.
Perry..." *Perry, I knew him.* I shook the thought away,

damp strings of hair touching my cheeks. "Devi says she's got a way for me to remember how the case ended up."

He stepped forward, stopped. Braced one shoulder against the wall. I thought of the bone underneath pressing out through wasted muscle and skin, how much that had to hurt. "Are you sure you want to?"

The only thing I'm sure of right now is that every bit of firepower I strap on makes me feel better. Oh, and that I'm going to put a bullet or twelve in the head of anything that hurts you. A good grocery list to start out with, right? "She says she can do it. She's got an idea, I guess, and as soon as she tells me I can get started—"

"No." A shake of his beautiful, wasted head. One of the charms—a silver wheel, tied in with faded red thread— moved against his temple. "Are you sure you want to re-member?"

"I...yeah. Of course." I backed up a step, shifted my weight as if I was going to turn. The fragile stick in my fist creaked a little, and I eased up on it. "I've got to. There was Perry, and Belisa was mixed up in it. The Eye, too— Gilberto's probably got that. Gil's at Galina's, I'm betting."

He thought this over, watching me, those dark eyes soft. Almost wounded.

"Yeah," Saul finally said, heavily. "Locked up tight, poor kid. Just let me get some more food, and we'll get going."

That might not be such a good idea—I opened my mouth to protest, but he beat me to it.

"Don't even start with me." His head dropped forward wearily, and he glared at my chin through his lackluster, silver-scarred hair. "If you're going, I'm going. I'm not losing you again."

"You didn't—" I began, but I couldn't finish. The words lodged in my throat, because I was suddenly sure that I had been lost, and in a big way.

Utterly lost.

"Here's what I know." He reached up, brown fingers gripping the doorjamb. "You told Theron to make sure the first thing I heard when I woke up was *She loves you.* And Devi, God damn her, always finding a reason not to be in the room when I showed up. Until I cornered her and she told me you'd been...that you'd bargained yourself away. For *me*."

I blinked. *Was that what happened? Who did I...*My brain shivered inside its bone casing. I shuddered.

"And I couldn't find you," he continued. His free hand flicked, and flashes of silver chimed as they hit the floor. My gaze didn't drop down to check, riveted to his face. "I couldn't find you anywhere. Even *inside*. You were gone. I went half mad looking for you. Then I came back to the barrio to die." He waved aside my instinctive protest, knobs and spindles of bone moving under his skin. "And now, here you are. Inside and out."

"Saul—" The thing in my throat wouldn't let anything else get past. Just his name.

He shook his head, so hard I was afraid he'd snap his wasted, scrawny neck. His fingers tensed against the jamb. Wood groaned. "No. Everywhere you go now, I'm going with you. *Everywhere.*" He turned on his heel, sharply, and stamped away. The hall almost rocked around him, one gaunt Were with the burned-candle smell of anger trailing behind him in eddies and swirls.

Even their anger is clean. It doesn't twist into hatred. You won't ever find a Were Trading.

But you might find a hunter Trading, a deep voice whispered inside me. *You just might. Especially for what she loves.*

What she can't do without.

I found out I was trembling. A wave of shudders went through me, but I bent over anyway. I found the charms and tweezed them up delicately. Three of them—a tiny silver shoe like the one from the Monopoly game, a Celtic cross, an exquisitely carved spider.

It was there, on my knees, clutching the eyeliner and the small bits of silver, that it hit me.

The blue-eyed mute who had paid for my breakfast and given me my gun. He had seemed familiar. Too familiar.

And now I knew who he was. The knowledge opened up another door in my head, but only halfway.

Halfway was enough.

"Shit," I muttered, there on the floor. "Oh, God. God." My arms came up, and I hugged myself, rocking back and forth.

God didn't answer.

He never does.

16

I stamped down the stairs and found everyone in the kitchen. Everyone, that is, meaning a crowd starting with an unhappy-looking pair of lionesses, Theron nursing a beer, Anya Devi chowing down at a table littered with plates, and Saul right next to her, doing his level best to destroy a mountain of beans and rice. A huge pan of what looked like beef enchiladas verdes heaped with cheese sat to one side, and between pulls off a Corona bottle he was doing very well at taking the whole load of food down without chewing much.

The house muttered and sighed, because there were other Weres now too. A bird Were bent over the stove, something sizzling, as another lean tawny cat Were—*Ruby*; I found her name with a lurching mental effort—set down a pair of grocery bags and stared openly at me. Several other cat Weres were crammed in the living room, and the only reason why more weren't in the kitchen/dining room was because it literally wouldn't hold any more. The first story was full to bursting, and I was lucky to be able to squeeze through the hall downstairs.

As it was, I stepped into the kitchen and let out a long breath. I had enough eyeliner smeared on to make me feel like a raccoon, and the long leather trench whispered reassuringly as I came to a halt, boots placed precisely and the three charms knotted into my hair with dental floss I'd found in the bathroom cabinet.

Hey, whatever works.

Everyone except the bird Were, feathers fluttering in the updraft in his dark shoulder-length hair, looked at me. I squared my shoulders and tried not to feel like a carnival sideshow.

Except it was too late for that. I was armed and dangerous now, and for the first time since I scrabbled up out of the sand with filth covering me I felt…

…human. Or, like I knew who I was. Or like I belonged in my skin. Even if the thought of a carnival sent another rippling shudder through me, ruthlessly quelled. I remembered *that* case, thank you very much.

Devi swallowed a forkful of paella and blinked at me. "Nice to see you up and around. Get some food, we've got to get out of here."

I shrugged, rolling my shoulders under the heavy leather. The T-shirt was vintage, and the lettering on it was going to give someone a perfect target to aim at, but I couldn't cavil. It would probably get shot off me or blood-drenched in no time at all. "I'm good. We're headed to Galina's?"

Saul stopped shoveling long enough to glare at me. "Jill." A rumble filled his thin, wasted chest. "Sit. Eat."

I dropped down into the only free chair at the table, and the bird Were was suddenly there, banging down a huge plate of steak, eggs, and crispy hash browns. Fragrant

steam wafted up, and there was a fork buried in the potatoes. He took a load of dishes away, table space magically
appearing. His long nose twitched once, the feathers in his
hair fluttered, and he hurried back into the kitchen, dis-
missing my faint thank-you with a nod.

Anya grinned, the corners of her eyes crinkling. The
beads in her hair chimed sweetly. "Now I *have* seen everything." She took another huge forkful of paella and washed
it down with a gulp of absinthe.

I shuddered at the thought, and stared at the plate.

Perry was trying to feed me, too. Everyone trying to
shove something down my gullet.

Which brought me back to my blue-eyed mute and the
diner. I still wasn't sure if that was a hallucination. But he
and Martin Pores had been the first to feed me.

It probably meant something, but what? No clue. I'd
wait until we got to Galina's and sort everything out.
Sounded like a reasonable plan, right?

Steam rose from the browned potatoes, the fluffy eggs,
the strips of medium-rare steak. Anya shoved a glass bottle
of ketchup over with one hand, then grabbed her absinthe
and took another long healthy drag.

*The sorcery will burn it out of her. Not like Leon and
his constant beer-swilling, to dull the something-extra he
came back from Hell with—*

My head snapped aside as if I'd been slapped. The
heavy butcher-block table rattled, my fingers curling
around its edge and sinking in, the gem giving a subsonic
thrill all through me. Plates and cups waltzed, chattering
together, and Anya was on her feet, the chair shoved back
with a squeaking groan that might have been funny if she
hadn't had both hands on her guns.

"Easy there." Saul barely looked up from his methodical shoveling-in. "Both of you settle *down*. Trying to *eat* here."

Ruby, in the kitchen, peered out with wide dark eyes. She'd gone down into a half crouch, but the bird Were simply racked dishes in the open dishwasher, hooked it shut with a foot, and twisted it on. "Pizza next!" he sang out in a light tenor. "Extra cheese. Rube, unpack those for me, will you? Then you're on drying duty."

I picked up the fork, awkwardly. A thin lattice of golden-fried potato hung from it, still steaming. My other hand still clutched the table. "I, ah." My throat was full of sand. "Just thought of something. That's all."

A long silence, broken only by the methodical chink of Saul's spoon against his bowl. The rice and beans were vanishing at an amazing rate, and the enchiladas were going down just as smoothly. You could almost *see* the food being converted into muscle, filling him back out again. His shoulders weren't hunched, but I thought of the way kids eat in juvie—protecting the plate, arm curled around it, and the blank look as they took it down as quickly as possible.

They eat that way in prison, too. You ate that way, before and after Mikhail found you in that snowbank. You only stopped when Saul started coaxing you to use some manners.

Another soundless explosion touched off inside my skull. "Mikhail. Something about him. And Belisa, that Sorrows bitch." I searched Devi's face. "And...Perry."

Her *bindi* flashed, a dart of bloody light. She lowered herself down gingerly. "Yeah." Just the single word, no more. And she, I noticed, almost hunched over her plate as well, before straightening a little self-consciously, taking another hit of absinthe, and going back to making the food disappear.

I took a bite. The hash browns crunched, salted and heavenly. I swallowed carefully. It scorched on the way down, and the bird Were came back out with another bottle of beer, so cold it smoked with vapor, and a king-sized mug of what proved to be thick black coffee.

From there it was easy. But I kept thinking of diner food, possible hallucinations, ol' Blue Eyes, the Sorrow who killed my teacher, the gaps in my memory…

…and Perry's snow-white table with its blood-clot rose in the crystal vase.

The burst of frantic loathing that went through me turned the food to ashes, but I kept chewing and swallowing. I needed the fuel.

* * *

The city drowned under sharp honey sunlight, dust rising on an oven-hot, unsteady breeze. A rattling, mottled-green Chevy pickup was our only transportation, Theron and Saul both hopping lithely into the bed and Anya twisting the key with a little more force than absolutely necessary. The engine roused, protesting, and I caught a shadow of movement from inside the house. Weres, peering out through the windows like frightened children.

War against Weres. I should ask about that.

Anya pumped the gas pedal, and the engine caught. "Only wheels we've got right now. Mine got torched, yours wouldn't run—"

"Sorry," I mumbled, staring out the window. Even with

the leather and the pounds of weaponry I wasn't hot, my temperature regulating itself with only a faint passing ghost of sweat touching my skin before I remembered I didn't have to. The deep rumble of the engine was soothing, and I caught myself thinking I could probably tune this beast up. Wouldn't take more than a couple afternoons, you can get Chevy parts easy enough. And they respond well to both threats and blandishments.

Not like that Pontiac. She was a lady, but damn she was hard to please. Something had happened to her engine, though. It was in the middle of that blank spot in my head. I'd been working that case pretty hard, and half mad with agony over Saul…

"No worries. Jesus." She dropped it into gear, and for a moment I considered grabbing for the dash. It wasn't a completely unwarranted thought, because she floored it, and we jounced down the street in a rumbling roar. I thought of glancing back to check the Weres, too, but they could probably hold on. Even if Devi did wrench the wheel and send us careening down an indifferently paved cross street.

This was familiar, too, only I was used to being behind the wheel as we bounced through negligible traffic. We certainly didn't stand out in this rig.

Not in the barrio.

Anya reached for the radio knob, drew her hand back. "So," she called over the wind rushing in through the windows, "we're pretty safe as long as we're in the barrio. Outside, though…"

I actually twitched with surprise. How could we not be safe? "It's daylight!" I yelled back.

"Of course it is." She fished a pair of Jackie O sunglasses out of her coat, slid them on, twisted the wheel, and we slewed and bumped up onto slightly better pavement. "But that isn't stopping *them*, Jill. Just relax. Coming back from the dead was the trick of the week, but I've got one better."

"Nice to know you have a plan." I grabbed at the door as she swerved wildly around another turn.

She must not have heard me right. "We're heading for Sanctuary," she called over the windroar, and reached for the radio. Snapped the knob all the way over, and the wail of a country song filled the cab.

Great.

17

The bells over the door jingled, and we piled in through a sheet of cascading redgold, energy flushing deep purple as it sealed us inside. With the Weres crowding behind we couldn't slow down, and I was halfway across the small occult shop before skidding to a stop, guns flicking out.

The ride here had been spine-tingling but uneventful— if by *uneventful* you mean "almost got into six different traffic accidents, lost a cop in the industrial district, and bailed out of the truck with the tires still smoking." Now I knew how other people felt when *I* drove.

It occurred to me to ask why the cops didn't recognize her ride, but with the radio going supersonic and her lips moving as she cursed steadily, it didn't seem like a good time.

Shelves of books and candles stood against the walls like good little soldiers, and there was a large rack holding crystals and stones in small bins. Another wooden rack held amulet-making materials—leather, bits of bone, beads, feathers, and less-nice things. Glass cases slumbered under falls of dusty golden sunlight, and the air quivered a little as the walls ran with purple light. My smart eye watered, trying to pierce the curtains of etheric force.

But that wasn't what was bothering me right now. Anya let out a short sharp yell, and the Weres behind me suddenly let loose with twin growls, shelves of books and candles and other assorted trivia—including the glass cases and the racks—vibrating as the Sanctuary's walls resounded like the curves of a gigantic bell.

Galina spread her arms, green eyes alight and her dark marcel waves slightly disarranged. She was in full robes, smoky gray silk glowing with pigeonthroat sheen, the medallion of the Order—a quartered circle inside a snake's supple curve, cast in some light silvery metal—running with white radiance against her chest.

But that wasn't why I had my guns out. You'd have to be crazy to draw on a Sanc inside her own walls. They settle, drive in their roots deep, and are near godlike inside their hallowed homes. Outside, they're a tasty, almost-defenseless snack. But hunters, Weres, and even most 'breed or Traders will smack you down *hard* if you attack your local Sanc. Neutral supply of necessities is the least they provide.

No, I had both guns out and braced because of the hell-breed near the sleek black cash register, his eyes glowing sterile blue and his pale hair ruffling as he saw me—and grinned.

"*Jill!*" Galina yelled, and the walls tolled their deep bell note of restrained power again. Each hair on my body stood straight up, my skin shrinking with reaction, and I found myself suddenly hoping she wasn't going to lose her temper.

It can get awful uncomfortable inside when a Sanc loses their temper.

"Darling." Perry's lip lifted, his pearly teeth bluntly human but too, too white. The silent snarl turned into a bright, bland, sunny smile, the kind a real-estate broker will use right before moving in for the kill. "*So* good of you to come."

Galina's open palm, flung out toward him, twitched. "Don't make me, Perry." Flat and loaded with terrible power, the single sentence turned the air inside the shop to frost. "Jill. Jesus Christ. *Pax*, hunter. Put the guns down."

My breath turned to a white cloud. Every muscle in my body protested. Anya Devi drifted away to the right, and I was suddenly certain she was getting a better angle on Perry. An angle that would leave Galina out of the line of fire.

My stomach cramped, my arms aching and tingling. If I needed to know how Anya felt about me, it was all in that subtle movement. We were hunters. If I was going to throw down, even inside a Sanc's hallowed walls, she was ready to back me.

"Stay where you are, Anya." Galina was having none of this. "Jill, put your guns *down*."

Perry took a single step forward. Galina's hand twitched and he halted, a ripple running under his pale skin. Like tiny mice, begging to escape. The pale linen of his suit was dotted with black ichor, hems and cuffs sending up little threads of steam, but he looked pristine under it.

Like he could just step out from under the spatter stains and they would fall to the ground with tiny little *plash*ing sounds.

Splashback. He's been killing other hellbreed. Because we got away? Maybe. I took in the spatter patterns as I lowered the guns, slowly. So slowly, my arms straining, every muscle locking and fighting me.

I walked right into the Monde with nothing but plain lead in my gun. Jesus. My skin chilled again reflexively, and I tasted copper. *What would have happened if I'd eaten something there?*

There was no deciding which was worse: being helpless and mostly unconscious of the danger, or looking back and seeing how badly things *could* have gone.

Perry's grin widened, the further down the barrels went. He shook his head slightly, white-blond hair sliding back from his face like raw silk. He changed hairstyles like some women change shoes, but very subtly. You had to look to see what he'd done each time.

And I did not like that I knew that, or how closely it meant I watched him.

"You left too soon, Kiss." The sheer good humor, as if we were at a party and he was dropping banal gossip. A hot draft of desert wind, laden with the scent of spoiled honey, brushed every surface. "Always in such a hurry."

Buzzing pressed itself inside my skull, tiny insect feet prickling over my hands and face. I even felt them *inside*, chitinous bodies and dragging stingers pressing behind my cheekbones, running lightly over the surface of my brain as the buzz became a roar. They were crawling and eating, and my fingers almost shook with the urge to rip at the skin of my face and peel them off—

"Back *off*, Perry!" Galina's walls shivered again, the bell-gong sound rattling through my bones. "If I toss you out, you're never coming back in. Settle *down*."

"I just want to talk to her." He sounded so *reasonable*. I blinked furiously, my left cheek twitching as if a seamstress had her needle in and was plucking at the flesh. "Just a little tête-à-tête with my darling one, surely it can do no harm?"

"Galina." Devi, her tone slicing through his. "Get him the fuck out of here, or I won't be responsible for what happens."

All those threats. Blandishments. Pulling on me like dogs with a bone, except I was armed and ready the way a bone never is. The machine inside my head started calculating whether or not I could aim and squeeze both triggers before Galina twitched and made all of us mighty uncomfortable.

The machine returned a number I didn't like, no matter how many times I ran it.

"Everyone just simmer down." The air hardened, pressing against all of us, Galina's temper fraying. "I can separate you all like toddlers at the lunch table if I have to. Perry, you're done here. Leave."

"I don't have what I came for." Soft, deadly, the sliding sound of another step. "Kiss. My dearest. I have all the answers you could ever want, and I *ache* to give them to you. All you have to do—"

I fought to keep the guns down. Because sooner or later I was going to chance it, no matter what the numbers in my head said.

It wasn't surprising someone interrupted him. What was surprising was that it was Saul.

Weres don't take on 'breed. Traders, yes, because Traders are still at bottom human. But there's no corruption in Weres that can track and anticipate a 'breed.

The thrumming growl under his words said very clearly that Saul didn't care. "Step any closer, hellspawn, and *I will kill you.*"

The world narrowed to a pinhole of light, darkness crawling around the edges. Galina's shop trembled like oil on disturbed water, afternoon sunlight suddenly brittle and chill through the windows. Air-conditioning soughed, the humming in the walls oddly distorted, shimmers of energy cycling up. Galina's arms tensed, and her green eyes flamed. Red-gold Sanctuary sorcery smoked in the walls.

"Little puss." Amused, disdainful, Perry's chin lifted. His face had changed, cheekbones turning to blades and severe handsomeness rising from under the blandness. Helletöng grumbled, its flabby fingers picking at the strings under the surface of the visible. "I will deal with you in my own time. Go back to lapping milk and clawing at walls. Kiss…" The sibilant turned into a hiss. "When you're ready, *come and find me.*"

When you're ready. Silver spat and crackled with blue sparks, bleeding free of the metal. My aura rippled, the gem vibrating against my wrist. The rattling hum rippled and crawled over my shoulders, sliding under my clothes. Leather rustled, my hair ruffling on a breeze that came from nowhere, Galina's shop trembling around us both. The wooden floor groaned sharply, once.

Perry *winked out*. A *pop* of collapsing air, a draft of rotting, spoiled honey, an obscenely warm breeze caressing my face. My guns jerked up, but there was nothing for them to track, and the Sanctuary shielding made a low overstressed noise, rocks shredding under contradictory gravitational pulls. Galina chanted something, low and furious, and my fingers cramped.

I was sweating, great clear drops of water standing out on my skin. And shaking too, like a horse run too hard.

"What. The fuck." Anya sounded puzzled. "Lina?"

The world righted itself. "Well, that was unexpected." The Sanctuary blew out a frustrated sigh. "Jill?"

I thudded back into myself. My arms were straight, and even though I shook, the guns were absolutely steady. They were up.

Maybe I would have been fast enough, after all.

Training. Goes bone deep. "Jesus," I whispered.

Galina skidded to a stop right next to me. I almost twitched. Hunters don't like it when someone gets too close. But I lowered the guns, and my fingers eased off the triggers.

And Galina, wonder of wonders, threw her arms around me. She hugged me, her walls suddenly tolling a greeting instead of a threat. She was rounded at hip and breast the way I was not, and her hair smelled of incense and green growing things. The murder under my skin retreated from that softness.

18

The Sanctuary gave up trying to shake me and hugged me again, and she was actually *crying*. Her soft, unlined face blotched up, and the defenses in her walls made another low, unhappy sound. She looked for all the world like a grade-school girl crying in the bathroom.

Galina was old, though. Old enough to remember the hunters before me.

Old enough to know things I didn't.

"—*worried* about you!" she finished up into my leather-clad shoulder. The rest of her smelled like fabric softener, smoky sorcery, apples, and an acrid tang of worry and tension. "What the hell happened? It's been *months*! One second we had Saul back, everything was wrapped up, and then—"

"Give her a second, Galina." Theron folded his arms, leaning against a glass case. Mummified alligators, a scatter of tarot-card packets, and wristlets with brass bells crouched inside the case along with statuettes and chunks of semiprecious stones. "Our Kismet's come back from the dead, it looks like. Saved my ass over at the Monde."

"And you should *not* have been there, Were," Devi piped up, with a meaningful eyeroll. "First things first, though. What the fuck was that asshole doing here? And Galina, while you're explaining that to me, I need one of your vaults. Altar and circle." The other hunter drew in a deep breath. "Jill's going *between*."

I blinked again. That was her plan?

Well, great. That's just peachy. Someone stop the world, please, I want to get off.

I slid each gun back into its dark home, quietly, my breath coming hard and high and my arms weak as noodles. *Jesus. Jesus Christ. Perry.*

You could've heard a pin drop. Galina held me at arm's length, peering up at me. Dark hair fell in my face, the silver spider weighing down a curl, and I just stood there and suffered it.

There really wasn't any other choice. And I needed a few seconds to get myself together, so to speak. Something was rising under the hole torn in my memory, and I didn't like the look of it.

Saul took two steps forward. He was still gaunt, but the sheer amount of food he'd managed to pour down his throat was showing. The dark circles under his burning eyes had gone down a little, too.

Or maybe I was just hoping they had.

Had he really been ready to throw himself at Perry? The thought of *that* particular dance number, even within Galina's hallowed walls, was enough to turn everything inside me cold and loose.

"*Between?*" He sounded mildly enquiring, but a rumble poured under the surface of the word. "That's it? That's your wonderful idea?"

"Oh, Lord." Theron sighed. "This is not going to end well." He leaned against the case like we hadn't just seen a 'breed wink out of existence. Of course, Galina *had* told Perry to leave. But still…I had never seen a 'breed do that before.

I'd never *heard* of a 'breed doing that before, either.

Come on, Jill. With the holes in your head, can you be sure?

Still, he'd done things before that made him different from the usual scion of Hell. The only thing I was getting any surer of was that Perry was a separate fish indeed. I had a cold, sinking suspicion deep down in my gut, and I wasn't liking it. As much as Mikhail taught me not to assume, this was looking very very bad.

Anya shrugged and slid past Galina, her leather duster creaking slightly. She was pale. "It's the only thing I can think of, Were. The bigger question is, though—"

"You'd better think again."

God, give me patience. But there was no answer. I was on my own, as usual.

I tipped my head back. "Stop it." I sounded very small. "I'm doing what she says."

"I've got a better way to bring a memory back. But nobody asked me." Anger glittered and smoked under Saul's tone, and that growl spread out, rattling the windows facing the street. The Chevy sat in a glare of afternoon sun, its pale patches leprous. The telephone poles up and down Jimenez wavered slightly in the heat. The air-conditioning kicked on, soughing cold air through vents, and the walls of the shop resounded again, but gently, all its power held in check. "And that hellspawn son of a bitch is here, *inside* Sanctuary, and gets close enough to touch her, and none of you *do* anything? What the fuck is going on?"

"Ease up, Saul." Theron, oddly conciliatory. Of course, he was a Were.

But Saul didn't sound like a Were. Saul sounded downright furious.

"I *lost my mate*." Saul was suddenly next to me, his fingers curling around my shoulder. "And the only thing you can think of is throwing her *between*? She *doesn't remember*."

"You..." Galina's hands dropped to her sides. She cocked her head, her marcelled waves falling just-so, and glanced from my face up over my shoulder, then at Theron. "What *happened*, Jill?"

I get the feeling I should be asking you *that*. "I *don't know*. Not much, anyway." I kept my hands away from the guns with an effort that threatened to make me sweat even under the AC. The shudder that went through me made my own leather coat creak, weapons shifting. "Devi says I can remember how I wrapped up that case. I'm down with that. So let's just get it over with." I made a lunging mental effort, trying to prioritize. "No. Wait. Wait just a second. Where's Gilberto, and goddammit, what was Perry doing here?"

"Gil's upstairs." Galina's soft mouth turned down at the corners. "With Hutch. I wanted them both safe and out of the way."

Well, hooray for that. One thing to be happy about, I guess.

"And Perry?" Anya had turned away, studying the fall of sunlight through the windows. Tension sang in the set of her slim shoulders. "I am very, very interested in why *he's* here, Sanctuary."

The Sanc actually shot her a quelling glance. It would've been magnificently effective, maybe, if Devi had been looking. "He was waiting." Galina's gaze darted to me, and for a moment, I could have sworn she looked almost frightened. "For Jill."

* * *

I plunged my hands into the stream of cold water. The upstairs bathroom was familiar, sun falling in through the skylight and caressing every surface. She'd chosen a nice soothing blue up here, with little Art Deco accents. Maybe she realized she looked like a silent film star, so she might as well have a stage set.

They were fighting down in the kitchen. Saul's voice, raised, rattling the walls. Galina's, unhappy but patient. Anya Devi throwing in a spiked comment every now and again, just often enough to keep it at a boil. She wasn't going to win any smoothing-the-waters awards.

It wasn't like her. Devi knew Weres better than anyone—they helped her hunt the scurf infestation in Sierra Cancion, keeping it as contained as possible. Weres are scurf's natural enemies, and Anya was close to a Were herself, what with the munchies and her disciplined ferocity.

Still, the situation here was enough to tax anyone's temper. And hunters aren't known for interpersonal patience.

The bathroom door quivered, and when I glanced up, a scrawny-tall cholo stood there eyeing me. Lank dark hair fell in his acne-pitted face, without a hairnet for once, and his dark eyes were even more flat and lifeless than they had been. He'd put on some more muscle and shot up a couple inches, and the way he braced himself, leaning lightly against the doorjamb, told me someone had been training him.

Anya. You asked her to. Or she just did what another hunter would have done, stepped in to finish what you started.

There was a gleam on his chest, a razor-linked chain holding a barbaric, bloody gem. It rested uneasily against his faded flannel button-down. If he'd been shirtless, his narrow face with its high bladed nose might've been a little less pizza and a little more Aztec.

My apprentice's hands twitched a little. Jeans and engineer boots, his fingernails were clean, and I was assessing him from top to toe before he even opened his mouth.

Weighing. Measuring. As if I was still his mentor. Small wonder—he'd chosen me, not Devi, and I winced when I thought of what this must be doing to him.

"Eh, *profesora*." He grinned. A shark's wide humorless smile, curving his thin lips, and in that moment you could see a flash of who he might have been. "Had enough vacation, gonna go back to work?"

I almost snorted. *Was I just worrying about this kid?* But there was a hair-fine tremor under his façade. Gilberto Rosario Perez-Ayala had a shark's smile, true. Even in the barrio's seethe that grin would make seasoned gangbang cholos step back and reconsider.

But on the inside, he was a hunter's apprentice. With the dangerous but exactly right mix of need, aggression, loyalty, a goddamn bundle of twitchy neuroses, and a need to prove himself big enough to get him into serious trouble if he wasn't trained hard—and trained right.

Which was my job, and I'd failed by dying on him.

"Gilberto." I dipped my chin at the bloody, sullen gem on his chest. "That needs to be drained. And soon."

I didn't ask how the Eye of Sekhmet had ended up on *him*. The last time I'd seen my teacher's greatest prize, its razor-edged chain had been hugging my own neck.

Because Perry had left it in my warehouse. A present. *In the nature of recovered property.*

That snagged a deduction out of the soup of memory. "Belisa." I stared at the Eye, and it responded, its humming almost breaking into the audible as etheric force tensed like a fist. "He got it from Belisa, somehow."

Gilberto shrugged. His long spider fingers worked at the chain, but it wasn't any good, he couldn't get any purchase. It was kind of funny, seeing such a male reaction to jewelry.

He finally gave up and lifted the gem carefully from his chest, gingerly sliding his fingers under and working the chain around his ears and the rest of his head. "Makes me nervous." Sunlight gilded highlights into his hair, but it was merciless to his pitted cheeks. "Devi, she say to hold it for you. She thought you weren't comin' back. *Estupida.* But I took it anyway. You hold what you got to, *profesora.* Learned that somewhere else."

You hold what you got to. He wasn't old enough to know how true that really was. "Yeah." The water slid over my hands. I scrubbed them against each other as if they had blood on them. Which, given my job, was a good possibility. The sink was chill white porcelain, and it felt good to just let the water carry everything away.

Jill, you're hiding. What the hell?

He offered it, the sharp links dangling from his fist. There was a healing scrape across the back of his left hand, looked like matburn. How was Devi finding time to spar with him, if there was a war on Weres and all sorts of other shit going on?

The Eye's gleam sharpened, and the stream of water over my hands warmed. I shut off the faucet and flicked my fingers. "Keep it. It's safer with you." *Because if I take that, I'm going hunting for Perry. And that is probably what he wants, so it's a Very Bad Idea.*

Gilberto shrugged, his shoulders hunching. "You went off to dance with *la Muerta*, *profesora*. Months you been gone, and things going to hell." He acknowledged the pun with a curled lip, and the Eye hummed slightly in his grip. The chain trembled a little, its links scraping.

Like lovers' fingernails. I knew what that felt like.

Gil watched my face. "What you gonna do? We drowning. Losing turf every day, and *la otra cazadora* ain't got time to see the half of it. Weres getting squeezed onto Mayfair and the barrio, and I'm not thinking Mayfair gonna hold out much longer."

I shuddered. Mickey's was out on Mayfair, the only Were-run restaurant I knew of. Plenty of nightsiders caught a meal or a cuppa joe there, and it was relatively neutral ground.

Neutral, that is, as long as the hellbreed hadn't declared open war on Weres and were making it dangerous during the *day*. This was all sorts of wrong, and it pointed to something big.

Trust Gil to put it in terms of a gang war, too. It actually wasn't a half-bad metaphor.

The Eye quivered, dangling from his fingers. Every inch of skin on me prickled, as if I were standing on a flat plain right in a thunderstorm's path, the tallest thing around.

"*Profesora?*" The trembling in him was more pronounced. "What we do now?"

Like this wasn't a disaster in progress I didn't have a clue about how to start solving. It was like five shots of espresso and a bullet whizzing past, like dusk falling, a jolt that peeled back layers of confusion and woke me out of a stupor.

My apprentice was counting on me. Every soul in this city was counting on me to figure out what the 'breed were up to, and fast.

Why else had I been sent back? I'd said that. *They sent me.*

Sent, brought, what the hell, didn't matter. I tipped my head back, rolled my aching shoulders in their sockets. Leather creaked, and the gem on my wrist sent a little zing through me, a needle-sharp nerve-thrill.

Vacation's over, Jill. Get back to work.

Everything clicked into place. My chin came down and my eyes opened. I tapped two damp fingers on a gun butt, thinking, and Gil's face eased visibly.

"*Profesora?*" No longer tentative, but he was waiting for direction. The Eye made a low, dissatisfied sound.

"Put that thing back on, Gil. You're my apprentice; it's yours. I've got to go downstairs and break up that fight." I took a deep breath. "If I'm going to go *between*, it's better sooner than later. Anya'll hold the Eye while I do; it'll even drain it and solve two problems at once."

It was a great plan. It might even have worked.

* * *

The kitchen wasn't quite in an uproar. Still, Theron had wisely taken himself off somewhere, probably to the greenhouse.

Weres don't like conflict.

Galina stood near the butcher-block island, her hands up, glancing from one end of the room to the other like a tennis spectator. Saul, near the door to the hall with his arms folded and legs spread, actually *scowled* at my fellow hunter. "You're not. And that's *final*."

"I am not even going to—" Anya halted, glancing at me as I appeared in the doorway. A curious look spread over her face, and she dug in a right-hand pocket, still frowning at me. She fished out, of all things, a pager, and glanced at it.

That's right. I was dead, so she took over the messaging service. Either that or it was transferred to hers. I wonder if Monty moans at her about replacement costs, too.

"Montaigne," she said, flatly, and I almost started. "*Shit.*" She stalked for the phone by the end of the counter, and Galina's shoulders relaxed slightly.

"Hey." Saul's arms loosened. The circles under his eyes were fading, and I wondered how long it would be before Galina started feeding him, too. He was still too damn thin. "You okay?"

"Peachy." I did what I should have done in the first place—reached out, touched his bony shoulder. Fever heat bled through his T-shirt, and I reeled him in. He came willingly enough, and when I closed my arms around him he let out a shuddering sigh. He's taller than me, but his head came down to rest on my shoulder, his entire body sagging, and I held him. Slid my fingers through his hair, and I was still stronger than even a strictly human hunter. Because he leaned into me, and I held him with no trouble, just a little awkwardness.

"You don't even smell the same," he murmured. "But it's you. It *is*."

Was he trying to convince himself? My heart squeezed down on itself, hard. What could I say? *It* is *me, don't worry*? That was ridiculous, and a lie, too.

I wasn't sure just who I was, right now. And even though I didn't want him to worry, there wasn't a hell of a lot else he could do.

And really, it was time to worry. It was time to worry a *lot*.

"It's me," Devi said into the phone. A long pause, and the tiny scratch of another voice over a phone line brushed at the tense silence. If I concentrated, I could hear it more clearly.

I didn't. I stroked the rough silk of Saul's hair. "It's okay," I whispered, and the sheets of energy cloaking Galina's walls lightened.

Go figure. For once, I was being soothing. Should've known it wouldn't last.

"Really." Devi tapped her fingers on the counter, once. Frustration or impatience or habit, I couldn't tell. "Okay. Tell Eva to keep them away from that place, have her hold Sullivan and Creary there so we can question them. Do *not* let them go any closer to that—yeah, okay, I know you know. And relax. I've got good news for once."

Another short pause, then a jagged little laugh. "Very good news, Monty. Keep your hat on and have faith. We're on our way."

Faith? That's not anything I'd ever say, Devi. Sullivan and Creary—that would be Sull and the Badger, homicide detectives. Eva was one of the regular exorcists working Santa Luz's nightside, handling standard cases and calling me in for anything out of the ordinary.

Devi smacked the phone down like it had personally offended her. "Galina? I need an ammo refill. And some grenades."

"Got it." Galina sounded relieved to be given something to *do*. The herbs in the bay window breathed out spice, basking in a flood of sunlight that was no longer pale and brittle with winter. She took off at a dead run, her slippers whisking the wooden floor as the house settled with an audible thump. Her robes swished lightly.

Anya's attention turning to me was a physical weight. "Jill?"

Saul stiffened, but I kept stroking his hair. "That was Monty."

"It was. Saddle up, change of plans."

"Good deal." I tried not to feel relieved, failed miserably. "What's boiling over now?"

"Missing rookie cop. Vanner. Something about him being at a crime site and going shocky-weird?" Anya's tone was light, but the inside of my head clicked and shifted.

I let Saul draw away. "Vanner. I remember him." *Called him Jughead. Was always running across weird scenes.* "Where did they find him?"

"Eva brought him in a week after you disappeared. He was up at New Hill—"

I blinked. *Goddammit.* "What was wrong with him?"

"Catatonic. I gave him a looksee, but there was nothing we could do. They kept him in one of the barred rooms at the Hill; two days ago he vanished."

Jesus. A chill walked down my spine. Vanishing from

a barred room at New Hill is a Houdini act and a half. The last I'd seen of Vanner, he'd been in shock, in the back of an ambulance, after seeing me fight hellbreed-controlled corpses. "Vanished. Out of a barred room. Okay."

Anya nodded, the beads in her hair clicking as braids fell forward. "Well, Creary found him. She called in Eva, and as soon as that Faberge-painting bitch showed up, the rookie made a beeline for guess where."

"Where?" But a sick feeling began under my breastbone, a spot of heat like acid reflux.

I had the idea that I already knew where Jughead Vanner was going. It made a sick kind of sense, like cases start to do once they heat up.

Anya's mouth drew down at both corners. "Where else? Henderson Hill. The *old* one."

I couldn't even feel good about guessing right. Of course. Of *course* it had to be the one place a regular exorcist—and many nightsiders—wouldn't go. A psychic whirlpool of agony, fear, and degradation, especially since the great demonic outbreak of 1929, when the inmates had ceased being prey for sadistic jailors and turned into a buffet for Hell's escaped scions.

Ever since '29 hunters have been not just mostly outnumbered. We'd been outright fighting a losing battle, for all that we give it everything we have—and everything we can beg, borrow, steal, multiply, murder, liberate, or otherwise get our hands on.

It is not enough.

And what the hell was Vanner doing heading for that place?

Anya watched me, very carefully. Like I should know something else.

I kept my hands away from the gun butts with an effort. My face was a mask. I *did* know something else about that place. Or, more precisely, there was someone I suspected I'd find at Henderson Hill. Someone I wanted to talk to.

If he would talk. If I could *make* him talk.

So I ignored the tiny chills walking all over me. "Let's go."

"Not without me." Saul's hands actually turned into fists, his shoulders squared as if he expected round however-many-they-were-at-now.

I reached, once again, for diplomacy. It was a goddamn miracle. "It'd be nice if I could go with Devi to watch my back, and you stay here and fuel up. I can pretty much tell you're not going to go for that."

I was right. Again. When I didn't want to be.

"What part of *everywhere* do you not understand?" The question was mild enough, but his hands curled into fists again, and weariness swamped me.

The old me would have argued, or at least given it the old college try. He was safest here in Sanctuary...but he'd been taken from the street right outside. I remembered *that*. I remembered Galina telling me to calm down when I found out, up in the greenhouse. I remembered burning rubber out to the Monde, and something there waiting for me. Something huge, a thing I bumped up against the edges of, my brain shying away like a skittish horse. The black cloth bulging over that memory was wearing thin, little bits peeking out through its moth-eaten, merciful darkness.

Right now he's safer right where you can see him, Jill. So you can make sure nothing happens to him. Or you can kill whatever touches him.

With this amount of ammo and my knives securely strapped in, not to mention the creaking-new bullwhip, it sounded doable. More than doable.

It sounded good.

And if it saved me from descending into the chaos of *between* to look directly at whatever had happened to turn my memory into Swiss cheese and kill me, then bring me back...well. Maybe I was a coward for feeling relieved, but it was getting to where I didn't care as much as I should.

"Fine." I didn't recognize my own voice. "Get ready, then. You'd better go armed."

19

Out of the four of them, Eva took it best when we showed up. Sullivan went even paler than usual, only his receding coppery hair under his bleached-out Stetson showing any color. His thin hands twisted together, and he drew himself up and back into the inadequate shade provided by a warehouse's side as if I might not notice him if he hid well enough.

Montaigne, in an ill-fitting sports jacket despite the heat, stared. His bulldog jaw dropped, and he hadn't shaved in a while. Cigar smoke drifted across his scent, and the tang of whiskey. There were bags big enough to carry a week's worth of luggage under his eyes.

The Badger was actually in a tank top and jeans, the white streak at her temple glowing and her round, pale face sweating. She is, like some heavy people, astonishingly light on her feet, and many a perp has been surprised when he thinks the rotund little lady cop's the easiest one to escape or overwhelm. She acquired her nickname even before her streak began, working a downtown beat and quietly, in her own unassuming way, taking absolutely no shit from anyone. Right now she stared, and I had the uncomfortable idea that coming back from the dead is not guaranteed to keep you any friends.

Eva, slim and dark, hopped down from the hood of Avery's Jeep and strode toward us. She gave Devi a brief nod, looked curiously at Saul, and swept her long hair back over her shoulder.

Devi contented herself with nodding back, for once, and moved over into the shade. Sullivan let out a sound that might've been an undignified *eep*, quickly turned into a cough.

"Nice to see you." Eva blinked under the assault of sunshine, wiping her fingers on her jeans. "Christ."

Thanks. I was dead. I didn't glance back at the truck, where Saul leaned against the hood. The silver in his hair was bright starring, and he munched slowly on an energy bar while his eyes took in the street in controlled arcs. "Vanner. He was catatonic the whole time?"

"About as long as you've been AWOL, sweets. Ave and the boys will be happy you've shown up."

"You still dating Avery?"

She shrugged, and a small smile lifted the corners of her cheerleader-pretty mouth. And she apparently got the message, because she glanced away up the hill. "Sometimes I let him think so."

Even in the sun, you could feel a suggestion of a chill draft. She was right at the edge of the Hill's etheric shadow, and the only surprise about that was how far the stagnant bruising in the fabric of reality had spread.

Should really do something about that. But what was there to do? Banefire might burn the whole place to the ground and leave a blessing in its wake...but that amount of bane might turn into just-plain-fire at the edges, and with the slumped warehouses and converted offices hunching around here, we could be looking at a huge burnout.

Before, the scar would have provided me with hellfire. But hellfire around this sort of stagnation and misery would just drive the scar in deeper.

And with all the Hill's accumulating force to fuel it, it would spread even further. No, hellfire was *so* not a good idea.

"Good deal. So, yeah. How did Vanner present?"

All the amusement fell away. "Catatonic. Both me and Devi scanned him, he was...inert. In every possible way. I checked him weekly over at New Henderson Hill." She glanced up the street and actually shivered, her tiny gold-ball earrings winking before disappearing behind her hair and her safari jacket rippling. "Now?" Her shoulders hunched. "I think something's riding him."

"Possessor?" It was a risk, but they didn't usually go for men. Well, it was about 60–40 in favor of females. But Possessors favored morbidly religious middle-class shut-ins, not reasonably irreligious rookie cops locked up in asylums.

Still, anything's possible, and he'd gone shocky after brushing up against the nightside. And even before that, Vanner had shown up at a fair number of odd homicide or burglary scenes, crimes with a nightside connection.

We'd even joked about it. Or at least, Badge and Sully had.

Eva shrugged. "I don't know how he would've caught one, and there's no marks. He disappeared from New Hill two days ago, hasn't slept or eaten that I can tell. Slippery little fuck, whatever it is, but altogether too active to be a Possessor. Plus, it doesn't *smell* right."

Out of the four regular exorcists, Ave comes closest to being a hunter candidate through sheer adrenaline-junkie insanity. It's Eva who comes closest through cool calculation and the tendency to be three or four steps ahead of everyone else.

They make a good pair. I was actually hoping Avery wouldn't let her slip through his fingers the way he usually lets women go.

"So. Smart, mobile, smells different than a Possessor..." I tapped at a gun butt. "All right. You can take the cops and head out as soon as Devi's done. And *be nice*."

She spread her hands, a plain silver band on her left index finger flashing. "Bitch is the one with the problem, Jill. Not me. Can I just register how happy I am to see you?"

Likewise. If you only knew. "Duly noted. Hey, how have cases been lately?"

"Hopping. We're all working for the cops now, not just Ave, and on shift so we can get some sleep. It's never been this bad." And there it was, printed all over her dusky, weary face. The transparent, slightly squeamish relief you see when you show up to handle the weird so people can go back to Happy Meals and vodka tonics. Or what passes for normal to an exorcist. They're good souls, fighting the good fight, and some of them could almost be hunters.

But not quite.

"No worries. We're on it." I restrained the urge to clap her on the shoulder. Eva most definitely did *not* like to be touched. I wondered how Avery managed it.

"Yeah, well, it's been getting progressively worse the

longer *she's* been here. I mean, she handles it, Jill. But she's not you."

Oh, for Chrissake. "She's a hunter, Eva. Come on. I want to talk to the cops and then send you guys home. Monty's not sleeping again, is he."

"Murder rate's spiked. The media's blaming it on the heat, but..." Another shrug, her hands spreading. "Not just murder but all sorts of fun. Rape, arson, assault, and enough weird to make it feel like thirteen o'clock all day. We've gotten to the point where even triage isn't helping."

"Well, fuck. Come on." It looked like whatever case had shot me in the head and left me out in the desert wasn't over. I half-turned, glanced at the deserted street. Something was troubling my city. Of course the legions of Hell flood in when a hunter goes missing. We're barely enough to stem the tide as it is.

But this was exceptional. And when the exceptional shows up, a hunter gets nervous.

Saul had gone still, looking the same direction I was, the empty wrapper closed in his fist. I headed for the knot of cops, my trench flapping a little and Eva drifting reluctantly in my wake.

"It's about goddamn time," Montaigne greeted me. He coughed, and it had a deep rasp to it I didn't like. "Where have you *been*?"

"Dead, Monty. You want to keep asking questions like that, or you want to tell me what you've got?"

"Hi, Jill." Badge folded her ample arms over her equally ample bosom. She blinked, as if dazed. "You look like shit."

"Thanks." I glanced at Sullivan, who visibly flinched. It wasn't like him. Of course, he would probably have been an accountant if he wasn't a cop; he had a feel for the nitpicky detail and he liked things neat. That was his trouble—he liked everything all *explained*. "Vanner?"

"He's..." It was Badge's turn to glance around uncomfortably. Neither of the guys gave her a hand. "He's changed, Jill. He's scrambling around on all fours, but it's definitely him. Fast, too. Guerrero here says we're not supposed to get any closer to the old Hill."

"Yeah, that's a good idea. You know the drill." Everything clicked into place. This situation, at least, I knew how to handle. "Relax, boys and girls. Kismet's on the job."

"Thank fucking God." Monty muttered. "I suppose you need another pager, too."

"It wouldn't hurt. But I'll be with Devi, just buzz her for the time being."

He hunched his wide shoulders. "Fine. Jesus H. Menace to property."

Well, that was good. If Monty was bitching about property, he was relatively okay.

"I haven't blown anything up yet today, Montaigne. Give it a rest." *But you should've seen me the other night. I busted up the Monde but good.* Another chill walked up my back. The gem rang softly, like a crystal wineglass stroked by a delicate, damp fingertip.

Devi was staring down the street as well. She'd gone completely still. "Jill?"

"Let's roll. Go home, everyone. Good work."

"I suppose I can't tell you to be gentle," Badger called after us.

She probably *had* to say it. She is, after all, a mother.

* * *

The county put up a concrete wall around the old Hill after the Carolyn Sparks episode. Which was a reasonable response, given that that had involved a Major Abyssal, an untrained psychic, and a string of murders that made even a seasoned hunter blanch. I've seen the file—even with only black-and-white photos it's enough to give you nightmares.

Someone even occasionally tries to put a fresh padlock on the front gate. Come nightfall, however, the padlock is always busted wide open, shrapnel scattered in a wide arc, and the iron gates stand open just a little.

Inviting.

The gravel drive inside the gate was moving. Little bits of it popped up and turned over with an insectile clicking, as if the whole expanse thought it was popcorn while it's still just bursting sporadically. Before the big explosion.

I cocked my head and stared, one hand loosely on a knife hilt. It was, I suppose, a hunter's equivalent of a nervous tic. "Jesus," I breathed.

Anya laughed, a jagged, brittle sound. The gravel settled down, little gray stones twitching in the sunlight. "Thank God dusk is a ways off."

"Look." Saul pointed. Scuff marks on the scattered ground, and smears of something on the gate itself. My eyes narrowed, and I didn't need to get any closer to tell that the stains were fresh, and crimson.

Anya and I both drew our right-hand guns, a weirdly synchronized motion. We could've been on the stage.

"Take point." Anya indicated the gates. "I'll follow in three. Were?"

"I'm a tracker." Saul crouched fluidly, the fringe on his suede jacket fluttering. It almost hurt me to see how it hung on him; he was so thin. "I'll be fine. This is just like spot-jumping scurfholes on the Rez."

I blew out a short breath. "Okay. Give me three, Anya, then come in. Give *her* three, Saul, then you come in. If something's going to go wrong, it'll go in the first few seconds. Christ, I've never seen it so bad here."

"You sure about that?" But Devi, tight-lipped, just shook her bead-weighted hair with a heavy chiming when I glanced over. "We're burning daylight. Do it."

Still, I took another few precious seconds to study the gates. Wrought iron, quivering just slightly, and the gravel moving uneasily behind them. It shouldn't have been this bad.

Something happened here. Something fed the Hill. Shit. Inhale, exhale, watching the gates with their seaweed drifting, just a little bit too quickly to be the wind moving them, just a little too slow to be anything else.

Some hunters say it's not the big weird that wallops you the hardest. It's the just-slightly-off, the subtly wrong. Because it echoes inside your head and builds until you want to scream. I've lost civilians to both. Some people crack just seeing a body-modded Trader. Some go screamingly, eye-clawingly, gratefully insane when faced with something that breaks all their base-level assumptions about how the world works.

Still others take the whole enchilada, seem okay, then walk home and ventilate themselves.

You just can't ever tell. You can only visit the grave afterward and feel the horrific tightness in your chest that means you didn't do a good enough job protecting them.

Personally I think both the big and the little weird are hideous, and depending on when they hit, they can take the legs right out from under a normal person. Even a hunter gets a chill now and again. We're trained, and we're ready, but nobody is ever *really* ready for the weird all the time.

At least a hunter has an explanation, and a job to do.

The gates clanged wide, my boots hitting them squarely, and I landed on popping, pinging gravel. Little chunks of stone rose, whirling, and my aura fluoresced into the visible, hard little sea-urchin spikes tipped with points of light. That shell flexed, a sphere of normalcy asserting itself, and a tide of whisper-screams rose around me. My hair lifted on a not-quite breeze, and my left eye turned dry and itchy, untangling tricks of perception and snarled etheric strings. The lines quivered, and I could almost-See the passage of *something else* through here recently. More spots and spatters of blood. Someone was moving fast.

Well, at least we had a trail. And for a hunter, blood's as good as neon arrows.

The buffeting increased, but I had my feet planted, and the gem gave another high clear hard ringing all through my bones. I *pushed*, bearing down as if I was ripping a Possessor out of a hapless victim inch by inch.

Most often, they code and you have to jump-start their hearts and get them to a hospital. It's a tremendous psychic shock—all your mental cupboards torn open, furniture hacked apart, windows smashed, the Possessor digging in with its little claws, woven into mental architecture over weeks or months of dedicated pawing and fingering.

Pushing, pressure mounting behind my eyes, hearing the snap of a leather coat as Devi landed, the Hill rousing itself like a sleepy beast. An almost-physical click as the compression vanished, it was work not to stagger. My left hand was a fist, cramping, I shook my fingers out.

Saul was beside me, stamping his right leg twice. It was like striking a drum, and the driveway shuddered before it settled. His eyes were lambent even under the assault of sunshine, and as he straightened it was suddenly easier to breathe.

Anya's *bindi* flashed, the beads in her hair rattling, and it was a relief to see the same speckled sea-urchin shape to her aura. She opened her eyes cautiously, and took a step forward. The gravel was still in a perfect circle around her booted feet, just as Saul and I carried an area of eerie stillness with us. Outside those calm patches, the gravel popped up, flinging itself about knee-high.

We waited.

The Hill calmed slightly. It was rumbling and unhappy, quivering on the edge of sentience. Before, it would have been cold and tricky during the day, active and dangerous at night.

Now, even under the sun, it felt *treacherous*. And the cold was not physical. It lay under the daylight with its own heavy weight, a prickling like tiny feet wandering all over me, probing delicately into every cavity, tickling every inch.

I shuddered, threw the thought aside, and a buzzing rose momentarily inside my skull.

Oh, you tricky bastard. No, thank you. Another *flex*, sweat popping out along the curve of my lower back. Even with a hunter's regulation of body temperature, a few things will make you damp up.

Sorcerous effort. Combat. Sex.

Terror.

The black hole inside my head yawned, and for one vertiginous second I was skating its edge as the walls between me and however I had ended up in a shallow grave crumbled.

Oh, Jill, you are fucked for sure. A soft, merry voice, my own, inside the dark reaches of my skull. *Fucked six ways from Sunday and hung upside down, too. This was where it happened.*

Where *what* happened, though? I returned to myself with a jolt. Saul's hand over my shoulder, claws needle-poking through the tough leather, just felt, not breaking the borrowed skin. His mouth was close to my ear, warm breath on my skin, and for a bare moment a tide of hot feeling rushed through me, too complex to unravel before my sightless eyes blinked and started relaying information to my busy little brain again.

"Kismet?" Devi, thinly controlled.

"Steady." The gun was pointed down and to the side, thank God. "Steady as a rock, babe."

"Doubt it." But she set off, soundless over the gravel, with a sliding, rolling, hipwise step. "Follow the yellow brick road, children."

"Ding-dong, the bitch is dead," I muttered. Only, if the bitch was dead, that bitch was me. Under the dirt with my socks rolled up.

Great. Now was a bad time to be thinking those sorts of things.

Anya laughed again, but softly, lighting with a feral intensity that turned her into a very pretty woman indeed, blue eyes firing and her mouth turning up. *Hides her light under a bushel,* her teacher had remarked to Mikhail, back when we were apprentices. The sort of girl who would wallflower at a party until you actually spoke to her and realized what a sharp mind was behind that pleasant face.

She led along the trail and I swept next, Saul behind and slightly to my left. It was like moving after Mikhail, stepping only where he did, breathing only as he did. You can't get closer to another human being than when they're trusting you to do your job and watch their back. Anticipating, guessing, responding to every breath of chill intent against the skin, taking over the angles like clockwork so each is covered, gaze moving in smooth arcs, the little hitch in Anya's breathing when the gravel began to pop like shrimp in a sauté pan. It evened out immediately, and I thought our hearts were probably matching beat for beat, too.

She was heading for the main steps, and I wondered if the air inside was still reverberating from my last visit here—or at least the last visit I remembered. If the front desk was still smashed, if there was still violence in the air—and if there was a room upstairs where I'd taken apart a hellbreed-built altar, bile burning my throat and the banefire whispering and aching to escape my control.

And the scar on your arm aching as it tried to burrow in toward the bone, Jill. Don't forget that. Another soft, sliding, nasty little voice. *The little scar Perry gave you. The mark of Cain.*

Cain shot his brother, though. I just shot my pimp. And oh, Christ, I did not want to go back to that night, to the hole in Val's forehead and the ticking of the clock on the wall. The ticking that would turn into a buzz as tiny feet crawled over my rotting flesh.

"Stop." My voice cut the thick, cloying silence. "Devi. The windows."

She glanced up. "What?"

Someone—probably the caretaker who lived in the boiler room, with his filmed gaze, scarred face, and his quart of rye—sometimes haphazardly nailed boards over the windows. They were Band-Aids on gunshot wounds, mostly, with the look of just being put up for appearances.

But now those boards were gone. The five floors of Henderson Hill's public front—offices on the two lower levels, progressively tighter security on the next three, but no heavy equipment, that was saved for other buildings—stared at us with compound centipede eyes. Some windows were starred with breakage, but the chicken wire mostly held everything up. Scarred, but not broken. On some hungry, avid little windows the cracks looked decorative.

Like war paint, or the crackglaze in the makeup of an aging hooker.

"The windows. Some were covered, before."

She was halfway through a one-syllable obscenity when chaos broke loose.

20

*H*enderson Hill's front door shattered and the gravel rose in popping, excited bursts. I caught a flash of motion— something pale and human-shaped, flung aside as the attacker streaked down the stone stairs, straight for us, its claws making deadly little snicking noises.

The thing was long, and low, and bullet-lethal. Anya hopped aside, whip already in her hand and flicking forward neatly, and I'd already squeezed the trigger twice as Saul faded behind me. It moved like a hellbreed, stuttering through space, and was between us in an instant, snarling and hunching, blood steaming on it. The sunlight drew lashes of scorch-smoke from its hide, but it merely bared broken, shark-sharp yellowglass teeth and snapped, ignoring the assault of that clean light. Its eyes were coins of diseased green flame, and as soon as they locked on me the thing let out a shattering squealgrowl and doubled on itself, flexible spine cracking as its back scythe-claws dug in.

This was not a *ronguerdo*, a bonedog made by hellbreed that never ran by day. No, this was one of the creatures of Hell itself, and it was—

"Hellhound!" Anya yelled, the word disappearing into a string of gutter Latin as she chanted, hunter sorcery rising in thin blue lines as every inch of silver on her flamed.

Well, shit, I could've told you that. A flash of annoyance like bright sour sugar against my tongue, but the hound was in the air, body stretched out in a lean unlovely curve.

Hit me, sound like worlds colliding, blood exploding from my mouth, something snapping in my side as we tumbled. I shot it twice more and had my knee up before we hit the ground, flung gravel pelting both of us. The hound snarled again, a low rumble of Helletöng boiling from its narrow ungainly snout, and the impact knocked me free.

Up on my feet, ribs howling, boot soles sending up a spray of gravel as the gem poured a hot tide of strength up my arm. Leather flapping—those curved claws are *hell* even on tough cowhide—I skipped to the side, gun coming up and my left hand shaking my whip free with a quick sine-wave movement from my shoulder.

It was a relief to have a clear-cut problem in front of me, even if I coughed and nails of agony cramped through my left side. Creaking pops as the ribs snapped out and messily fused together, etheric force jolting through my bone structure like an earthquake through a skyscraper, and when the hound leapt again, steaming and smoking and howling in 'töng, Anya's chanting reached a fevered pitch behind me. If I could keep it busy enough, she could slow it down, then we could tear the goddamn thing apart.

What was in the door? But Saul was already gone, scrambling past us up the stairs and plunging into the Hill's maw. I had to forget about it, trust that he would take care of himself and—

CRACK. It hit me again, and this time we simply

blinked through space and smashed into the stone steps. The gem rang, a piercing overstressed note, and my scream was cut short.

If I'd been paying fucking *attention*, I would've used the whip instead of letting it smack me that time. More bones snapping, my head hit sandstone with stunning force and I actually pistol-whipped the thing instead of shooting it, my left fist coming up too, freighted with leather whip handle, and clocking it on the other side of its head. 'Breed mostly have a hard outer shell you can breach with silver, but hellhounds are elastic over hard bones, the skull a titanium curve under a gooshy, slippery-thick layer of congealed darkness birthing yet more scorchsteam as the sun lashed it. It reeked of corruption, and the gem hissed angrily on my wrist.

Anya's chant spiraled up into a scream. My left arm was up, and the thing's jaws closed, teeth driving in. It had its back legs braced and snaked its misshapen head, hot bloody foam spattering as it shook me like a piece of wet laundry. Lines of blue sorcery bit, driving deep, and Anya yanked back. If the thing hadn't been loosening up to take another bite of me, I would have gone with it as she whipped it back away from me, a hawkscream of effort escaping her as she pivoted, hip popping out and boots scraping through hop-bouncing gravel.

The thing howled like a freight train with failed brakes on a steep grade. Warm trickles sliding down my neck because the noise was *wrong*—it reverberated through the ice bath of the Hill's charged atmosphere and tore at sanity itself, an amplified squeal of psychic feedback.

"*Inside!*" Devi yelled, and I was already scrambling to my feet, letting out a scream of my own as broken bones

ground and my left arm *burned*, if its bite was septic we
were looking at fun times.

Never a dull moment around you, Jill. Get UP!

She didn't grab me to haul me up, but she didn't bound
past me, either. She covered as I made it, awkwardly, up
the stone steps, struggling into the building.

It was good tactical thinking. One-third of our force was
inside here, we had a civilian we needed to track and lock
down, and inside a building the number of approaches a
hellhound could use were reduced.

Blood spattered the scarred, ancient black-and-white
linoleum squares. I scrabbled through on all fours, rolled
while sweeping, and was on one knee with the gun braced
as Anya plunged through behind me.

I was right. I could see the damage from my last visit.
The monstrous wooden reception desk had a hole blown in
it, a jumble of wooden chairs and trash at one end of the
room vibrated uneasily, and Saul was on the stairs holding
down a writhing, spitting mass of paleness that had once
been Jughead Vanner. The hellhound had tossed Jughead
aside to deal with us, the bigger threat.

Might have saved his life. Goddamn.

One booted foot off to the side, his coppery fingers
clamped on Vanner's nape, my Were glanced at me and
his dark eyes widened slightly.

"Status!" Anya yelled.

I coughed, spat. Etheric force tingled all through me,
and my left arm cramped up as the gem fought whatever
toxin had been smeared on the thing's teeth. Or in its
blood-foaming saliva. Or whatever.

The world trembled and came back, the Hill shivering
all over. "*Jill!*" Anya didn't sound happy.

Buckle up, Kismet. Just buckle up. "Fine!" I barked, and shook the whip slightly. I had to swing my shoulder back and forth to do it, my arm had seized up. "Ready to tango. Saul?"

"He's strong." Quiet, clinical. "You're bleeding."

Well, no shit. That's how these things always end up. "I'll live, it's closing up. Devi?"

"What do you wanna bet that hound isn't coming back?" She moved back and to her left, finding a good angle, both guns covering the door. Outside our little spheres of normalcy, the air was thicker. Almost opaque, like dust-fogged glass. Paper trash twisted and ruffled at random, half-seen shapes flickering and my blue eye burning as it tried to focus *through*.

"I don't take losing bets." I levered myself up, coughed rackingly again. *Move it, Jill.* "Saul, what's wrong with him? Is he bit?" A hellhound bite could do any number of things to a person.

Bad things.

"Don't know." Saul's back tensed as Vanner writhed, bare toenails scratching the linoleum. The stairs groaned sharply, once. "Steady, friend."

It was hard work to lever myself up and turn my back on the door, even though I knew Anya was watching. My ribs ached, and my left arm flopped a little, huge jagged waves of pins-and-needles cramping up from my fingers, exploding in my shoulder, sliding down to grip at my ribs, grinding in my knees each time my boots hit the floor. Half-heard voices rose in a whispering tide, little unseen fingers tickling the edges of my vision. The bright spangles tipping each spike of my aura winked uneasily, little stars. "It's *bad* in here. Jesus."

"Something happened." Devi, carefully neutral. "My guess is that fucking blue-eyed 'breed was in it up to his neck." She paused. "And Belisa."

Yeah, I noticed my apprentice had the Eye. Subtle, Devi. "So it would seem." I approached cautiously, each step tested before I committed my weight. Thin traceries of steam rose from my flayed sleeve. "I'm cuffing Vanner."

"You sure it's him? Maybe it's his cousin."

"I'll revise my assumption when I get to him." The banter was supposed to soothe our nerves. I don't know how well it was doing for her, but for me, not so good. My arm came back to life in a scalding rush, and the flechettes on the whip's end jingled merrily as I stowed it. My fingers were finally obeying me again.

She magnanimously didn't mention that I'd pulled a rookie mistake and gotten myself hit. Nice of her.

Saul had our victim's right arm twisted up behind his back so far it looked ready to separate the ball joint; along with the knee in his back and the lock at his nape it looked reasonably secure. Which was wrong. Because even a weakened Were should have no trouble at all holding down a human, especially one that presumably had been lolling catatonic in a chair for months and shagging ass all over the city for the past couple days.

Oh yeah. This just keeps getting better.

21

It *was* Jughead Vanner, and something was seriously wrong with him. There was so much blood I couldn't tell if he'd been bitten. The reinforced silver-coated cuffs went at his wrists and elbows, and I flipped him over while Saul straightened, glancing mildly around like he was interested in the scenery.

"Jesus," I muttered, and the memory of the last time I'd seen Vanner hit me right in the gut. It was that house. The one with the dead girls a hellbreed had harvested organs from, the girls that got up and started moving while I was there. Vanner had come in—maybe to help, maybe to gawk, even though he knew the rules.

They all did. When I say *stay*, they stay like good little boys and girls.

Back then Vanner had been a big lumbering rookie, blue-eyed corn-fed All-American steak with a habit of blushing and stammering whenever I spoke to him. Now he was wasted down to pasty skin, bruised crescents of shocky flesh under his rolling eyes and the remains of a filthy, bloodsoaked hospital johnny covering a skinny torso that had once been an advertisement for weightlifting. He'd found a pair of canvas pants, too, and God alone knew what color they were originally. Now they were stained, smeared with sixteen different flavors of street grease and claret, and he'd lost control of some very basic functions most of us get a handle on before we're three.

Wonderful.

I grabbed Vanner's unshaven chin. The hair on his cheeks was more stubborn than the mop on his head, once leonine blond and high and tight, but now just a few soft strands over a naked white domed scalp. His jaw worked loosely, spittle drooling down his chin, and he shrieked.

The Hill shrieked back.

Mottled rashing burns spread down Vanner's throat, a distinctive bright-red wattling. Like radiation. The other skin was dead white, and it rippled as his back bowed and he shrieked again.

Ohshit. "Vanner?" I snapped. "*Vanner!*" I found his first name with a lurching mental effort. "*Christopher!*"

He moaned, far gone, eyes rolling up, their whites yellowed as old teeth. His bare heels drummed into the linoleum as I wrestled him back down. "Something in him all right. Can't tell what it—"

"Jill!" Devi moved forward, light even steps. "Incoming!"

Poor Vanner. He'd run so hard, and so long, and he had reached the end of it. There was a boom and a snarling of Helletöng as the hellhound hit Henderson Hill's front door, and the skin over the parasite-thing breeding in a Santa Luz cop, one of *my* cops, peeled back and burst.

The unhuman shape came up out of him in a looping stream that resolved itself into a narrow canine head, sharp

needle teeth made of basalt and slick eggwhite ectoplasm
clinging along it. Bones crackled, forelimbs lengthening
and hindlegs shortening, muscle roiling and shifting as it
assumed its shape. The 'plasm splattered, and the bits of it
that hit the Hill's turbulence hung in midair, spinning little
milky spheres. I was chanting myself now, bastard Latin
strung together in an ancient prayer pagans had stolen and
Christians had stolen back, and thin blue lines of sorcery
snapped into being. My apprentice-ring sparked, the three
charms in my hair did too, and I went over backward.
The whip doubled and looped, caught just over the thing's
head, locked up as its teeth champed an inch from my
nose. It had mad, wide blue eyes burning with unholy fire,
and it was slick-wet with the noisome fluid of its birth.
Short blond hair bristled all over its hyena-shaped body,
and for a single sickening moment my blue eye saw Vanner himself in the thing, his hands turned to needle-fine
but lethal razor claws and his entire body a lean compact
weight. Like a nightmare the thing scrabbled at my chest,
and another massive sound was the hellhound and Anya
screaming at each other, gunfire popping and Saul's en-
raged roar.

This is not good not good not good—my fingers, slick
with ectoplasmic goo, didn't slip. I tightened up, shoving
the thing back, and it choked, spraying me with more
foulness. *Goddammit, get up and help them! That's a hellhound! Saul's over there! Fucking kill this thing, get up
and kill the other thing, and let's get this* done*!*

The gem shrieked, a crystalline, overstressed note, glass
tearing apart instead of breaking. Red pain jolted up my
arm, exploding in my shoulder, and for a long moment it
was Perry with his lips on my skin again, the scar melting

with sick delight, him fiddling with my nerves and trying to make me respond. To jump in any direction, as long as he could just get a reaction, *any* reaction, from me.

It's not the scar it's something else the scar's gone ohGod the scar's gone where—

The hole in my memory gaped, yawning...and I fell in with the hot breath of the beast on my face. The Hill screamed like a woman in labor, and time...stopped.

The Sorrow rose. She cast a glance back over her shoulder, her face slack and terribly graven. Bruises crawled over her skin, the shadows of Chadean sorcery doing what they could to ameliorate the damage. But she was in bad shape, bleeding all over, her tangled hair smoking at each knot.

Each inch of silver on me ran with blue flame. My head was full of screaming noise.

"Kill," Perry hissed, from where I'd kicked him. "Kill it now!"

I lifted my gun, slowly. It was a terrible dream, fighting through syrup, my muscles full of lead.

Belisa's chin dipped wearily. She pitched forward just as the egg stopped spinning.

The thing that slid its malformed hand through the barrier between this world and Hell twitched. I heard myself screaming, sanity shuddering aside from the sight. They do not dress when they are at home, and when they come through and take on a semblance of flesh it's enough to drive any ordinary person mad. Wet salt trickles slid down from my eyes, slid from my nose and ears.

They were not tears.

There was a rushing, the physical fabric of our world

terribly assaulted, ripping and stretching. My screams, terrible enough to make the Hill shudder all the way down to its misery-soaked foundations. Perry, hissing in squeal-groan Helletöng, and under it all, so quiet and so final, Mikhail's voice from across a gulf of years. Long nights spent turning over everything about his death, remembering him, all folding aside and compressing into what he would say if he was here. Or maybe just the only defense my psyche had against the thing struggling to birth itself completely.

Now, Mikhail said. Kill now, milaya. Do not hesitate.

My teacher's killer was in the way.

The scar crunched on my wrist. I squeezed the trigger. Both triggers, and I saw the booming trail of shockwaves as the bullets cut air. Belisa's fingers had turned to claws, Chaldean spiking the soup of noise, and she tore at the not-quite-substantial flesh of the thing. Blue light crawled over her as if she wore silver, the same blue that the caretaker's eyes had flashed. The shadows of the Chaldean parasite flinched aside, for some incomprehensible reason.

I was still screaming as the bullets tore through her and the egg as well. The collar made a zinging, popping noise, the golden runes sliding over the collar shutterclicks of racing, diseased light. Her body shook and juddered as she forced the thing behind the rip in the world back, and the physical fabric of the place humans call home snapped shut with a sound like a heavy iron door slamming. The bristling, misshapen appendage thumped down to the floor.

Belisa's fingers, human again, plucked weakly at the collar. She was a servant of the gods who were here long before demons, the inimical forces the shadowy Lords of *the Trees trapped in another place long ago. It was a Pyrrhic victory; the* Imdarák *didn't survive their victory, either. And the Sorrows are always looking to bring their masters back. The 'breed? Well, they're always looking to bring more of their kind. It's like two different conventions fighting over the same hotel.*

If anyone could have slammed a door between here and Hell shut, it was a Sorrow.

But why? And the caretaker, what was he—

My knees folded. I hit the ground. Henderson Hill whispered around me like the end of a bell's tolling, reverberations dying in glue-thick air.

Oh, no.

Belisa folded over. I'd emptied a clip. Sorrows can heal amazingly fast, but she was probably exhausted after all the fun and games.

Her knees hit the concrete in front of the altar. Blood flowered, spattered on the floor. She shook her head, tangled hair swaying. The golden runes on the collar snuffed out, one by one.

"Ahhhhh." It was a long satisfied sigh, escaping Perry's bleeding lips. "Oh, yes. Yesssssssssss.*"*

The scar drew up on my wrist and began to ache. This wasn't the usual burning as I yanked etheric energy through it. I tore my eyes from Belisa's slumped form and turned my right wrist up.

The print of Perry's lips was not a scar now. It was black, as if the flesh itself was rotting, and it pulsed obscenely. As I watched the edges frayed, little blue veinmaps crawling under the surface of my flesh.

And I knew why. I could have shot around her.

But I'd chosen not to.

* * *

The dog-thing that used to be Vanner hung motionless
over me. Further away, seen through vibrating, glassy air,
Anya Devi extended in a leap, her long dark hair a silver-
scarred banner. One of the bullets was just exiting the gun
in her left hand, the explosion behind it clearly visible.
Saul crouched on the grimy black-and-white squares, the
fringe on his jacket unsettled, standing straight up. They
were utterly, eerily still.

The hellhound itself was leaping for Anya. It was
wounded, sprays of black ichor hanging behind it like fine
lacework scarves.

"We have a little time," he said.

Henderson Hill's caretaker crouched easily next to me,
stroking the sleek head of the canine thing on top of me.
Same faded coveralls, with the snarl of embroidery hiding
his name. His eyes were bright clean blue, no longer
filmed. And the shadow of scarring on his face was clearing up nicely. Alone of all the things at the Hill, he'd
always just looked solid.

Normal.

Well, this sort of shot the idea of *normal* in the head,
didn't it? He wasn't any species of nightsider I'd ever come
across. He was something else. I'd been wanting to talk to
him, and I'd thought I might find him here. Or even just a
clue to where he was likely to be hiding once he dropped a
quarter in me, pulled my arm, and set me spinning.

He'd brought Belisa to the operating room and turned
her loose on the hellbreed in there. He'd also bought me
breakfast right after I clawed my way out of my own
grave. He'd given me my gun and my ring.

Which made him a question mark, at best.

I blinked. *What the fuck?* My fingers cramped on the whip, I kept the tension up. Everything stayed still, the movie of life paused and nobody thinking to warn me about it. So I wet my lips and wished I hadn't, something foul was spread on my face. "What. The fuck."

He grinned, a boyish expression, while he scratched behind the dog-thing's ears with his expressive, callused hand. The shadow of sorrow in those blue eyes didn't lighten. "Do you know how liberating it is to actually *speak*? Don't worry," he added in a rush. "I mean you no harm."

Oh, I'm not so sure about that. "Get this thing off me." A harsh croak, something stuck in my throat.

"Can't. I can only break the laws of the physical so far. Little Judy, listen to me."

I went stiff. Resisting. My jaw creaked when I finally loosened it enough. "Don't. Call me. That." *That's a dead girl's name, and I've had enough of people saying it to me.*

"Very well. Kismet, then. You named yourself for Fate, didn't you. As a holy avenger. Much the way your predecessor Jack Karma did. You're rather amazingly alike; all of you choose those like yourselves. It's…" He shrugged slightly. His tan workman's boots made a small sound as he shifted, their rubber soles grinding on dust and dirt. "It hurts to see, sometimes."

"What the fuck *are* you?" I breathed. Because the gem was making a low, satisfied note, and the flood of etheric energy up my arm had turned warm and caramel-soft.

Well, that answered *that* question, didn't it.

"Call me Mike. I'd shake your hand, but you're busy. Kismet, Hyperion must be stopped."

Hyperion?

My brain did another one of those sideways jags. *Perry. That's what other hellbreed call him. Galina calls him Pericles, because he's old. Mikhail just called him "that motherfucker at the Monde."* My breath jagged in, with a ratcheting sound. "No kidding."

"You don't understand. *Everything* has been according to his plan. Everything. Except your final act—the little break in the pattern. Do you remember what you did?"

My head ached, fiercely. The buzzing came back, rising inside me on a black tide. "No." I struggled, achieved exactly nothing. I was nailed in place. I could breathe, and my heart was a live wire jumping and sizzling inside my chest. I could even tighten up on the creaking leather of the whip.

But I couldn't move.

"You sacrificed yourself, Kismet. For the sake of many." He was grave now, a blush of color high up on his cheekbones. Before, he'd been horrifically scarred, the gray film over his eyes somehow making him gentler. This man looked like the caretaker's handsome older brother, his hair lifting and curling, taking on a richer gold. "That makes…certain things…possible."

Now it was a laugh, tearing free of my resisting chest. "What things? What the hell?"

He leaned down even further. Those eyes were pitiless, terrible. They were not burning with a hellbreed's fire. No, they were simply sad. A sadness like a knife to the heart, numb grief when the night rises and the bottle is empty and the voice of every failure and weakness starts to rumble in the bottom of your brain like a bad earthquake.

Cops get that look after a while, sometimes in stages,

sometimes all at once. Other hunters, too. Sometimes, looking in the mirror while I smeared eyeliner on, I've caught glimpses of it.

It's the look of seeing too much. Of being unable to turn away.

"Go to Hyperion. Do what is necessary to convince him you're intrigued. Pretend your friends have thrown you out, whatever you like. But *go*. I am asking you to play Judas to a hellbreed, so that when he laughs in the moment of his triumph you can strike him down. You can be our avenging hand."

Which brought up the very first question I needed to ask, the first of many I wanted fully answered. "And who the hell is *we*, white man?"

I didn't think he'd get the joke, but he smiled. It was a terrible smile as well, that sadness staining through the expression, and a sick feeling began right under my breast-bone. A low, nasty buzz mounted in my ears, little sticky feet probing and tickling all over my face, down my throat, down my aching, immobile body.

"You know who we are." His shoulders set.

"I don't know a single—" I began, but my heart was skipping triple time, and his hands were coming forward. He was going to *touch* me, and everything in me cringed away from the notion. "No. Don't. *Don't.*"

"I'm sorry," he whispered. "I would bear this for you, if I could."

I strained, black spots dancing at the edges of my vision, sweat rising in huge pearly drops, terror like wine filling my veins. I made a helpless sound, and I hated it immediately. It was the gasp of a very bright, very needy dark-haired girl huddled in her bedroom or shivering on a street corner, a girl under someone's fists. A girl begging and pleading. *Please. Please don't. Oh please don't.*

"I have been with thee from the beginning," he said very softly, and his fingers clamped on my head. White light exploded inside my skull, and it *hurt*.

It was like dying all over again. Or mercifully—or maybe just practically—I can't now say what it felt like. I can't remember.

And I don't ever want to.

22

*H*ip popped up, heel stamping down, massive lung-tearing effort and the doglike thing spun to the side as I wrenched its head and flung it. Shove at the head and the body will follow; it's a basic law of anatomy. My whip reeled free, flechettes spilling out with a jingle, and I was up in a hot heartbeat, whip end snaking out and me right behind it. Throwing myself across space to crash into the hellhound at the apex of its leap, whip looping and turned taut, straining. Gunfire popped, bullets splattering behind us, and I wasn't quite sure why I'd done this.

Then I remembered. Saul.

We hit the shipwrecked desk, and my right hand was full of knife hilt. The blade slid in, twisted, the silver laid along its flat flaring with sudden blue radiance, and the warmth on my chin was blood as the thing snarled in my face. It couldn't get any purchase; the whip was now wrapped around it and pulled tight, my legs clamped around it too and the tearing in my side was ribs broken, *again, dammit, can I just go five seconds without another bone snapping please God thank you—*

I bent back as the head snaked forward, teeth snapping near my throat, rank hot breath touching my chin and Henderson Hill shuddering again on its foundations. The knife punctured its gluey hide, cut deep, drag on the blade as unholy muscle gripped it, silver hissing and sparking as it grated hard against ribs. Tearing it free, rolling, splinters shredding against my coat's surface, the cubbyholes behind the desk exhaling dust as a current of bloodlust foamed up their surface, and I cut the thing's throat in one sweep.

Arterial gush sprayed, thin black-brackish and stinking. I blinked it away, knee coming up, and realized I'd almost taken the hound's head off. The neck broke with a glassy snap as I heaved it aside, dusty corruption racing through its tissues; it slumped off the desk and fell.

The voices in the air around me sighed, a hundred little sharp-toothed children all exhaling in wonder. For a moment the Hill pressed down, the psychic ferment shoving against my aura like it wanted to get *in*.

I pushed air out past my lips, *hard*, blowing through a thin scrim of hellbreed ichor. The shit was all *over* me, dammit. But there was that second thing to worry about too, and I was already rolling, dropping off the desk with a jolt, legs and ribs protesting as etheric force hummed through me and I shook the whip, the knife spun and held with the flat of the blade back along my arm. Anya could shoot the fuckers all she wanted, but my forte was knife-work, and it was looking like I could take a hell of a lot more damage than she could.

You know what we are, he whispered inside my head.

Mike. What kind of a name was that for what I suspected he *might* be?

Anya was covering the door. Saul stood, brushing his shoulders gingerly, as if he'd been showered with dust.

"Where?" One clipped syllable, but I said it too loud and the foyer rippled. The spangles of Anya's aura, their spines popping out and shifting uneasily, roiled as she sighed and slowly lowered her guns. Her coat creaked a little as she did, and the tension humming through her made lines of force swirl in the thickened, dusty air.

"It ran off." She spared me one swift, very blue, very annoyed glance. "You want to tell me what the *hell* just happened here, Kismet?"

"Something was *in* Vanner. It busted free, I slapped it pretty hard and took out the hellhound, and Vanner... Jesus Christ, what *was* that? I haven't seen anything like that before."

"I have. Dogsbody." Tight and unamused. "Why the fuck did it run off?"

Gooseflesh rippled under my skin before training clamped down on my hindbrain. I shivered. *No fucking way.* "*That* was a dogsbody?" *Should've taken my head clean off. Jesus Christ.* "It can't be. Nobody's bleeding." I shut my mouth, realized how absurd it sounded. "Well, except for me. But that's normal."

"Take a look. That rag laying on the stairs is just skin. That rookie's a day-running dog full of hellhound venom now, and we'd better get going if we're gonna track him."

"No need." My mouth was numb. The knife slid into a sheath, I slid my right-hand gun free just in case. Everything inside me was shaking and shivering. An internal earthquake, bits popping and shattering inside my skull, puzzle pieces dropping into place.

Still too much I don't know.

"No need," I repeated. The Hall quivered, and a cold draft blew between us, rustling paper trash with a sound like drowned fingers slipping free of their skin. "I know where he's going."

* * *

We made it back to Galina's just as afternoon shadows began lengthening. The heat was a hammerblow, the worst of the day, and Anya was white-knuckled on the steering wheel. The way some of the shadows were twisting oddly, I didn't blame her. And with Saul riding terribly exposed back in the truck bed, it was a nerve-wracking slalom for me, too. Especially since I could swear we were followed, or at least *watched*. I just couldn't tell who was doing the watching.

Anya slammed the absinthe bottle down on the butcher-block table. Venomous green liquid sloshed inside it. "All right. I've had it. Talk."

Galina still kept the Jack Daniels in the cabinet above her ancient Frigidaire. I had to go up on tiptoe to get it, and I left a smear on the fridge's chilly white enamel. The hellhound's ichor was drying to a gummy black paste on me, and I was filthy with the ancient dust of Henderson Hill.

Low golden light fell over the herbs in Galina's kitchen window, and the Sanctuary was in the door watching both of us, her hands tightly laced together. Her tone was soft, conciliatory. "He's downstairs pacing. Theron is watching him. Gil's trying to escape through the sunroom, and Hutch won't come out of the vault."

"Vault's a good place for him." I worked the top free, considered the bottle, and took a long pull. It burned going down, and I could pretend it was the alcohol heat making my eyesight waver. The gem purred on my wrist. "Nervous type, our Hutch. Has anyone told him I'm alive?"

"Jill—" Galina, trying to forestall the explosion.

It didn't work. Anya Devi had waited long enough. "Kismet, start *fucking talking*. I've been keeping this town on the map since you disappeared, and now this? *This?* You just vanished and reappeared across a whole fuckload of empty space. Not even hellbreed are that fast. And why didn't that dogsbody tear you up, huh? What did you *do* out there?"

The world stopped, and I had a visitation from a hallucination. I grimaced at the fridge. My hair hung in long strings, matted with hellbreed ick, and I didn't have nearly enough silver to tie into it. "Do you believe in God?"

"What?" My fellow hunter sounded about ready to have a heart attack.

I didn't blame her. "It's a simple fucking question, Devi. Do you?" I took another hit off the bottle, to stop myself from saying more.

"No." Sharply, now. Liquid sloshing inside a bottle. "I believe in booze, and in ammo, and in being prepared. But God? No. *Fuck* no."

"Neither do I." It gave me no comfort to admit it. "I pray like everyone else, when my ass is going to be blown sideways. But I don't believe. Hellbreed I believe in, and they predate anything we might think of as *God*, right? By a long shot."

"I like history." Anya drummed her fingers on the tabletop. "Really I do. And philosophy's a great discipline too. Foundation of the humanities. But for fuck's sweet everloving sake, Jill, not *now*."

I held out my right hand. It shook, slightly, the tremor running through my bones making the flesh quiver. I didn't have a lot of flesh on me to shiver, still scrawny as hell. My stomach twisted on itself, and I was guessing my metabolism was burning as hot as a Were's for a while to speed the healing. My ribs were tender, and my shirt was a blood-soaked rag.

Also, I needed to calm down. Unfortunately, that didn't look like it had any goddamn chance of happening.

I stared at the Frigidaire and the smears I'd left on it. I fouled everything I touched, didn't I. I had from the beginning, from the moment I ruined my mother's rootless life by being conceived. Then there were her fist-happy boyfriends, and the street boys, and Val. So many shapes of men.

And Mikhail? If I'd been better, faster, stronger, maybe he could have told me about the bargain he'd made with Perry. He wouldn't have hidden it from me, which meant maybe Perry wouldn't have been able to jerk me from one end to the other and play me so neatly—and finally, finally trap me.

"I remember what I did now," I whispered. "I damned myself. Didn't I."

"Galina." Scrape of a chair as Anya stood up. "Give us the room, huh? And keep the boys downstairs."

"But—" Galina must have swallowed any objection, because the next sound I heard was her bare footsteps shushing away.

They sounded, for the first time, like an old woman's shuffle instead of a girl's light step.

Devi approached, softly but definitely making noise. "Something on your mind, Jill? You bleed clean, and I don't know what that thing on your wrist is, but it isn't hellbreed. I bet you went out into the desert and played one last game with Perry, and got free the only way you could." Reasonable, even, spacing out the chain of logic. "That far, at least, I can get on my own. But what the fuck else, Jill? What else happened?"

I blinked, a trickle of warm salty water easing down my filthy cheek. The booze wasn't doing any good. It might as well have been milk.

I am asking you to play Judas to a hellbreed. Either it was a hallucination who'd bought me breakfast and slipped Belisa's leash, or it was real. If it was real, I was just given my marching orders, wasn't I?

But orders from who, and why? And if it *wasn't* real, was it because I wanted to go back to the Monde? Or because I was looking for a way out, any way out of what was going to happen next, so I could ease my conscience and go riding off into the sunset with Saul? Leaving Anya to pick up the pieces. If she could.

She'd certainly try. She was *hunter*.

What did that make me?

"Belisa's dead." I weighed both words, found them wanting. The rest stuck in my throat, but I had to force them loose somehow. "I shot her because I wanted to. It wasn't a clean kill, Devi."

"Yeah, well." She paused. I sensed her nearness. "I don't blame you. But that's not the point, is it."

Thank God she understood. But of course she did.

She was a *hunter*. We commit the sin of murder every night, we who police the nightside. When you're trained to do that, when mayhem is an everyday occurrence, you have to have something to keep you from going over the edge. From making you worse than the things you hunt.

There's a lot of words for it, but I've only ever found one.

"No. It's not." I capped the bottle again. "Perry's planning something big. The caretaker out at Henderson Hill is in on it somehow. I've got to dig further." The half-formed idea that had been trying to wriggle its way out from under a bunch of soupy terror finally came out into the light, and I let out a long sigh.

Thank God. One card in my hand, at least.

Devi folded her arms, leather creaking. "Okay. What do you need me to do?"

Because this was my city, right? I was the resident hunter. Even if I'd clawed my way up out of a grave and couldn't remember my own fucking name, I was *responsible*. There was no getting away from it. If I did drive off with Saul, sooner or later I wouldn't be able to live with myself.

And we all knew where *that* ended, didn't we. With me between the rock and the hard place, where I had all the freedom in the world—but I could only make one choice, because of who I was. How I'd been made.

Oh yes, God exists, even though I don't believe in Him. He absolutely exists. And He is a sadistic fuck.

I gave myself a mental shake. *Focus, Jill.* "Tell Galina to keep Saul here. Keep him in the vaults if you have to. He's going to go nuts, but if you let him outside alone, he's going to die." *Perry will kill him. Just to show me he can.*

He wasn't even safe with me, no matter how much I wanted him right where I could see him. How craven of me was it to let him come along to the Hill, even?

Self-loathing turned to spurs right under my skin. It was difficult to think through the noise in my head, but I managed.

Anya didn't hesitate. "Done."

Well, that was the easy part. "Call Montaigne and have him list Vanner as a line-of-duty casualty. Full honors and a memorial service. We don't have a body and we never will." The rag of skin left behind at the Hill wasn't anything we could bury, and was eaten by banefire now anyway. A thought occurred to me, I went up on tiptoes again to put the JD away. If I kept looking at it I was going to finish the whole damn bottle, and with a metabolism running this hot it wouldn't do any good. "Get hold of Badger. Have her pull every car Vanner's owned in the last four years off the DMV and list them for you. Keep my pager, I'll use that number and Galina's to check in." *If I'm still alive to check in. If I pull this off.*

"Okay."

I wasn't imagining it. She actually sounded relieved I'd started firing on all cylinders again. *Stop it,* I wanted to say. *You're a full-blown hunter too. What the fuck do you need me for?*

Well, I was Santa Luz's hunter. I was also the only damn person who could possibly worm Perry's big plan out of him.

Lucky, lucky me.

"Get Hutch on the computer." I couldn't believe I was saying it, staring at the fresh smudges and smears I'd left on Galina's cherished icebox. It looked like a thirties-era rendition of a spaceship, all rounded and solid, the Frigidaire logo polished but still showing little signs of age. Rusting and flaking, its chrome giving up the battle.

Evan a Sanc can't completely stop time. "Have him beg, borrow, hack or tap everything he can about Perry. Especially about what Perry was doing in the twenties. Tell him not to worry about anything, I'll authorize whatever he wants to do retroactively. You understand? Give Hutch the T1 line and carte blanche. Get *everything* on Perry, but don't let Hutch leave Sanctuary either, even if there's books he needs at the shop. Have him find them in some other library, twist whatever arms you have to."

"Jesus." It was the first time I ever heard her sound shocked. "All right. What else?"

"Saul. Tell him…"

She waited.

"Tell him I'm coming back. Tell him even dying won't stop me, and he's not allowed to let himself waste, because I'm going to need him."

She said nothing. Maybe she knew it was a lie. But when I finally turned on my heel and looked at her, I found out her cheeks were wet too. Her hands were fists. The scar down her cheek flushed, and for a moment she was so beautifully ugly my heart threatened to crack.

"And you be careful. I'll keep Perry as busy as I can, but this is likely to be nasty."

She found her voice. "What about Gilberto?"

My conscience squirmed. I clamped down on it as hard as I could. "Gil's coming with me. We're going to visit someone." *If he wants to. If he decides to.*

But he was my apprentice. I already knew what he'd say.

23

Melendez still lived on the north edge of the Riverhurst section, where the lawns were green and wide under the bloody dye of dusk. Sprinklers were going full tap among the fake adobes and the few Cape Cods, the expensive mock Tudors and other ersatz-glitz refugees. If you wanted truly antique houses you would go over to Greenlea where the yuppies elbowed each other over twenties mock-Victorians and organic boutiques. Or toward the edge of the suburbs, where there was a belt of poverty-stricken structures from the forties and fifties hanging on from before the blight of tofu housing development started.

Gilberto yanked the hand brake. I didn't ask where he'd gotten the small black Volkswagen from; in return, he didn't ask me what we were doing. He kept it below the speed limit, obeyed all traffic laws, and generally piloted the thing like an old granny. He even whistled tunelessly below his breath. Like he was having a good time.

Since Mama Zamba had disappeared, Melendez was no longer jester of the local voodoo court. He didn't have Zamba's appetite for gore and grotesque, but he did have a stranglehold on power—and he was in very good odor with his patron Chango. Anyone who parlays with a non-human intelligence is suspect in a hunter's book, but I was living in a glass house at this point. Not only that, but Melendez had been...helpful, once or twice. In a limited sort of way, when he could see his own advantage.

Or when I had him by the balls.

The noise in my head had cleared a little, and I was feeling more like myself. Gilberto ghosted behind me, stepping only where I did, his pulse slow and even. I glanced back, and the half-grin fell off his face, almost shattering on the sidewalk.

This is serious business, I'd told him, *and there needs to be no goddamn funny stuff. No face, no insults, no nothing. You keep your manners on, your mouth shut, and you don't draw unless I do.*

Si, senora bruja, he'd said, and it looked like he meant it.

Melendez's faux-adobe hacienda sat behind its round concrete driveway. A brick bank in the middle of the heat-shimmering concrete held heavy-blooming rosebushes, a monkey puzzle tree, and a bank of silvery-green rue. Lemon balm tried its best to choke everything else in the bed, but aggressive pruning held it back. The fountain in the middle of the driveway was bone-dry, the concrete cherub who was usually shooting water out of his tiny little peeper looking sadly dejected. My smart eye watered, but I detected nothing other than the usual febrile etheric congestion.

Afternoons Melendez was usually ministering to the faithful at his storefront out on Parraroyos, nonprofit under the tax law but donations encouraged, drumming and chicken dinners pretty much every night. Today, though, I was pretty sure he'd be here. That's one thing about being psychic—sometimes you're home when someone wants you.

Gilberto hung back as we approached the wide iron gate, until I motioned him forward. I very pointedly did not ease a gun free of the holster. Busting in shooting and yelling wasn't going to be necessary, no matter how much I liked the idea.

"Be cool, Gil."

"I am very fuckin' cool, *profesora*. Don' worry bout me none."

I shouldn't be bringing you here. I swallowed hard and crossed the driveway, checking the sun. Not much daylight left.

Everything around me rippled, chills spreading down my spine. The gem sang, vibrating on my wrist. I kept going, stepped through the gate, the courtyard closing around me. Another fountain here, seashell shaped, also dry. Was he having trouble paying his water bill? Not likely.

I didn't even get to ring the bell. As soon as I stepped up to the door, there was a sound of locks chucking open. The door creaked as it swung inward, and a rotund little Hispanic male eyed me. He wore a bowling shirt festooned with pineapples, a pair of jeans, and there was a hint of a smile around his wide mouth.

"Senor Melendez." I kept my hands where he could see them.

He studied me for a long, tense-ticking fifteen seconds. His gaze traveled up over my shoulder, and I knew Gilberto was staring back. Melendez waved one pudgy hand, as if shooing away an insect. He examined me from top to toe, taking his time.

I suffered it.

"*Ay de mi*," the little butterball finally breathed. "*Ay, mamacita*, you took *El Camino Negro*. And you come back."

No shit. "I've got a few questions."

He nodded thoughtfully. "Bet you do. I just bet you do." He seemed content to just leave it at that, sucking at his upper lip, and didn't move. The heat was a thick blanket, I tasted sand and rot, and buzzing rose inside my head. A ghost of sweat touched my back, training clamped down and I kept my hands loose with an effort.

"Melendez." I didn't raise my voice. "Your cooperation is *not* optional."

"And what about *mi patron*, eh?" He grinned, his teeth shocking white. The spirits paid for good dental care, at least.

"His isn't optional, either." I stepped forward, Gilberto following silent behind me. Melendez retreated, and the cool and quiet of the voodoo king's house enfolded us.

* * *

The kitchen was stainless steel and sharp edges, a blue-tiled floor and every surface painfully scrubbed. The light was warm and electric, even though there was a wide window looking out onto the blue shimmering jewel of the pool in the backyard. A faint tang of cigar smoke hung in the air-conditioned breeze, and the tall silver fridge stopped humming. Uncomfortable silence rose, and when I pointed Gilberto dropped onto a tall stool at the breakfast bar. His shoulders hunched before I gave him a meaningful look; he straightened and buttoned his lip.

Nice to know I still had the quelling glance.

Melendez opened the fridge. Glass clinked, and he came out with a couple brown bottles of expensive microbrew. He cracked the beers with practiced twists, and handed me one. "You got to know," he said finally. "You owe Chango a bullet, *bruja*. Don't think he forgot."

"I haven't forgotten either. This is about something else." I took a long pull off the bottle. "Time's a factor, Melendez. So spit it out."

He took a pull off his beer, made a face. "I ain't got much to spit. It ain't pretty out there, *bruja*. Faustina on Seventy-Third, she dead. Mark Hope, he dead too. That cocksucker on Martell Avenue with his fancy cigarettes, gone. Luisa de la Rocha, Manuelita Rojo, that Dama Miercoles bitch, they gone too."

"Wait. Hang on." I stared at him. *That's every big mover in the voodoo community, for Christ's sake.* "All of them? You're telling me they're dead?"

"Well, they ain't in fucking Baja, fuck." He took another pull. "*Es Los Otros, los diablos.* No warning. *La Familia*, they gave no warning. Just, one second everything fine. Then bam! Dead, dead, *muerto*, and the spirits screaming about the treaty broken."

Gilberto shifted uneasily on his stool, his hands cupping his sharp elbows, and under his sallowness his pitted cheeks were pale. He stared at me, and I was abruptly reminded of just how young he was. Had I ever been that wide-eyed?

"No warning? When was this?"

"Couple months ago." Melendez's eyes glittered sleepily, hooded. The cigar smell drifted across the room, and a thin thread of smoke curled up from the open mouth of the beer bottle.

This just keeps getting better. "So the hellbreed all of a sudden started killing voodoo practitioners. The movers and shakers. Why are you still alive?"

A sneer twisted his plump face. "I in *strong* with Chango, *bruja*. You know dat. He tell me long as I stay inside he protect me. Now here you come. What you want, eh?"

It took several long throat-working swallows to get the beer down. I didn't taste a single bit of it, which was a shame. Nothing like getting an unexpected gift to make a cold beer go down nice and easy.

"I want to talk to Chango." Might as well get it all out in the open. "About several things, but we can start with Perry."

"*El Diablo Rubio?*" Melendez paled and set the bottle down with a click. Beads of condensation on its surface glittered. The pool sent dappled reflections through the window, making a pattern-play on the roof. "Aaaaaah."

The lights flickered. The reek of cigar smoke thickened, and my hand dropped casually to a gun butt. Gilberto hunched on the stool, his eyes wide, and as much as I wanted to give him a reassuring glance, I didn't. I watched Melendez, who seemed to swell inside his chinos and blinding-white shirt.

"*El Diablo Rubio,*" I echoed softly. "*Si. Buenas tardes, Senor Chango.*"

A long, low, grating laugh, too big to come from Melendez's chest. Smoke rose from his cuffs, eddying in swirls that opened like crying mouths. Little fingers of vapor threaded across the tiles, reaching for me. "*Buenas tardes, hija.*" It wasn't the little man's voice—it was richer, deeper, and crackling with authority. "Still owe me *una bala*, bitch."

"I haven't welshed yet," I reminded him. My bitten fingernails tapped the gun butt. "Perry, senor. I'm looking to hand *los diablos* a world of hurt, and I haven't forgotten the help you gave me last time."

The spirit riding Melendez's body rolled his shoulders back in their sockets, his rib cage oddly torqued. Tendons popped, creaking. The smoke billowed, knee-deep now, but swirling uneasily away from me and Gilberto.

It eyed me, a spark of red inside each of Melendez's dilated pupils, before his eyes rolled back in his head. Still, the spark remained, burning against the whites, a tiny blood-gem.

My right wrist ached, force humming up my arm and shaking my shoulder. I waited.

"*Una bala*," he said finally. "In *el rubio diablo's cabeza*. You kill him for us."

Well, isn't that handy. It was my turn to shrug. "That's the plan. What can you tell me about *El Rubio*'s little game?"

The bloody pinpricks rolled, fastened on Gilberto. "Why you bring him here? Little man in a big man's house. He got too much brag in him, *bruja*."

"Don't you look at him." Snap of command, I straightened, and my fingers had curled around the gun butt. "You're dealing with me, *padre, no me chingues*."

And God help me, but it reminded me of the first time I'd seen Perry down at the end of the bar in the Monde. Mikhail had said very much the same thing, and at the time I hadn't wondered why they seemed to know each other, since Perry had been new in town. The old hellbreed who used to run Santa Luz had just died a bloody, screaming death, but I hadn't seen it. I'd been locked up at Galina's during *that* whole set of events, still an apprentice, prowling and trying to escape through the greenhouse too.

Nothing ever changes, Jill. Ever.

The spirit twitched. Melendez's whole body jerked, knees bending. His boat shoes scuffed against the tiles, a sad, squeaking sound. "We lost too many, *bruja hija*. Not weak, but you on you own. I look after *mi hijo* here much as I can, and him *only*, when dat *rubio cabron* come callin'."

"Understood." And it was probably for the best, too. "What's Perry planning, senor? Tell me everything, leaving nothing out." That was the most important question, and I didn't know how long the *loa* would ride his horse. The smoke thickened, curdling.

Melendez's body let out a long slow hiss. "*La Lanza.* Yes. He aims to use *la Lanza*, and open the door all the way."

My skin chilled, gooseflesh threatening to rise. "Open the door?"

"Between here and *there*, *mi hija*. Between you and them. Like they did before, *mi hija*. This time they have *la Lanza*, and it will prop door open like broomstick."

Oh, my God. There was only one thing that could possibly mean. I went cold all over, and glittering little insects with sharp tiny feet prickled me everywhere. "*Y la Lanza? Que es eso?*"

"*La Lanza.*" Another long hiss of escaping air, another frothing billow of cigar smoke. "*El rubio*, he hide it under the eyes of *los santos*, and he lie to keep you away from it and from *los padres*, *sus amigos* no more. *Es la Lanza del Destino*, and *los diablos* can't touch it. Only *las marionetas de carne*, the ones they bargain with."

Oh, Jesus. Jesus Christ. I hadn't realized I was gripping the counter with my right hand. Indigo tiles groaned as the gem made a low melodic sound, and I had to work my fingers free with an effort. I'd left splintered marks. "Tell me where, *senor de los parraroyos. Where* are they going to throw the party?"

But Melendez swayed. "Owe me a bullet, bitch," the spirit rumbled through his mouth, and the entire kitchen rattled. "Go serve it to *el rubio.* And if you die before you do it, I find you, and I make you *pay.*"

Oh, no worries about that. "Don't threaten me." I couldn't kill a *loa,* but I could make things very uncomfortable for his followers.

If I survived this.

"*La puerta no debe abrirse, bruja.* Stop him. They send you back for this."

Really. Thanks. I would never have guessed. My mouth was so dry I had trouble forming the words. "*Gracias,* senor."

Melendez sagged against the fridge. He held the beer bottle like it was an artifact from another civilization, and I was momentarily grateful Chango hadn't been in a glass-chewing mood. You don't get hurt doing something like that—the spirits take care of their own—but it can be uncomfortable. Afterward.

His eyelids fluttered. Normal human eyes now, dark, their pupils humanly round but flaring and constricting wildly. His knees buckled, I caught him before he hit the ground, the empty beer bottle flung away. Gilberto was off the stool, his hand flashing out and closing around the neck, neatest trick of the week, and the Eye on his chest sent a dart of bloody light splashing against the window.

Melendez lay in my arms like wet washing, curiously boneless before consciousness flooded him again and he stiffened.

"Easy." I braced him, he was so *light*. A breakable doll in a breakable world. "Easy there, senor. Everything's co-pacetic."

You're in shock, Jill. But I just held him until sanity flooded his dark gaze again, conscious of the smell of his aftershave—something heavy and orange-musky, expensive Florida water. I got him on his feet by the simple expedient of pushing myself up, strength humming in my bones even if my knees were suspiciously mooshy. I got him propped against the counter, and I think it was the first time I'd ever seen Melendez actually, honestly terrified.

"Gil." I glanced through the thinning smoke. It smelled like a bar in here. "Get us a few more beers, huh?"

"*Si.*" My apprentice was still pale, and the Eye gleamed against his narrow chest. His flannel shirt flapped as he straightened and headed for the fridge.

"*Madre de Dios,*" Melendez breathed.

"No shit." I made sure he was steady enough to stand. My brain thrashed like a rat in a cage, I took a deep breath and forced stillness. *I need a plan, and a good one. Don't have one. So I guess we just wing it. As usual.* "We need to talk, Melendez. I'm leaving Gil here for a while."

24

Night fell hard on Santa Luz, sinking her teeth in and shaking a little. Neon greased the dry streets, and the whole city was restless.

I walked into the Monde like I owned the place, steel-shod heels clicking and my coat swinging heavily. I hadn't stopped to clean up, so I was covered in hellhound filth, but I had borrowed a handful's worth more of charms from Anya. I tied them into my hair while sitting in the parking lot, in Gilberto's little Volkswagen.

As armor, they sucked, even though they ran with blue light the deeper I penetrated the etheric bruising laying over the nightclub. But I had my gear, and my coat, and my aura flaming with bright spikes. I had the eyeliner, now smeared and messy enough to make me look bruised under the scrim of decay. I had all the ammo I could carry.

I even had a couple grenades; they'd been packed in the trunk. Gilberto was a sneaky little boy, but right now, I wasn't going to scold him. No, I was just going to hope he was sneaky enough to stay one hop ahead of everyone.

Just like me.

The damned pressed close. All hellbreed tonight, and all beautiful. Every single one of them aware of me as I forced my way to the bar. And it was time for another shock, because in addition to the two Traders dispensing libations there was a familiar, lined face and a pair of filmed, sightless eyes. Riverson's hair was a shock of white, and he moved with jerky, mechanical quickness. Every motion looked painful.

Serves you right, motherfucker. Still, he'd tried to warn me. Too late and too little, but he'd tried.

Unless that was part of Perry's royal mindfuck, too.

Riverson went dead still as I approached, one of his hands holding a bottle of Stoli, the other cupped around a delicate fluted glass. I didn't quite turn my back on the mass of 'breed writhing on the dance floor. The damage from my earlier visit had been repaired, and the disco ball was sending little screaming jets of light all over. Whenever the lights paused, you could see they were shaped like skulls. Laughing little skulls.

Well, that's an interior decorating trend that's never going to hit the big time. At least, I hope it won't. It's so fucking tacky. I reached over, quick as a snake, and grabbed the Stoli bottle. Took a healthy slug, saluted Riverson. "Well, hello, you helltrading sonofabitch," I yelled over the noise. "How's tricks?"

His mouth worked wetly for a moment. One of his teeth had been broken, a jagged stub that must have hurt like hell. His fingers tightened on the glass. "You shouldn't be here!" he finally yelled back. "God *damn* it, Kismet, you shouldn't *be* here!"

I took another belt. As a bracer, it didn't do much. The thought of Gilberto out in the dark, deep in Riverhurst with a voodoo king who made most Traders look sweet and innocent, was better.

Still, Melendez was at least as frightened of me as he was of Perry. He'd keep Gil safe tonight and put his part of the plan in motion. More than that I couldn't ask for—and if he didn't take care of my apprentice I would come back and do more than break a few dishes.

I was *through* with fucking around.

Riverson stiffened. The glass shattered in his hand, and all expression left his face as blood welled between his clutching fingers.

I felt him arrive like a storm front, a flash of paleness and his fingers were over mine. Perry took the vodka bottle, raised it to his lips, and grinned at me, the blandness dropping for a moment. High cheekbones, bladed nose, sterile beauty shining briefly before the screen of average came back up. His bright blue gaze fastened on me, indigo threads staining his whites with an inky vein-map, and the music took on fresh frenetic urgency.

The disco ball sped up, and the assorted hellbreed leapt and gamboled. They drifted away from the bar to pack the dance floor, faces blank and beautiful, the twisting of rot underneath candygloss corruption flickering through them like wind through high wheat.

The woman, Mikhail had reminded me so often, *has advantage in bargain like this.*

And God, I was hoping it was true.

"You shouldn't be here." Perry's lips shaped the words, they sliced through the jet roar with no difficulty at all. "Not yet."

Come on, Jill. This is just like working a sharkjohn. The kind that will pay double if you perform according to his little script. The cold calculation wasn't a hunter's totting up of percentages and averages—no, this was an older feeling.

It was the mental scrabble that lights a ratlike gleam in a quarry's eyes. The *how can I make this work for me* gleam, the one my mother used to get when her boyfriends got too drunk or too loud and she started thinking about how to make their attention fasten on something else, anything else.

Even me.

My right hand flicked forward. I grabbed the bottle, slid it out of his hand, and took another hit. The glass was too warm, body-warm, and the thought that his lips had touched it sent a bolt of hot nausea through me.

I tipped the bottle further. Liquid chugged and churned. I kept swallowing, and Perry's gaze dropped. Not high enough to be watching my mouth, not low enough to be watching my chest.

He was staring at my throat as it worked, the liquor sliding down and exploding in my stomach, a brief heat lightning. The tip of Perry's cherry-red tongue poked out, for just a bare second, gleaming wet and rough-scaled.

The last of the vodka vanished down my throat. I slammed the bottle down, a gun crack that managed to cut through the music. My apprentice-ring spat a single spark, bright blue and quickly snuffed.

"*Do svidanye,*" I yelled, and I grinned with all the sunny good humor I could muster. "Hello and good night!"

Perry cocked his blond head. The light ran over him, the tiny skulldapples screaming as they touched the pressed linen of his suit. He was even wearing bleached suede wingtips, for God's sake.

You're carrying this much too far. Maybe the vodka was affecting me after all. But no, I just felt cold all the way through. Making myself ice, the real me curling up inside my head and a stranger taking over.

The stranger was hard and cruel, and she had no trouble surviving. She'd shot Val in the head, and she was the one Mikhail had rescued from a snowbank that night. It was probably *her* who made me refuse to die. Certainly she'd been the one who had pulled the trigger in that circle of banefire, breaking my skull and brain open for the hornets to devour.

I might be weak, but that bitch never gave up. And I was going to need all of her to pull this off.

Okay, Jill. It's time to start the game.

Still grinning like a goddamn fool, I reached out.

And I grabbed Perry's hand.

25

The room upstairs was no longer so white. Maybe I was just seeing it through a screen of vodka heat, or my own hopelessness. The carpet was softer, dove gray, and the bed was still crisp but cream instead of a bleached cloud. The mirrors all looked dimmer, not hurtfully clear and bright, but the television screens still held their familiar news feeds, static crawling from one to another in blinking, random loops and whorls.

I let go of Perry's feverish, marble-hard fingers and took perverse pleasure in stamping smeared tracks across the carpet. Vaulted the mirrored bar, my dirty hand leaving a streak on its surface, and examined the bottles. "Not much of a choice here, you know. I've always wanted to ask what's in these." *Talking too much, Jill. Bring the focus back to him.* I looked over my shoulder.

Perry shut the door, and his fingers flicked. There was the *chuk* of a lock engaging, and he stood for a moment with his pale head down. The hand I hadn't touched was in his pocket, and for a moment he almost looked human.

Almost. Except for the little ripples passing through him, as something else twitched under the surface.

I selected one bottle, full of shimmering sapphire liquid. It looked oily. I touched its slim neck, pulled it forward a little. A little more. It teetered on the edge of the glass shelf for a long heart-stopping moment, plummeted.

The crash went right through the room. Perry didn't move. Blue liquid spread out slowly, gelatinous. Steam lifted from its surface.

I selected another bottle. This one held shifting gray smoke, a screaming face in its depths becoming a picture of dismay as I tugged, sliding it exquisitely slowly across the shelf. Again, the teetering, the will-she-won't-she.

Oh, she will. She always will, but on her own terms.

It was so easy to break. I flicked a dirty, chewed-down fingernail, the bottle plummeted, and the smoke oozed up with a small sound, like a cricket's breathless chirrup in the distance.

"Stop," Perry said mildly.

But he didn't move, so I did it again. This time I selected a tall thin bottle full of a milky white liquid that spun strangely when I scooped it up and hurled it across the room.

Before it hit the wall he was suddenly *there*, but I'd anticipated and was on the bar again, boots grinding as I landed cat-footed, and he skidded to a stop.

I didn't go for the whip.

He was on the other end of the counter, his wingtips placed just so on the glass surface, solemn-faced as he hardly ever was. That was wrong—I wanted him smiling, but still. I'd rattled him.

Good for me.

We examined each other, standing on the bar like a couple of cheesy B-movie gunfighters. The indigo was gone from his eyes. They were very blue, shadows moving in poisonous depths. "Dangerous," he said, again very quietly. "For you. Here."

Well, let's see if we can't get you interested. "I'm for sale, Pericles. Bid high."

His gaze had fastened on my throat again. "What is this, Kiss? A misguided attempt at sacrifice?" He cocked his head, his cheek twitching just slightly before it settled. "What do you remember of the last time you tried?"

All of it. The hornets buzzed and prickled, pinprick mouths chewing at my flesh. Eating my brain, scouring my skull. "Enough."

"Really." His fingers flicked, and a silver chain dropped from them, running with blue sparks. His face was set in a grimace, like he was smelling something hideous. It was in his shadowed hand, the one he'd tried to reach through the banefire circle with.

I wondered how long it had taken for the fingers to uncurl and uncramp, if it had hurt when the skin started to grow back.

The chain held a rose-carved ruby as long as my thumb. I'd used it as a key for the sunsword after Mikhail was dead and the Eye of Sekhmet stolen by his killer. The stone was cracked now, but still alive with clear crimson light. It sizzled, still vibrating with the shock of its wearer's death.

My death. I tasted vodka fumes and bitterness, the sharp metal tang of fear. If you're not afraid when dealing with hellbreed, you're not paying attention. Inattention is just *asking* to get fucked up six ways from Sunday, and all the way to breakfast too.

"For you," he said lightly. "A memento, worn next to my heart. The only thing I allowed myself to keep."

You buried me. Well, isn't that sentimental of you. For a moment we stood, sizing each other up.

"I remember enough," I repeated. "Come on, Perry. I'm sure there's other buyers. I'm a useful tool."

"How do I know you'll stay bought?" Whimsical, now. "Oh, darling Kiss. Don't play this game with me. You'll lose."

That's yesterday's news. I already lost. But we've already established I don't know when to fucking well quit. "You don't know *what* game I'm playing, Perry." It was time for a bit of truth turned sideways. That was a hellbreed specialty—just enough honesty to bait the lure. You can't deal with them, night after night, and not know it. Know it—and know how to do it yourself. "I spend my nights killing hellbreed, but there's always more and more of you. And all of them, all those oblivious fucking people I kill you to protect, they fall all over themselves making deals with you night and day. The world threatens to end and I yank it back, I break every bone in my body, I even put a bullet through my own head and you know what? Even then I'm not allowed to rest. I'm *tired*."

He dangled the necklace, ignoring the silver biting at his hand. Sparks popped. "As are we all. The point?"

Shit. "You're not interested. Fine." I hopped off the counter.

Or at least, that's what I had planned. He hit me in midair and we slammed into the wall near the door with a rattling crunch. The gem hummed on my wrist, sleepy under the weight of honeyed etheric corruption.

Perry inhaled, his nose buried in my throat, his hands

clamped around my wrists. He only had an inch or so on me, if I dropped my knee and brought the other one up I could nail him pretty hard, or I could kick and take out *his* knee and wrench myself sideways, breaking free, my hand slapping on a gun butt.

But I didn't. I just hung there, silver pressed against my right hand dangerously warm, responding to hellbreed contamination. The ruby dangled, scorch-bright, and my breath came in shallow rasps. Heat rolled off him, a terrible cold fire, and even if the thing inhabiting his skin wasn't human it felt like he had a pretty respectable hard-on. Shoved right up against me.

Oh, we've been here before. At least he's interested, right? Good sign, wouldn't you say?

I told that rabbit-jumping part of me to shut the fuck up and struggled to control my pulse. My heart settled into a high, hard thumping, ready for fight or flight, adrenaline touching the back of my tongue with a copper finger.

"I didn't say I had no interest," Perry breathed against my throat, obscenely warm and wet. Condensation gathered on my skin, and every inch of flesh on me crawled. "I didn't say that at *all*. Please, continue."

Sure instinct ignited in my head. *Now* I could bite back. I gave him a love tap to the knee and shoved him, and he stumbled away. I punched him, too, a good hard crack that snapped his face aside, and I finished with a ringing open-handed slap on the other cheek. Just like I hadn't taken the next step to turn this into more of a fight, now he did not. He simply stepped back another foot or so, making a quick sideways motion to resettle his jaw. Then he dropped his chin and looked at me.

The dirt on me had smeared on his linen, too, but the

grin was back. It was wider than ever, his patented old
I-could-buy-this-if-I-cared-to expression, its sheer amoral
good will capable of sending a shudder up even a hunter's
spine.

I met it with my own fey careless grimace, defiance and
terror gasfumes just looking for a spark. My pulse settled
down, dropping into the high-spaced gallop of impending
action, and I knew he could hear it. The music thudded
away underneath us, but neither of us paid any attention. I
straightened, shook my right hand out once, fingers loose
and easy. The gem had gone quiescent, but etheric force
hummed through my bones.

"Don't fuck with me," I said tonelessly. "I'm *this* close
to walking out, Perry, and you'll never see me again. I'll
retire to fucking Bermuda while you're still here thumbing
your ass and playing little hopscotch games with whatever
hunter comes along to replace me."

He took this in. Swung the ruby in a tight, tense little
circle. It sparked, once, a bloody point of light. "What am
I buying, my lovely? I seem to remember being cheated
once before."

"*You* welshed. Not me." It was out before I could stop
myself, but his grin widened. He spun the ruby, the chain
making little groaning noises as it whirred, faster and
faster. "Don't you ever want to find out what would happen if I was willing? Or are you one of those stupid
bastards who just likes the chase?"

A little moue now, the flush on his cheek where I'd
hit him dying down and leaving him pale and perfect
again. "It *has* been a long chase. And full of such tender
moments. I find your homicidal little displays charming,
darling, and you know how much I...*love*...you." The

snarl drifting over his face sent a ripple through the entire room. Behind him, television screens fuzzed with static.

Oh, good Christ, if this is love, I don't want to see hate. "It's not love." I folded my arms and raised my chin. The air tightened, and I knew this dance. If he jumped me again we were going to have a hell of a tango. It wouldn't stop until one or both of us were bleeding, and once I started beating on him, I wasn't sure I would stop.

Or vice versa.

So I pulled out my last card and threw it on the table. "You're the only one who understands, Pericles." Soft, as if the admission was pulled out by force. "A fucking hellbreed, and you're the only one. You *know* me."

And like all good lies, it was true. I hadn't gone on mortgaging bits of myself for the glory of it. Sometimes I hadn't even for the speed and strength a hellbreed scar could give me.

No, sometimes—*plenty* of times—I'd done this just to see if I could. To walk right up to the edge, to prove I was different from him, to make him respond. To get out the razor and make the mark, and laugh at the sting.

There was no way he could play with me so effectively, otherwise.

Idiots, Mikhail sneered in my memory. *They think we do this for them. Is only one reason to do,* milaya. *It is for to quiet screaming in our own head.*

Every time I walked away from Perry breathing, it was like walking away from a car wreck, leaving an old life behind and striking out for parts unknown. Like being pulled out of a snowbank by a pair of hard callused hands and told *Not tonight, little one.*

Maybe it took shooting myself in the head before I could admit I *liked* having the power to play with him, too.

God help me. But there was no help for this. I was on my own. Like always.

Perry stared. The tip of his wet, red tongue slid out again, touched the corner of his bloodless lips. His eyes glowed, twin blue infernos casting shadows down his cheeks, and the air behind him ruffled into two points of disturbance high over his shoulders. The reek of spoiled honey trembled around us both. A buzz of chrome flies in chlorinated bottles mounted, matching the wasps' singing as their little mouths and feet prickled all over me. The cracked ruby swung, its circles shrinking as his slim hard fingers curled.

He's not going to bite. "Fine." I took two steps toward the door, sliding along the wall. "See you."

"You actually surprised me." His fingers flicked, the necklace vanishing into his palm. Now the dark threads were in his eyes, spreading from his irises, eating the whites. "I thought you would love life too much, like all those other insects." His fist tightened, a narrow artist's hand clutching at a coin for a magic trick. Shadows slid over the skin like clouds reflected in a glass of milk, and blue sparks struggled between his clenched fingers. "But not you, my Kiss. No. You were already dead, so pulling that trigger was no trouble at all." Quietly now, the softest and most seductive of all his voices. "You've been dead a long time."

There was no way I could argue. I was dead long before Mikhail plucked me from that snowbank. I'd been born dead, and fighting it didn't make much difference. The whole thing was pointless, except for Saul.

Oh, God. I couldn't think about him right now. At least he was safe.

Perry took a soft, gliding step closer, infinitely slow. "They suspect you, don't they. Your fellow hunter, your Sanctuary, the beasts you call your friends. You can feel the suspicion breathing on your back, and it *twists* in you, doesn't it. Knife in the wound." Another step.

It wasn't true. It *wasn't.*

But I was shaking. Because Anya had checked to see if I was bleeding clean. Theron hadn't been suspicious at all, Weres weren't like that. If I'd still been tainted somehow, if I hadn't had the strength to pull the trigger, it would have fallen to Anya to hunt me. To keep me from doing any more goddamn harm.

It wasn't true.

So why was I trembling? In great waves, weapons shifting and leather creaking a little as they slid through me. The closer he got, the more I shook.

It was because I knew that tone, the soft reasonableness. He was about to slide the knife in, and I had to stand there and let him do it.

"Or maybe it's that you suspect yourself," Perry murmured. "You always have, Kiss. You push yourself so hard, because down at the very bottom, *you* understand *me.* We're twins, my darling, and I waited so, so long for you." A soft sigh, and he was so close now the exhalation touched my hair, too warm and too damp. "We are the ones crying outside their circle of light. We are the ones they cast away. We are the sufferers, and on our backs they build golden cities." His fingers were on my shoulders, very gently, and he eased me forward.

It's not true, I reminded myself. *Perry never suffered a day in his hellborn life. Never.*

"Do you remember your visits to me?" he whispered into my hair.

Another shudder went through my bones, this one violent, and his heavy, marble-hard arms closed around me, cold water dragging at a swimmer's boots.

Of course I remembered.

Most often, he would have me strap him into the iron rack in the other room, and the rosewood case with the blades was always on the little gurney. He would order me to start cutting, and he wouldn't make a sound as the bright metal parted his flesh and made hellbreed ichor run in thin black stinking streams.

"Do you remember what I said, each time you stopped?"

More, he would whisper, or let out with a breath like a sob. *More.* The shaking had me all over now. Great, clear drops of sweat cut through the filth on me, one of them tracing down my cheek like a tear, another fingering the shallow channel of my spine.

"If I atoned enough, my darling Kiss, do you think I would one day bleed as red as your oblivious ones? I've tried. You've *seen* me try."

Oh, God. The water was closing over my head. He sounded so reasonable, and I was exhausted. There was no way this was going to work.

"You're hellbreed," I whispered, but it was the last gasp of a drowning woman.

"Even a hellbreed can dream." So softly, into my hair, a spot of condensation on my scalp. When he stepped backward I didn't resist, I came with him. He walked me across the room, and he loosened the coat from my shoulders. It fell away like a heavy skin, and he unbuckled the weapons-harness and let that fall, too. The ammo belt lay on the floor like a snake, and the bed was cloud-soft. I sank into it like I was falling through heavy water, and the mattress didn't creak as it accepted his weight next to mine.

You can do this. It's Judas to a hellbreed, you can do this.

But I was horribly naked, and on a bed with him. The worst part was that it felt...familiar.

Not safe. And not comfortable, even though the bed was soft and I was filthy and hungry and so tired. And most definitely not like lying next to Saul—

I stiffened, shut that thought away.

The hellbreed made a small, soothing noise. He held me, arms like flexible stone, his chin atop my head. "Rest," he said, very softly. "Just rest, Kiss. You're so very tired. Sleep."

The music coming through the floor was a heartbeat, and we floated in the bed. He even stroked my dirty hair, so gently, despite the silver that hissed and crackled at his nearness.

"Or if you can't sleep," he murmured, "simply close your eyes, and I will do the rest."

And I did. We lay there, hunter and hellbreed, and he made soothing little noises while I sobbed.

26

There was a shower in the white-tiled room I'd often cut Perry up in, and my skin crawled at using it. But the water was hot, the towels were fluffy, and I kept an eye on my coat and my weapons the whole time. I probably didn't have to, because the hellbreed was playing house with a vengeance, humming to himself while he brought the towels in, arranging them just so. He brought me a stack of black silk T-shirts—medium, V-neck, three-quarter sleeve, just what I liked to wear in cotton. And leather pants, too, and I had to shudder when they crawled up my hips. They fit like they'd been made for me, and wasn't that thought-provoking?

He even watched me get dressed, but that wasn't a huge deal. Dating a Were will give you a whole new definition of nakedness, and I've been tied down naked to an altar and almost-sacrificed. Skin doesn't bother me.

But the way he licked his lips with that rough cherry-red tongue was disconcerting. And even more disconcerting was shrugging into my coat and finding it clean. It also reeked of candyspiced wickedness, just like the whole

Monde. My hands roamed, finding the pockets full of ammo, everything as it should be, my whip at my side and my guns heavy at my hips and everything right with the world.

When I turned around again, blinking under the sallow glare of fluorescents, Perry was holding something. A flat case, rosewood, balanced on his palms. "For you."

Another present? My stomach turned over, hard. The case was just the right size for one of those shiny knives, the kind that weren't silver because they didn't react to him. Light and razor sharp, with hatching on the handles for a better grip.

They were so *cold*.

I froze. The iron rack was set off to one side against the wall, but if he sauntered over to it and ordered me to strap him in...

He actually rolled his eyes. Back in the linen, immaculate, but even his tie was raw pale silk now. Those shoes of bleached suede were creamy against the white tile. "It's not going to *bite* you, darling. That's past."

Oh, is it? It would be idiotic to relax now. So I just stood and looked at him until he made a small amused sound and passed one hard, narrow hand over the top of the box. There was a click, and the lid opened like a flower.

There, on rich red velvet, were the charms. Honest silver, each one running with blue light in the choked atmosphere, and a spool of red silk thread to tie them with. Nine of them, twisted shapes, fluid and somehow-wrong, creatures that walked under no earthly sun, clawed and furred and winged, vibrating against the velvet.

The silence from downstairs was deafening. Was it the

middle of the day? My internal clock was all wonky, and I hadn't slept. Or had I? I'd drifted in and out, rocked in Perry's arms. The familiarity bothered me.

Well, I had so much else bothering me at this point, it was pretty academic, wasn't it?

"A hellbreed giving me silver." I addressed the air over his head. "Now I *have* seen everything."

"Not quite." Did the bland smile falter slightly? It came back as soon as it slipped. "Do you like them?"

On the one hand, all the silver I could get my hands on was a good idea. On the other, I wouldn't put it past Perry to make them start crawling over my scalp, digging in with their sharp little pinprick feet.

"They're gorgeous." And they were, in the twisted way the damned are beautiful. I swallowed. "Thank you."

Did he actually look *pleased*? "Well." A slight cough. "I thought, perhaps..."

I braced myself, hands loose and ready.

"*Will* you relax?" he snapped, before taking back that honey-and-butter tone he liked so much. "My dearest one, you are here of your own will. As my *guest*, and my own darling, lovely, oh-so-unbending Kiss. Furthermore, you are a very particular piece of a very particular plan, and I will be *very* vexed should you come to any harm."

"You wanted to kill me the other night." I probably shouldn't have reminded him.

The snarl drifted its way across his face like a thunderstorm coming down from the mountains. "I don't like it when you consort with beasts."

I've heard that before. I watched, fascinated, while his skin rippled a little. As if tiny little insects were running underneath the poreless, elastic stoniness.

It drained away, the indigo threads vanishing from his whites. "After all, jealousy is a besetting sin, isn't it. Such a lovely sin, either soft or hard, such an *instructive* tool." Quiet, reflective, he tilted the case. "If you don't like them…"

"I do." I even sounded like I did. "Perry—"

I don't know what I was going to say. But he interrupted me.

"Good." He offered the case. "I would tie them in your lovely hair, my dearest, but, well. *Silver.* Soon that will cease to matter."

I avoided touching him, but I took the flat length of wood. It was surprisingly heavy. His hands dropped to his sides, and I studied the charms. Bile rose briefly in my throat, *Why would silver not matter? Because you're going to do what no hellbreed ever has, and if you pull it off, well, you're right, it won't matter.* "And why is that?"

"It's a surprise." He pressed his hands together, a parody of praying—but then he bowed slightly, and his lips pursed in that bland face. Like he wanted to say more, like he held a secret too delightful to contain.

Cold sweat broke out all over me. The box tipped, I righted it, and he backed up two silent steps.

"Tie your shinies on, my darling, and come downstairs. We have guests, and it doesn't do to keep guests waiting."

"Soul of politeness," I muttered, and the hellbreed *laughed.* A deep, rich chuckle, like he was having a fantastic time. He headed for the door, while I stood there like an idiot. The blue glow running under the surface of the silver submerged, thin threads of it remaining like healing sorcery, reacting to etheric contamination.

Halfway there, he stopped. He did not *quite* glance

over his shoulder, but he did turn his head, and the three-quarters profile was chillingly beautiful, some trick of fluorescent light and passing shade.

"You recall Belisa, of course." Level and dead serious. "Always treacherous. Which is a woman's own sort of constancy, isn't it? And it earned her a bullet to the head. After she'd been so *useful*, too."

The sweat turned to ice. I opened my mouth, but nothing came out, and the hum of the fluorescents dug at my skull.

Perry's profile turned to a grinning satyr's mask. His shoulders moved briefly as he settled himself further inside his human shell. "And cover up that *thing* on your wrist, darling. It's distracting."

He swept the door shut, still grinning, and I found out I was shaking again. The charms rolled on the velvet and chimed together, sweetly musical. The red thread fell and hit like a blood clot on the white, white floor.

III: Libera Me

Deliver Me

from prayer for The Dead
after Requiem, before burial

(Have mercy on The deceased
at The Last Judgement)

(choir speaks for The dead
person)

Also said on All Souls Day

27

The worst part wasn't going down the stairs with the charms tied in my hair. It wasn't even opening the door and stepping out into the vast daytime cavern of the Monde, tiny golden shafts of sunlight struggling through the dust and thickening. It also wasn't the sight of Riverson flung backward over the bar, his mouth slack in an upside-down scream and his hand still dripping blood. His filmed eyes were closed forever, and the terror frozen on his dead face was enough to give any reasonable person nightmares.

I barely glanced, storing it away for later, because the worst thing was the ripple that went through the assembled hellbreed packed into the Monde's throat. They filled the dance floor, brushing against the bar and its bloody cargo. The Traders at the door were grotesque slabs of muscle with submachine guns and slack mouths. There were no other Traders; it was strictly a 'breed affair.

Hellbreed lips parted, the female mouths candyglossed and the males' merely sculpted, and they smiled at me like a collection of dotty old aunts beaming at a favored family baby.

"There she is." Perry stood on the stage, his hands in his pockets. It spoiled the lines of his suit, but he didn't look like he cared. Since he was grinning ear to ear. "Our lovely one, our own Kiss."

Oh, great. Every inch of silver on me ran with blue light, and the gem on my wrist muttered softly, buzzing in my bones. The hellbreed smiles didn't cease, and under their hard, flexible skins little ripples churned. Their eyes burned, glowing with excitement.

I swept the door closed. The sound of it catching shut was loud in the sudden murmuring stillness. The crowd was utterly still. *Here during the day. Perry must have called a meeting. Why? So he can impress me?*

Only one of them didn't look happy. He was a tall stocky 'breed with glare-yellow eyes, his skin dappled with inky stains. Frayed designer jeans, sharp bony claws, and the handsome face of a pimp who can afford to slide the knife in once a wrinkle or two shows up on a working girl's face. He stared at me, his lip lifting, but before he could open his mouth there was a low, rumbling growl.

The dogsbody lumbered out of the darkness behind the bar, slinking along. It had matured, and its close blond pelt was wiry and glossy. Its eyes were crystalline, flicking over the assembled 'breed as it placed its paws just so. There was something wrong with those eyes, but I couldn't think of just what.

The gun drew itself free, my finger on the trigger and my pulse dropping into the steady rhythm of impending action. It would be just *like* Perry to have a dog attack me in full view of his little throng.

But there was a whisper next to me, and Perry's fevered fingers on my wrist. "Hush, darling one. Wait."

I could still feel the thing's throat against my whip as I choked it, my coat was still flapping from its claws, and he wanted me to *wait*?

The dogsbody padded forward, its claws snicking softly on the floor. Perry's hand tightened. It was too close, if it bunched its hindquarters and sprang...

It was terrible, the way you could still see the shadow of human hands under its paws, and a weird roll to its humpbacked gait showed you it had been bipedal once. Its head dropped, snaking at the end of its adapted neck, and it slowed. It was close enough to spring, and I didn't want to die here in the Monde. It would mean breaking Perry's arm, or worse, but—

The dogsbody gave a sigh, settling down on its haunches. It lowered its front end, and it crawled belly-down on the floor, whining, until it reached my feet. Its tongue was black, too, and it lapped at my boots, still stained with hellhound ichor. The slimy trails it left behind glistened, and revulsion jolted up my legs to engulf the rest of me.

A huge retch filled my stomach, crawled up my throat. I swallowed so hard the effort left me blinking. A sigh went through the hellbreed, and a mutter of Helletöng like far-away thunder in the middle of a flint-cold night.

"See?" Perry, slowly releasing me, one finger at a time. "We're *all* at your feet, my darling." More loudly now, playing to the audience. "Do any of you worms doubt me? She's hunter, she's human, and she's *mine*, here of her own will. With her to wield it—"

"It's a long way from owning one of the monkeys to coaxing it to wield *that*," the piebald hellbreed piped up. "And she stinks of the Other Side. What are you playing at, Hyperion?"

Perry turned, and there was a general drawing away. The 'breed were packed in here like sardines in a can, but they managed to find the space to leave the piebald standing alone.

Dominance, I realized. *This kid's looking to take a bite out of Perry. Interesting.*

What was even more interesting was that he was a 'breed I hadn't seen before. I knew all the players—or at least, I had a couple months ago.

"Oh, the *Other Side.*" Sarcasm dripped from Perry's words, and the floor groaned sharply. "When have they ever taken an interest? Fear of them restrains us, is that it? I am no longer content to be restrained."

"Your lord father—" Piebald hesitated, because the Monde had gone still, and hot air breathed along every surface.

Father? Oh, my God, you mean someone actually gave birth to that? Hellbreed reproduction is not my area of expertise—I just kill the motherfuckers—but I supposed it was possible. And the thought made my stomach turn over again, harder this time.

"Oh, yes, my dear Halis. Let's mention *him.* Really, you're a bad guest." Perry's smile was wide and utterly chilling. He bore down on the piebald, hands still in his pockets, his shoulders square. The dogsbody had finished licking my boots and whined, deep in its throat. The sound was a glassy squeal, diamond claws on a mirror.

The Other Side. Wield it. Betcha ten bucks he means la Lanza, *according to Melendez, and I have to find out where he's keeping it.* I couldn't look everywhere at once, and I didn't want to. I watched Perry's linen-clad back, and when the dogsbody hunched itself up to crouch against my leg I almost retched again.

The piebald 'breed seemed to shrink, hunching his shoulders as sallowness rose on his pale parts. Even his hair was patchwork. "Don't be hasty." He swallowed, visibly. "I know where it is, I'm the one who can get it for you—"

"Oh, but I think we'll do quite well without you." Perry's sheer goodwill was terrifying. I still had the gun in my hand, loosely pointed at the floor. "*I* know where the Lance was, too, and even now I know where it *is*. Because it happens to be in my keeping, along with my darling Kiss."

Stop him. Judas to a hellbreed. The caretaker's eyes, bright blue now, and the dogsbody's teeth at my throat. He'd been stroking the thing's head, scratching behind its ears. Its eyes had been blue, Jughead Vanner's eyes with hellfire dripping through them, but now they were colorless crystals.

Just like the gem in my wrist.

"Really, Halis. Did you think to challenge me? Here? *Now?*" Perry made a little clicking sound, tongue against teeth, and stepped mincingly past the piebald 'breed. "Kiss?"

It took two tries before my voice would work, because I knew what was coming. "What?" At least the word came out right, bored and flat.

But whatever it was Perry wanted, Halis decided it was better off unsaid. He was deadly silent about it too, blinking through space with the stuttering speed of a hellbreed who means business. I was already tracking him with my right-hand gun, whip loosened and chiming as it flicked forward, one hip cocked and ready to swing back.

28

I didn't even see the dogsbody move. One moment it was right next to me. The next, it hit the flying 'breed with a boneshatter crunch, and several 'breed shrank back as ichor splattered. The dogsbody's jaw crackled, and it made a sound like a hyena late at night.

I ignored a cramp of nausea, backed up a few more steps to get some room in case the piebald threw off the dog-thing and came for me.

I shouldn't have worried. Because a dogsbody, like a hellhound or a *ronguerdo*, knows its work. The crunching of teeth settled into wet chewing slurps as it settled down to its feast, crouching, only the gleam of one colorless gemlike eye as it watched me. One flat ear was pricked, too, standing alert.

Like a good dog with a bone, waiting for his master's call.

Oh, Jesus. The world paled, came back in a rush of color. I actually staggered back, regained my footing, and gave myself a sharp mental slap. Looking weak in the middle of a crowd of 'breed is not a good way to go.

"How nice," Perry murmured. "Our Kiss has a pet. Well, would anyone *else* like to dispute our little plan? No? Good. Then you are all excused to work my will."

They didn't move. Some of them stared at me, avid, mouths slightly open and eyes burning. Another ripple ran through them, titters and half-heard whispers.

"Oh, yes. That reminds me." Perry half-turned, looked at the stage. "I want that Were's head. If the other beasts will not give him up, move into the barrio." His grin turned wide and white, his tongue flickering once. "Kill them too."

"It'll be difficult." This from a tall female, so skinny the alien bones rubbed against the inside of her parchment skin. "That's their ground, they know it better than we—"

"Nevertheless." Perry waved a hand. "Children, children, you are Hell's scions. I trust you'll find a way."

I found my voice. "Perry—"

"You may leave us now," he said quietly, and Helletöng filled the spaces between the words with misshapen drowning things bubbling in a cold vault. The hellbreed moved for the exits in a wave of seashell hips and painted eyes, chitterings and moanings and sighs behind them.

"Perry." *I am still a hunter. And this is my town.* "Leave the Weres alone."

"If they would hand over the one that shared your bed, my dearest, I would. But no, they're intransigent."

I almost choked. "What do you—"

"I had him once before, and I would have kept him after you were mine. Now I don't need him, so I won't keep him, but I want him for just a few moments, Kiss. Can't you guess why?"

"So you can take lessons on how to be a decent human

being?" I probably shouldn't have said it. Judas to a hell-breed, sure, but he wasn't going to touch my Weres.

Especially Saul.

The hellbreed were slipping away, and I still had my gun out.

But Perry had simply hopped up on the stage. 'Töng grumbled and swirled through the sun-pierced dimness, and all the hellbreed were scurrying to their cars under the assault of the cleansing light of day. "Too late now."

Salvage this, Jill. Assert some control. "Perry. Go after the Weres, and the deal's off."

"You should have said that earlier." He spread his arms, a paleness against the dark cavern of the stage. "All they have to do is hand over your kitten, my dove. Wouldn't it be nice to see him again? They move him from place to place, but sooner or later they'll see reason."

"Fine." I turned, and the dogsbody lifted its snuffling head from its snack. The piebald 'breed was rotting quickly, and my gorge rose again. The smell was something else, and to have your nose buried in it... "You send 'breed into the barrio, Perry, and you'll never see them ag—"

"Do you honestly think you can threaten me now?" He had my arm, suddenly, fingers biting in, and the dogsbody growled. "And you'd better leash that thing, before you lose it. There is a *limit* to what I allow you, Kismet."

I hit him hard, a good solid crack to the face. His chin snapped back and the gun was level, pointed into his chest. The whip jingled a little, and the dogsbody growled again.

"Shut up," I said, and the thing that used to be Jughead Vanner did.

The silence was immense. The hellbreed had drained

away, and the dripping from Riverson's outflung hand had stopped. *Why kill Riverson? This isn't like you, Perry.*

None of this made sense. Had I just made a huge mistake, or was I doing what I was supposed to? Had I thrown away any advantage over Perry by letting him think I was here willingly? Did any of this fucking *matter*?

Of course it matters. Melendez's loa wants the debt repaid, but I can't do that until I know where and when Perry's planning his party.

"Sweet nothings," Perry hissed. He wiped at his mouth with the back of one narrow hand. "Oh, I've *missed* you."

"You won't miss me if you declare open season on Weres. I'll be right up close, once I finish with the hellbreed you send into the barrio." The shaking had me again, but the gun was solid. *Fuck this, fuck everything. I'll kill them, then I'll take Saul and—*

And what? Ride off into the sunset while Chango got a hard-on for me and Anya braced herself for the next wave of hellbreed to come in? Because there were always more.

Or even, here's a thought, what if Perry had a little plan for Anya too? Or if something fatal happened to her? Hunters were tough, but also as mortal as everyone else.

And what would happen to my city, all the oblivious who liked signing deals with hellbreed and the others who had no idea they even existed? What *then*?

Stop, little snake, Mikhail whispered inside my memory. *Anger is no good. It makes things distort, yes? It makes you stupid.*

Hearing him used to be a comfort. Now it had teeth. I'd signed myself up for the scar because Misha had said it was a good idea.

He hadn't told me he needed someone to take his place

in the deal with Perry. Would he ever have told me? Couldn't he find the fucking words?

I would have done it anyway, for him. If he just would have *asked*. Add that to the list of my sins.

I swallowed. *Be clear and cold for this, Jill. You have to be.* "Besides, what does it matter? I left him, Perry. I'm here."

"Here, yes. Now." His mouth was flushed, a bruised scarlet line. "But I want you *more* than here, Kismet. I will take everything you love, everything that has ever loved you, and I will break it until there is only me. *Only* me."

Oh, for fuck's sake. Great. He's gone insane. "Well, that's a great Christmas list, Perry. Too bad it's summer. Why don't you tell me about the Lance instead?"

It wasn't very elegant, but at least it got his attention. He was still for a full ten seconds, Helletöng groaning and rumbling under the surface of the visible, and I knew I had his complete attention.

"Oh, that." He waved a hand. "It's not important. Yet."

"If you're wanting me to do something with it, it is." The gun was level, but he seemed to take no notice of it. My fingers tightened on the whip's handle.

"Oh, Kiss. Never bored while you're near me." The grin was back, and wider than ever. "You may go now, my lovely. Tell your friends I am coming for them. And tell whoever sank that stinking thing in your arm that they are welcome to try and stop me." He spread his arms. "It is *my* time, now."

I backed up a step. Two. My heart beat thinly in my chest, echoing in my wrists and temples. "You seriously want me to leave?"

"Take your dog. That's a nice trick, too, I'll ask how

you did it sometime. Later, when I'm not so busy." He watched me as I took another step. "Yes, I want you to go. It's Wednesday now. Come back tomorrow, we'll dance and dine. The world will end, and you will help me end it."

Fuck it all. I can't do it. "I should kill you now." My finger tightened on the trigger. I knew exactly how much pull would send a bullet through him.

But one bullet wouldn't do it. I'd have to start shooting, then I'd have to hack him in pieces, and call the banefire. And hope to hell it put him down.

Don't. You can't kill him yet, there's something even worse waiting in the wings. Play along, Jill. "I should," I repeated. "I should ventilate you right fucking now."

His grin turned savage, and the shadow of handsomeness was back, burning away the screen of blandness. "Likewise, I'm sure. But my primrose path, my darling, you can't afford to. You don't know nearly enough about what I want, or how I'm going to get it. So run along and ask some questions, and meet me tomorrow. About dusk, I should think."

This is not going well at all. "Perry—"

A thin tremor passed through him. A draft of spoiled honey brushed along the tense air between us. "For the love of your pale little God, my darling, go. I find myself growing murderous." Perry headed for the second door, the one leading to the red-neon hall. He left a scar behind him, viscous darkness peaking and eddying. The Monde grumbled, settling lower into itself, like an animal in a dark cave.

You've only got one more, Jill. Make it good. "Why Riverson? Perry, why Riverson?"

He snarled, a deep throbbing noise. "Go. Away."

"Why Riverson?" I yelled. "God *damn* you, answer me!"

"Because he robbed me of you!" Perry screamed, and the whole place shook. Dust pattered from the ceiling. His head dropped forward and his shoulders heaved, linen stretching and rippling as it fought to contain him.

For a second I was sure he was going to turn around and leap on me, and that would have made it all right to kill him according to the abacus inside my head. The *conscience*. The thing that kept poking me no matter which way I turned, the stranger who had made me a hunter in the first place. And then I would go tell Melendez that Chango should be satisfied, collect Gil, and go find Henderson Hill's caretaker, with his blue eyes and his vanishing scars.

And I would get some answers. All the answers he would give me willingly, and any others I felt like beating out of him.

"He robbed me of you," Perry said again, but very softly, like a killing frost creeping down from the desert. "There is my first warning, Kiss. All your friends. *All.* Even those who are not quite your friends. Everyone you have cast your eye upon, they are marked for death. You will have only me." His tone dropped, confidential and musing. "And I will have everything."

He stood there for another moment, while everything around him shook, spiderlines of reaction etching themselves on the Monde's floor—concrete covered in hardwood, the dance floor something else entirely, glimmering black.

I waited, hoping. And I was right. Perry had to throw one more bone in the pot to make it boil.

It was a good one, too. "And when you see my brother

Michael, ask *him* about your resurrection. Ask *him* about
the game you're so blindly stumbling through."

Call me Mike. The hornets buzzed, speaking to me with
their pinprick feet, a tattoo of warning.

I got out of there. The dogsbody padded after me, and
the sunlight didn't smoke on its wiry blond hide.

* * *

"Oh, thank *God*," Galina breathed. "He's gone mad, Jill. I
can barely—"

"Shut it." It was rude, but I was beyond caring.
"Where's Devi?"

Sound of movement. "Here," Anya Devi said, carefully.
"Jill?"

"Perry's got something big planned for tomorrow
night." I braced my hand against the phone booth's
scratched, clear plastic. Sarvedo Street was deserted even
this far up, and the sunlight was too thin. I kept seeing odd
shadows, my blue eye hot and dry.

"Hutch is running on coffee and nerves. He says he's
found an old etching or something, prior to any knowns.
Saul's tearing up whatever room Galina locks him in—"

"Devi." My throat was dry. "Tell Hutch to drop everything. Instead, get him on the horn and call every hunter
we know of. *Everyone*, do you hear me? Every single one
of us. This thing Perry's planning has something to do
with a portal to Hell, possibly *huge*, and have him cross-
check with a 'breed called Halis, spelling unknown. And
something else. *La Lanza de Destino*, Spear of Destiny.
Lance of Destiny. Whatever."

"There's so many—" she began. She was about to say

there were plenty of things masquerading as Spears of Destiny, and some of them were even Talismans. Every long piece of wood around in the Middle Ages with some etheric force in it was a goddamn "Spear of Destiny," it was a needle in a historical haystack.

"I know there's a million of them knocking around, but have him dig. And there's..." I almost choked. How could I even begin to explain? "Never mind. Get everyone we can for tomorrow before dusk."

She swore, but under her breath. "What else?"

Of course, you knew there had to be more. "The hell-breed are moving to take the barrio. Get everyone under cover. The Weres on Mayfair, too."

She cursed again. "Of course. Perry's been trying to get his hands on Saul for months, and now that you're back...Jill, what *is* it with you and that hellbreed? Mikhail had a deal with him and you took it over, sure, but he never played for Mikhail this way—"

"I don't know." The words stung my chapped lips as they slid free, and I didn't sound truthful even to myself. *Oh, you know all right. It's because deep down, you're the same thing. Twins. You proved it yourself, didn't you?* "Did the Badger come up with anything?"

"Vanner's cars? Let's see. A red Dodge pickup, two motorcycles—he was a Honda dude, fucking poser—a blue Buick four-door, a—"

"Blue Buick. Four-door. License plate?"

She reeled off a string of numbers and letters.

It matched up. One more question, then, to keep me warm. "When did he get rid of it?"

"A couple months before you disappeared. You need the date and the buyer?"

"No." I shut my eyes briefly, leaning against the phone booth's shell. My memory was cruel now, showing connections in a pitiless white glare, like the sun beating down or the wide white carpet in Perry's bedroom. "Jesus," I whispered. That tied up *that* loose end. Vanner hadn't been nervous around me all the time because he had a habit of walking in on the weird.

He'd been nervous because he'd tried to kill me once, during the case that lost me one of my cops and almost, *almost* turned my city into a wasteland. Only the 'breed pulling the strings hadn't warned him to use silverjacket ammo on a helltainted hunter. And doubly nervous afterward because he hadn't killed me, and he was in deep to that same hellbreed. I hadn't smelled any corruption on him, but it wasn't out of the question. Most likely he'd been full human and angling for a Trade...

...and that was a question mark, too, wasn't it? Perry's enemies were likely dead by now, if his treatment of Halis was any indication. Shen An Dua—the 'breed who I would've pointed the finger at—was dead, and so were Rutger and that pajama-masked psycho who'd been trying to kill me last time. There was nobody left to send a poisonous hellhound after one crooked cop.

Except Perry. Who would have wanted me down but not out, since my agreement with him kept him at the top of the hellbreed food chain in Santa Luz. He very well might not have warned a stupid human slave to use silverjacket. And Perry could *always* use a pair of eyes on the police force, couldn't he.

Or maybe Vanner had just been a crooked cop, tried to kill me, found out he couldn't, and went looking for something on the nightside that would keep him safe in the event that I kept digging and found out who'd been driving that blue Buick. Especially since Harvill, the DA who had been the prime node of corruption on that case, had ended up dead, too. Just how Vanner connected to Harvill I didn't know, but someone could probably tell me if I cared to find out. Now that I knew where to look.

I glanced out into the street, where the dogsbody padded back and forth, sunlight drenching its blond hide, its colorless jewel-eyes glittering. I tasted bile, and the gem on my wrist twinged sharply.

Why was a hellhound chasing him? Unless Perry wanted him back. Or maybe...

Devi's tone crackled with thinly controlled impatience. "Jill? Throw me a bone here. Give me something, anything, come on."

I'm having hallucinations about Henderson Hill's blue-eyed caretaker. Only they're not hallucinations, because he bought me breakfast and gave me a gun. "If I could, I would. Just get everyone you can, Devi, and watch your ass. Put Saul on the line."

"I'm not your fucking secretary." But she laid the phone down, and I heard Galina's murmured questions, Devi's sharp reply. "She wants to talk to him. If it'll stop him doing this crazy shit, I'm all for it." Bootheels coming down hard as Devi stamped away. "*Hutch!* Get your skinny ass up here!"

I waited, breathing deep. Fed another eight quarters into the phone. Devi had probably tucked a phone card into my coat, but it didn't matter. The coins dropped in, pieces of silver to pay the ferryman.

Cells are expensive and finicky, and the more advanced they get the more sorcery messes them up; once pay phones

were a thing of the past I was going to have to figure something else out. Right now, breaking and entering to use
someone's phone sounded like the most satisfying option.
As well as the most educational and entertaining.

Always assuming I survived long enough.

Static burst over the phone line. Then a listening silence. I could hear him breathing, deep even swells, a
sound of effort temporarily checked.

"Saul?" I always sounded breathy and silly over the
phone with him. "Saul, please. You've got to calm down."

"Where. Are. You?" The words vibrated over the lines
and carried all the fury in the world into my ear, and
gooseflesh spilled down my back.

"Galina's going to keep you there, Saul. I can't afford
to lose you."

"I *told* you—" he began, and it wasn't like every other
fight we'd ever had. Usually I was the one losing my shit
while he tried to stay rational. This time it was him losing
his shit, and if he lost it enough, it wasn't going to be easy
to slow him down.

I had to get it all out at once, before he got his head up.
"Saul. *Perry will kill you.* If he does, I'm damned and he
will have no trouble getting me to do anything he wants.
You are the only goddamn thing that matters to me, all
right? The *only* thing. *I don't even care about my fucking
city, Saul.*" I let that sink in, and wonder of wonders, he
was quiet. I swallowed, expecting the world to rock out
from underneath me from the blasphemy.

What did that say about me? Santa Luz could get wiped
off the map, and as long as Saul was alive I'd count
it chump change. That was *wrong*, because I was a
hunter...but that was the way it was. And if it stopped him

long enough for me to get a word of sanity in edgewise, I didn't care. "Just stay put and when I'm done with this, you can yell at me all you want. But I need you to rest, I need you to eat, and I need you to be strong so that when this is done you can load me in a car and get me the hell out of this godforsaken town. *Please.*"

Silence. The rage crackling over the line didn't abate.

"Please." It was a little girl's whisper. "Saul, *please*. I came back from Hell for you."

And here I was, racking up the lies. I didn't remember where I'd come back from. I had a suspicion that I didn't want to, and another sneaking suspicion that it hadn't been Poughkeepsie.

Hell was as good a guess as any.

Besides, I know Hell exists. The evidence is all around, every day, rubbed in your face. And the descent into hell-breed territory is the final step that makes a hunter—no, wait. The final step is the *return*, with your teacher holding the line and the souls of the damned screaming in your ears.

Heaven? Never been there. Unless being in Saul's arms on a sunny afternoon counts. Which it probably does, if I'm lucky.

If I deserved it. If I pulled this off and saved the weary world for him one more time.

A clatter. Footsteps stamping away. A low, rumbling growl dying out.

"Jill?" Galina, softly. "He's calmer. Theron and I are taking turns cooking; now he might even eat. I won't let him out. Are you all right? Is Gilberto okay?"

She was such a gentle soul. My stomach turned over hard. The dogsbody lifted its head, crystalline eyes fixed on the middle distance down Sarvedo Street.

"Gil was fine when I gave him his marching orders. Galina, *keep Saul there.* I don't care what you have to do, just keep him safe."

"I already promised." Solemn now. "What's going on? It's Perry, isn't it. What's he doing?"

Taking me apart one piece at a time. And repeating the worst part of modern history, thank you very much. "Something big. Look, I need you to do something for me."

"Of course."

The dogsbody slunk closer, still staring down the street. Under the golden wires of its hair, sharply defined muscles moved under black skin. "Start making silverjacket bullets. Get the Sanctuary ready for all the hunters who can reach Santa Luz in the next twenty-four hours. And Galina?"

"What?"

"Do you pray?"

She sounded surprised. "Well, the Order's quite catholic, in the old sense—"

"Good. Start praying. Maybe it will help."

29

The warehouse was full of ghosts.

It stood on the wrong side of the tracks, and from the outside it was just another dusty, decaying bit of urban infrastructure. Inside, though, it was space and light and the stamp of Saul's presence everywhere. It looked just the same as it had the last time I'd been here.

When I'd been preparing to go die.

I'd left the bed tangled and some cupboards open; the huge orange Naugahyde couch with the pretty slipcover Saul had made was dirty; I'd been covered in filth, as usual. Thin blue lines of etheric protection hummed in the walls, fading until I stepped inside, gathering strength from my presence. Dust lay thick over everything, and even though Gilberto or Anya had been out to lock up and keep everything tidy, it still smelled like an abandoned house. Places start to rot very quickly, etherically and physically, once they're uninhabited. It smelled sour and stale, and that would just about drive Saul nuts. He'd start scrubbing everything he could reach.

My eyes blurred, hot water brimming. I blinked it away.

The dogsbody padded behind me, whining softly to itself, and ignoring it wasn't making it vanish.

Not that I thought it would, but I didn't have the heart to shoot the damn thing.

Yet.

I strode through the empty rooms of our life together and stepped into the wide, wood-floored sparring room. Mirrored tiles along one side, a ballet barre firmly bolted to them; weapons hanging on the other three. There was one empty spot—a fall of amber silk crushed on the floor, and I don't know why I was surprised. Of course someone had taken the hunk of pre-Atlantean meteorite iron, with its dragon heads and scythelike blades.

I had a moment's worth of unease, wondering...but no, the weapon Mikhail had handed down to me couldn't possibly be called *la Lanza de Destino*. For one thing, it was too old, and it wasn't wooden. Anya would have taken it to store in Galina's vaults.

No windows, but skylights drenching everything with late-afternoon honey, dust motes dancing as the gem gave a hard piercing note, like a crystal wineglass right before it shatters.

My guns leapt free, trained on a column of sunlight. Dust coalesced, a single spark flared white, and he was suddenly *there*.

I didn't shoot him. But it was close.

Call-Me-Mike the caretaker regarded me mildly, his blue eyes glowing. The sun picked out fine threads of gold in his no-longer-dishwater hair, and instead of the jumpsuit he wore jeans and a plain white T-shirt. All he needed was a duck's-ass pompadour and a pack of Lucky Strikes rolled up in his sleeve.

The dogsbody whined and slumped next to me, shivering.

"What the fuck *are* you?" I'll admit it, I yelled. The words cracked, bounced back from the mirrors, set the dust swirling in tiny tornados.

Mike shrugged, a loose easy movement. "It's not important."

"It is to me." I didn't lower the guns. The idea that I could just start shooting every nonhuman or non-Were involved in this whole scenario was wonderfully comforting. I wondered if I had enough ammo. "Perry says hello, *brother Michael*. He's planning something for tomorrow night to send the world down the drain. But you know that, don't you. What was the point of sending me there?"

Mike shrugged, spreading his hands. The light made him insubstantial, just another ghost here with all the dust and the memories. "It was...necessary."

You son of a bitch. "Was shooting myself in the head necessary too? You're the *Other Side*, Perry says. We're bleeding and dying down here, where the fuck are *you*? Why are you just showing up now?" My ribs heaved. I didn't realize I was shouting until the echoes came back, the entire warehouse creaking like a tree in a high breeze. The triggers eased down a millimeter, another. Squeezing off a few rounds would just about start this conversation off right.

Sorrow, then, darkening those blue, blue eyes. Not sterile like Perry's, a warm summer color. But so terribly sad. "It's not that simple. I'm bending the rules enough as it is. So much depends on you, and of course..." Another slight movement, hands spread. "Of course I wish I could do more. It...it's painful, to see such suffering."

Well, isn't that big of you. "Wind me up and set me loose, right? Just throw me at the enemy. I've been fighting this war for years, and it never gets any better. I've been down in the streets trying to hold back the tide. There's no goddamn hope at all. And you've been sitting up at Henderson Hill the entire *fucking* time, doing *fucking* nothing, just waiting for... for what? For Perry? Is that it? You're in cahoots?"

"I wouldn't say that. He's part of the Pattern, as you are. As I am. But... there are disturbing signs. He's..." Another helpless shrug. "Even if I had the words, you wouldn't understand. I can't even offer you a dispensation. If you do this—stop Hyperion, save your fellows, and recover the Lance—you will not be rewarded. There is no glory, no recompense."

A harsh cawing laugh shook its way free of my chest. *Well, shit, that's par for the course.* "So why should I bother, huh? Because you brought me back? Is that it?"

"It's part of the Pattern, but I can't explain that either. *Kismet.* Did you really expect to name yourself that and not be called upon?"

It was like talking to Mikhail in one of his vodka-soaked philosophical moods. Baffling, opaque, and frustratingly-familiar enough to drive me to the heavy bag. I searched for something that would wring an answer out of him. I'm used to dealing with hellbreed, where you question them, then you hurt them, then you question them some more.

Something told me that would be a bad idea with this guy, whatever he was. "Perry called you his brother. You're related?"

Another gentle, rueful smile. "Is a mirror related to the image it holds?"

Oh, for fuck's sake. Disgusted, I lowered the guns. I was shaking again, and all I wanted was to lie down and sleep. Next to Saul, if possible. Let the world end, it had been lurching along before I came along to be a hunter just fine.

Focus, Jill! I blinked. A puzzle piece snapped down inside my head. "He needs me for something. *La Lanza de Destino,* Melendez called it; the only trouble is, there's several of *those* floating around. I at least know it's not the chunk of meteorite Mikhail left me. The important thing is, Perry can't use it. What does he want it used *on?*"

Mike nodded, the patient teacher beaming at a recalcitrant but gifted student. "*Very* good. But your task is simply to strike him down when he has achieved the first half of his purpose. It's very important, Kismet."

"So he wants me to do something for him, and you want me to murder him but you won't tell me exactly why." The guns lowered slightly. "I'd do it for free, you know. That bastard has gone too far." *And so have you.*

The caretaker crouched, suddenly, a fluid movement. I twitched, stopped myself at the last moment.

The dogsbody whined and leaned forward. It glanced up at me, colorless eyes suddenly pleading, and the sickness revolving behind my breastbone rose another notch. "Jesus Christ," I whispered, suddenly very sure. "The hellhound was chasing him to shut him up. Perry was just cleaning up a loose end."

"This one has paid for what he's done." Michael held out a hand, just touching the edge of the sunlight. Stroking it, the finely drawn border where light met air. "And it's fitting that he should protect you now, isn't it?"

God, there's not much difference between you and a hellbreed, is there. Maybe I should start killing you both.

"This isn't getting us anywhere. What the fuck are you, and why are you here?"

"I came to give you comfort, Kismet." He cocked his head, glancing up at me. The dogsbody didn't move, but its shaking slid up my leg. The gem groaned, etheric force thrumming up my arm. "And to explain, as far as I am able, what Hyperion wishes to do."

"It's about fucking time." I lowered the guns, nice and slow. "I'm waiting."

So he told me, in plain words. And I listened. By the end of it his voice was a brass bell, stroked softly in a forgotten chapel, and I was cold all over. The dogsbody whined even louder, crouching next to me and shivering. The sunlight dimmed, and by the time he finished I was on my knees too, hugging myself, staring at him.

"Saul," I whispered.

The caretaker was glowing now, his skin burnished and his eyes burning feverishly. My own blue eye ached, piercing the veil of the visible—his outline rippled, eddies and currents passing through the snarled fabric of reality. "Do it for him. Do it for love. Please, Kismet. You are the only one who can."

"I . . ." *But Saul. I promised him.* "I promised."

"If you will not do this, we are lost." He shrugged. "The Pattern will right itself in some other way, I suppose. But there will be terrible suffering, not just among those you love. I can only ask, Kismet, Jill, whatever you want to name yourself. You are free to refuse."

Oh, fuck. "You know I can't." Hopeless, pale little words. "You have to know I can't. That's not a way out, you know I was *made* this way. So I can't turn you down. *God* made me this way, and don't you dare fucking tell me He didn't."

"Do you believe in such a cruelty?" Michael sighed. "You're so willing to hurt yourself." The rippling through him was more pronounced now, bits of him wavering as if under clear, heavy water. Sunlight dimmed further, a cloud drifting between us and heaven's eye. "Goodbye, beloved."

Metal clattered somewhere, but my eyes were full of light. Just like that, he was gone. The dogsbody shuddered, pressing against me, and unhealthy heat boiled from its hide. I swallowed several times, and the world spun. When I came back to myself I was hunched over, my forehead against cool hardwood and awful knowledge beating inside my brain.

I was probably going insane. Coming back from the dead will do that to you, I guess. Or maybe this was a different version of Hell, one I'd been extra-special nominated to.

One that felt just like my life.

Get up, little snake. Mikhail, in my memory. Why hadn't he ever told me about his bargain with Perry? Could he just not find the words? Did he not care enough to...but no.

No.

Mikhail was my teacher. He'd held the line when I made my first trip to the hellbreeds' home, the one that turned me into a full-fledged hunter and gave me my smart eye. He'd loved me the way only a hunter can love another hunter, right down to the bones and back.

He must have had a reason.

I had my marching orders. Ol' Blue Eyes had been a busy, busy boy. He was just so helpful, feeding me and giving me weapons, showing up to push me in another direction, poking and prodding.

I made my legs straighten by the simple expedient of cursing at them, levered myself up from the floor.

"They want a sacrificial lamb." My voice sounded odd. The dogsbody stopped whining and made an inquisitive *rrowr* sound that might have been funny if it hadn't been so pathetic. "Boy, are they going to get a surprise."

30

*D*awn found me in a cemetery.

The northern side of Beacon Hill's lush greenness looked out over the valley, the mountains rising in the distance and the river a bright colorless ribbon as the sky lightened. I sat on the wet grass, sprinklers going overtime in the dark to compensate for the desiccation that would hit later in the day. The water had stopped, thank God, but everything squelched underneath me.

I put my chin on my knees.

The dogsbody slunk closer. It settled down with a sigh, its unhealthy heat steaming in the predawn chill. Around sunrise Santa Luz always smells like metallic sand as the city inhales, filling its lungs from the wasted desert all around, mixing it with exhaust and the effluvia of thousands of people going about their lives.

The gravestone shimmered, polished white rock. I'd dug up Mikhail's ashes a while ago and had Galina put them in one of her vaults. Still, it was here that I felt his presence most strongly, and it was here I sometimes came to talk to him. Galina's perfectly polite, but I don't like having conversations with my dead teacher where other people can hear.

Call me secretive.

I held myself absolutely still. The sky slowly turned gray, stars winking out and a few birds warming up for their morning chorus. What a waste it was to water the ground here. In the first place, water's a great psychic conductor, and the grief soaking this place echoed in every molecule. And in the second, why not spend some of that water on the living? They needed it more.

The only need of the dead is to sleep unmolested.

You're kind of sucking at that, aren't you, Jill. I squeezed my eyes shut, opened them. The gravestone was just the same.

Mikhail Illich Tolstoi. Nothing else, not even the years of his tenure on earth. Why bother, when I would remember it and it was in the files? It wouldn't matter to anyone else. Except maybe Gilberto, when he finished his training.

I wouldn't be around to see that, would I.

I stirred a little, shifting to relieve muscles threatening to cramp. The dogsbody was still, its weird eyes closed and its breath softly chuffing in and out. Just like a hound, really.

I'd never had a pet.

Are you crazy? This thing's dangerous. Plus, it's basically hellbreed, even if Call-Me-Mike did...whatever he did to it. A shiver went through me.

I was stalling.

"Misha." The word rode a breathy scree of air. "Mish, Misha-Mik, if you're there, I could use a friendly ear."

Well, strictly speaking, listening was all he *could* do,

right? He was fucking dead. Passed on. Joined the choir eternal. Had I met him, wherever I'd been after I pulled the trigger and broke my skull open like a pumpkin dropped off an overpass?

If I rubbed under my hair, I only felt the bumps and ridges anyone's head acquires after a few hard knocks. No shrapnel. Just a tenderness in places, like old bruising. A faint twinge.

"Why?" I whispered, staring at his grave. "Why didn't you tell me you had a deal with Perry and you needed me to take your place? Why didn't you tell me about Belisa? Why didn't you take me with you? Why did you pull me out of that snowbank in the first place? Why *me*? And Jesus Christ, Misha, why could I come back if you couldn't? Or is it just that you didn't want to?"

I go to Valhalla, he'd told me more than once, *where fight is like play. Like movie.*

I guess that was his idea of a good time.

"Why, Misha? I would've done anything you asked. Hell, I would've given Perry a lot more to buy you free. I would..." I ran up against the wall of what I *would* have done, what I'd've given if he'd just asked me.

Why hadn't he?

A while ago, I'd visited Melendez and Chango had deigned to speak to me. It had been a different case—the circus had come to town, and someone was looking for vengeance. Voodoo and hellbreed don't mix, and I'd been looking to get the whole thing tied up and safely stowed before open warfare broke out and the Cirque was given free rein in my town.

You meatpuppets, Chango had snorted with magnificent disdain. *You always got to know why.*

"It would sure fucking help," I muttered, and wiped at my cheeks with callused palms. Why the fuck was I crying? Another *why* question.

Shit.

"Was it worth it?" That was a new question. I sounded ridiculously young, and I stared at the white blur of the headstone. "Melisande. *Belisa.* Did you love her? Or were you just looking to get free? Was *she* worth it? You had *me*, Misha. Was I not enough?"

Of course I wasn't enough, never had been. I'd been born without some essential thing everyone else seemed to have. There was an emptiness in me, way down deep, and even if it had been the reason everyone who should have loved me couldn't, it was what kept me alive long enough to escape. Long enough to survive and meet Mikhail. And even then, I hadn't been enough.

The only person who shouldn't have loved me was Saul. And go figure, he did.

At least he's safe. But if you end up dead again, Jill, what's that going to do? He'll starve. He'll get matesick, he'll go down. Weres don't go to Hell, and you know that's where you're bound. If there was a heaven you'd've seen it by now. Hot water flooded my eyes, trickled down my cheeks. My nose was full. I'd given up wiping my cheeks.

"It's not fair." Lo and hallelujah, I was five years old again. "It's just not *fair*, God damn you."

The eastern sky was rosy. The birds burst into song, a great swell of twittering music. It stopped, started again. The hush returned, this time threaded with liquid birdsong. It was funny how noise could be a component of early-morning silence.

I was on my feet before I knew it, steel-shod heels sink-

ing into wet grass and mud. "I should leave it here to rot.
All of it. Everything. Including you, Misha. You lied to
me."

By omission, yes. But still a lie. Hunters aren't supposed to lie to each other. When you've been loved so hard
that the love turns into a rope that pulls you free of Hell's
cold shifting borders, you can see it in another hunter's
eyes. It's raw and bloody and it aches, but you can't lie to
someone who's been loved like that.

Mikhail *had* loved me. He'd pulled me out of Hell.
What if his lie had been a mercy, instead of deceit? Why
would he have done that?

Fuck. We're back to the whys.

I held up one finger. "You loved me." Another. "So you
lied to save me. You couldn't hold Perry off much longer.
But you thought *I* could."

A third finger. "Mike. The caretaker. Judas to a hellbreed. He can't interfere much more than he already
has."

A fourth. "A Lance. And Perry planning a repeat of
'29."

1929, the Black Year. The year when the hellbreed had
opened up multiple doors, and escaped en masse from
Hell's embrace.

Unwilling, I glanced up.

The eastern horizon was a furnace. Caught in the valley,
Santa Luz turned over, sighed, and began waking up. The
skyscrapers glittered, and for a moment the whole city was
open inside my head, the streets that made its arteries and
the buildings its bones. The people moving through it, the
city's dream made flesh, but so vulnerable. They had no
idea what abyss was yawning under their feet, and every

night, even since before Mikhail's death, I'd been fighting
to keep them safe. There was no reward, no prize; few of
them even knew my name.

So why did *I* do it? Why hadn't I taken Mikhail's other
offer—therapy, education, a way off the streets, my past
wiped clear and a fresh chance at life as a civilian? I'd
never even considered it.

Because I'd wanted so badly to be worthy of what he'd
done when he pulled me out of that snowdrift. Funny, that
year it had snowed; I couldn't remember a single white
winter in the time since.

My thumb popped out. "My city."

My city.

Now I looked at my callused palm and fingers, the lines
running across flesh, the bones of my knuckles. My hand
curled into a fist, and the gem muttered sleepily against my
wrist. When you got right down to it, was it any different
from the scar of Perry's lips on me?

Do it for Saul. Do it for love.

"I can't." There it was. "There isn't enough left in me.
You made sure of that. All of you fighting for a piece of
me, pushing me around like a rat in a maze. Jesus."

What did that make me? If I couldn't do this for love,
what did it make me?

*Who the fuck cares? I'm going to do it anyway. None of
it matters. Except Saul.*

Even if he was going to go down after I threw myself
into this losing game, at least he'd be going down in a
world where he had a *chance*. Where the hellbreed were
checked. Not permanently, that would take a goddamn
miracle. But I could keep the world spinning a little longer,
and make it a little safer.

It didn't matter if I was doing it for them, or for myself. At least, I wasn't going to let it matter.

"I love you," I told Mikhail's headstone. For a moment I had a crazed hallucination of my right fist punching, the shock grinding the white stone to powder. I could do it, I was suddenly sure of that. Before, it had been hellbreed-jacked strength. Now the power came from somewhere else, and I didn't have a clue what I would do if it deserted me. "Mikhail," I whispered. "I hate you, too."

I didn't recognize my own voice. Irrational, sudden fear drilled through me. I hunched my shoulders and waited. One breath. Two.

Nothing happened.

I looked up again at my city. The sun's limb lifted sleepily from the horizon, swords of gold piercing the sky, and I felt dawn in my bones like the ocean must feel its tides.

Another idea hit me. I actually rocked back on my heels, my brain jolting inside its heavy bonecase. The dogsbody lifted itself up, the imprint of its scorch on wet grass steaming, and shook itself. The flat ears pricked forward, and it stared adoringly up at me. It actually *did* look like a hound, and even my blue eye could find no trace of Jughead Vanner left in its long lean body.

"Shit," I breathed. "Shit shit *shit*. Come on."

The absurdity of talking to myself on Beacon Hill was enough to make me grin as I spun on my heel and left Mikhail's glowing headstone behind. The dogsbody loped next to me as my stride lengthened, my coat flapping, and I broke into a run as the day came up like thunder.

31

HUTCHINSON'S BOOKS, USED & RARE, glowed in faded gold leaf on the wide dusty front window. I remembered how proud he'd been when we'd changed the name over from Chatham's, and how soon the gold leaf had started to look dry and dusty, like it had never been anything else.

He'd left the desktop, and while it booted up I grabbed a couple references from the *other* part of the store—the climate-controlled bit where he kept a hunter's library. That library earned him some nice tax breaks and justified me saving his bacon when he was caught hacking something he shouldn't be. Weedy little Hutch thought he was ten feet tall and bulletproof in cyberspace, and it didn't help that he was usually right.

I stacked the D'Aventine and Miguel de la Foya on the desk, sweeping aside a clutter of paper and setting a cup of moldering coffee higher up on the file cabinet behind his antique cubbyholed desk. The place was beginning to smell of sharpish rot and neglect, the dust and paper covering the peppery tang of a refugee emergency. I hadn't given him much time to pack.

I was grateful I'd sent him off, however.

Everyone you love. Every one you cast your eye upon.

Was Perry really that jealous? Or was it just a way to distract me? To keep me running until—

The monitor blinked. I flipped open the D'Aventine, checking the binder that had been right next to it—a laboriously cross-checked index, and an old one. Hutch had bitched endlessly about the old dot-matrix even after he'd gone through two new laser printers by now, the same way old ladies complain about beaus who jilted them in youth. I'd learned to just make another pot of coffee when he started in on that.

I wrote down page numbers and checked the de la Foya and the *Scribus Aeternum*, tapping a pencil while I scanned. I checked Kelley's *Habits of the Damned* and Carré's *The Outbreak of 1929: Its Causes and Effects*. Also, Hartmann's *Catholic Myths* and Artur Fountaine's *La guerre d'Inferne*.

I knew what I was looking for. Confirmation and explication instead of a needle in a haystack. Still, I came up empty. Nothing about a particular Spear of Destiny that would fit the bill, and nothing about Perry even in Carré, who was generally held to be the authority on '29. Even if he was a terrible writer, he was pretty much always dead-on.

The constellation of intangibles that made the Outbreak possible—astronomical and astrological energies aligned to weaken the walls between the Visible and the other worlds, the Infernals collecting Talismans used to power the Portals in different locations, the carefully nurtured scurf infestations and overheated economy—were monstrous enough. Some Infernals have admitted there was a

Leader who forced an alliance long enough for the portals to be achieved synchronously on different continents; there are even whispers of a full-blown hellmouth that stood for hours, admitting a flood of Infernals to our helpless world—

He goes on for *pages*, refusing to speculate further but giving tantalizing hints, reporting rumors and in the next breath reminding the reader to rely only on the things that can be verified. The trouble is, 'breed don't like appearing in the historical record. Carré had been a researcher much like Hutch; he'd disappeared in 1942. The hunter he'd been attached to—Simon Saint-Just—had also gone missing.

It had not been a good time to be a hunter in Europe. Hell, things had been bad all over, and it wasn't until the mid-sixties that we got some sort of handle on things.

A hellmouth. A full-blown hellmouth, instead of the barriers between here and the hellbreed home gapping for just an instant to let a single monster through. Perry certainly didn't dream small, and if it had happened once before, it could be done again.

A Leader who forced an alliance . . . What had Perry said to me, more than once?

I cannot hold back the tide forever. I'd stopped one of his bosses from coming through twice now. Or more precisely, Belisa had stopped him last time, before I'd shot her.

And damned myself.

Each time, the big bad boss had been struggling to step through a fractional gap, sliding into the fleshly world. That was bad enough. A full-blown hellmouth—a passageway to Hell held open for God knows how long—was going to be exponentially worse.

How's he going to power it? Ten to one says this Lanza del Destino. Major Talismans of a certain type can power a hellmouth for a while, but I can't think of a Spear that applies. I sighed, rolled my head back on my sore, aching neck. The dogsbody dozed near the front door, seeming content just to lay there.

Was I going to have to feed it soon? Did they stock hell-breed dog chow at the supermarket? I wondered briefly if that was tax-deductible and closed Carré with a snap. Hutch was going to have a fit if I didn't reshelve every-thing.

Well, if he has one, it'll mean I'm around to see it. That'd be nice. I considered the screensaver for a moment—pictures of cats with weird captions, shuffling by in random order. It vanished as soon as I tapped the space key.

"Okay," I said to the dusty silence. The air conditioner kicked on, cool air soughing through the store and Hutch's silent, dark apartment upstairs. "Let's hope digital is better than analog for this, huh?"

It took me two hours of hunt-and-pecking and cross-referencing, broken only by a trip upstairs to make some coffee. Hutch's fridge was unhappy in the extreme, so I left it closed after grabbing the canister of espresso-ground. I considered taking the garbage out, but one peek under the sink convinced me it was best left to it-self. I was trying to stop a catastrophe here, not playing Molly Maid.

Halfway through that pot of java, I leaned toward the computer screen. I'd finally signed into Hutch's remote worktop, seeing what he'd pulled up recently. It was eerie that I could see what he'd last been looking at and when—

he'd been up late last night, not going to bed until near dawn. I would've been on Beacon Hill by then.

All excited about a woodcut, Devi had said. There were plenty of files in the image folder, I started going through them methodically. They bloomed over the expensive flatscreen monitor, and most of them were Perry.

Bingo.

Here Perry was caught by a telephoto lens, a black-and-white of him getting out of a car on a city street. The back of the photo, part of the same image file, held Mikhail's spiky backward-leaning script: *1969, Buenos Aires.* Another, this one in glaring color, clipped from a newspaper archive, all about new management at the Monde Nuit, decades later.

I stared at the date.

It was right after Mikhail had pulled me out of the snow. I shook my head, silver chiming in my hair. *Huh.*

Another black-and-white, Perry leaning against a bar and smiling, white fedora pushed back on his head, his shark smile showing up in the mirror between gleaming bottles. *Berlin, 1934.* Back when the first Jack Karma was working Germany. That was pretty much the first mention of him I'd ever been able to dig up.

I found the woodcut just as another scalding cup of coffee was going down. Mid-sixteenth century, originally from Bremen, now part of a museum collection. Thick black inked lines; the carver had been a genius. It was small as such things went, but exquisitely detailed—two cavorting figures under a full moon, facing a tall thin man in a long dark coat, his broadsword slanting up and flames running along its edge. He was unquestionably a hunter, and a long thin casket lay on the ground behind him. The title was *Der Schutz der ersten Spear,* and an electric bolt shot through me.

The two attackers leered. One of them was unquestionably the late and unlamented piebald Halis, floppy hair and all, claws and teeth bared.

The other was Perry, a spot of white in the woodcut's florid lines, a slim orchid.

"Oh, you son of a bitch," I whispered. "I've got you now."

Only I didn't. It took most of the afternoon before I had him, and when I did I was sweating, my teeth were chattering, and Hutch had run out of coffee.

32

I dialed Galina, but she didn't pick up. Which was odd.

I paged Anya from Hutch's shop too, but there was no answer. Of course, she was probably in the barrio, trying to get the Weres to safety. I dialed my own answering service, but it just rang endlessly. I even tried ringing Monty, but after getting his voice mail for the fifth time I just hung up.

From not remembering a single damn thing, I'd gone to being able to pull phone numbers out like I was shuffling through a card file. It was a goddamn pity nobody was listening, and the sun was past its apogee. The shadows were lengthening, and the dogsbody was nervous. At least, he *looked* nervous, pacing back and forth in front of the shop door, muscles rippling under blond hair. Whining while I dialed and dialed, getting no response.

"Galina should be picking up," I muttered. "What the fuck?"

He couldn't give me any reply, black-skinned ears fuzzed with blond fur laid flat against his ungainly head. Just that grumble, deep in his throat, spiraling up to an inquisitive at the end. I was still sweating, every nerve in me jumping and frayed raw.

"*Fuck!*" I finally snarled, and slammed the phone down. Just then, someone tapped on the glass, and the dogsbody growled, deep and low.

I stalked between bookcases, my hand on a gun, peered at the dusty window.

He tapped again. I almost fell over myself unlocking the door, grabbed his collar, and dragged him in. "What the hell are you—"

Gilberto's sides heaved. His face was painted with bright blood, and he was shaking. For all that, his dark eyes were alight, no longer flat and dead, and he looked completely, fully alive.

"*Mala suerte,*" he gasped. "*Mala* fuckin' *suerte, chingada.* Melendez, he prolly dead."

I locked the door and dragged him further into the shop. The air-conditioning soughed on again, and I smelled burned coffee and the flat copper tang of human fear and blood over the dust and paper.

I propped him against a bookcase in the Classics section and took a deep breath. "Why aren't you at Galina's, then? That's where you were supposed to—"

"Been there." He closed his eyes, gulping down air. "*Chingada, mi profesora,* the whole place burning."

"Burning? A *Sanctuary*?" I stared at him like he'd gone mad.

"Barrio too. City's rollin' like Saturday night. *Estamos corriendo en la chingada, mi profesora,* we are fucked for sure. Was *el Rubio* at Melendez's. Old man tole me run, tole me you'd be here. Almost din't make it out." He was gaining his breath rapidly, eyelids fluttering. "Ran for

Lina's, but it was on fire. Crawling with 'breed. Hopped away. Had to steal a horse."

Considering what he was telling me, I didn't even want to take him to task for minor auto theft. "Galina's shop was burning? The whole thing?"

"Blue flames, *profesora*. Screamin'." He'd regained his breath by now. "Whole goddamn thing. Looked bad."

Saul. Everything inside me turned over hard. *Oh, God. Saul.*

But Galina had the vaults. It would be simple for her to just get everyone downstairs and rebuild. Blue flames, though. And whoever heard of someone burning down a Sanctuary? It would take the equivalent of a sorcerous nuke to do it. Not worth the trouble when they could just rebuild like a tree growing in fast-forward...

"The fire. Blue. Hellfire, Gil?"

"Looked like. Listen, I ain't sure I'm clear—"

Meaning he wasn't sure if hellbreed had followed him. "It's nice of you to be worried. Don't be." The machine inside my head clicked on, calculating, assessing, weighing. "It'll take more than that to keep Galina down." *He wants her incommunicado.* It was the only explanation. And without Galina to hold messages and ammo, Anya and I were looking at some difficulty. "Go upstairs. Bathroom's second door on the left, grab the first-aid kit and wash the blood off. Then come down here, be ready to roll."

"*Si.*" He took off down the hall with enviable speed. Guess the young bounce back quick. And it was probably a relief to have someone giving him orders so he could just put his head down and *do*.

I remembered that feeling from my own apprentice days.

I peered out the front window, surveying the street. The shadows were clustering, the sky hot blue and cloudless. All the same, static electricity prickled under my skin.

"Fuck," I said, stupidly, under my breath. Like it was a secret. "*Der ersten Spear.*" The Prime Spear. The first spear-shaped Talisman. "Perry, you son of a bitch."

Well, Jill, what did you expect? He's been planning this for decades.

Another thought hit me, so suddenly I actually jerked and a half-amazed laugh burst out of me. "Of course. It's Black Thursday, all over again."

The dogsbody made a short barking sound, like it was echoing my laughter. Outside, the shadows sizzled, and several of them lengthened. I didn't like the way they were creeping toward the store, the world behind them warping into a colorless fuming wasteland. The blue of the sky was lensed with smoke now, and I snapped my fingers at the dogsbody. Its ears perked again.

"Come on, you. Guess we're not letting Gil come back down after all."

* * *

"Where we goin'?" Gil yelled, clutching the bandage to his upper arm. His torn sleeve flapped in the wind roaring through the broken windows, I slewed the wheel to the right and shot us through a red light with half a foot to spare, ignoring the blare of a horn from a semi and nudging us over into the left lane. Oncoming traffic was a bitch, but the tingle of intuition running along my nerves told me left was the way to play this part of our run.

I've never been in an accident. Basic precognition is

good for *something*. Besides, the rush of traffic might slow down pursuit.

It was nice to be behind the wheel again. Sort of.

"Sacred Grace!" I yelled back. The blue Nissan didn't have much pickup, but it was maneuverable, and that counts for a lot. Still, it was making a knocking noise I didn't much like, and if I sent it over another few railroad tracks at high speed the tires weren't going to be happy. "Where'd you get *this* car from, anyway?"

"My cousin!" Thin blue lines of healing sorcery crawled under the bandage on his arm, knitting flesh together. He was armed, too, and grinning so widely I could see his fillings. "Discount *por la familia*! Got it cheap!"

"Next time tell him to sell you American, for Christ's sake!" I twisted the wheel again, we skidded around a corner, I feathered the brake and stamped the accelerator and we were off again. Gunfire erupted behind us, perilously close to our tires. *They probably don't know I'm driving. Perry needs me to make his little plan work. Or was he lying about that, too?*

"Why we goin to church, eh?" Gilberto had a 9mm out, sunlight sparking viciously off its edges. "Father Gui owe you money?"

He owes me a lot more than that. "He's got something Perry wants!" I yelled. "Now shut up and put that thing away!"

He whooped as we smoked into a turn at the north end of Salvador Avenue, near Jordan's headshop. I hoped to hell she was under cover. Gil's pulse was jackhammering, but I didn't have the breath or time to get on him to calm it. The dogsbody was flattened in the backseat, and if it was making any noise I couldn't tell. A thundering *pop* and the car slewed wildly, of *course* we'd lost a tire, it was the way these things went. I hit another corner, floored it, ignored the grinding, wished it was a stick instead of automatic for the fiftieth time, and realized I was cursing steadily, a song of obscenities as familiar as breath. Tendons stood out on the backs of my hands as I fought the steering, forcing the car to do what I wanted as it bucked and shuddered.

We cleared the curb with a bump and soared, hit the steps and the car teetered for a long moment. "No no no *no no*—," I chanted, willing it to stay upright, and we thudded back down, listing terribly. I'd bought us a few seconds. "*Inside!*" I barked. "Move your ass!"

Gil was already bailing. The dogsbody wriggled out through the back window and I covered them, skipping backward up the stairs as the shadows down the street warped. Bullets chipped and plowed up the steps behind me, Gil hit the doors like a bomb and the dogsbody leapt, its claws scratching on stone. I flung myself back and Gil kicked the door again, neatest trick of the week, slamming it shut. The lock was broken, deadbolt wrenched free, I bounced up and swept the church's interior with both guns.

Sacred space, won't hold them for long though. Not when they're this motivated. "*Gui!*" I yelled, a harsh cawing in the sudden gloom. "Guillermo! Rosas? Ignacio?"

"*Dios,*" Gilberto breathed, and crossed himself. My eyes finished adjusting, and I let out a short frustrated sound. The dogsbody shivered, hunching next to me, steam drifting from its blondness.

The priests had taken refuge here, instead of the chapel attached to the school. This late in the day, maybe they'd sent the kids home. I *hoped* they had. Their rooms—they still called them cells, a sort of monastic joke—in the parsonage building would be empty too. Here was safest.

Only it hadn't turned out to be safe after all. Not when the forces of Hell were this goddamn enthusiastic.

Old thin Ignacio was in the middle of a jumble of broken pews, his body contorted into an enthusiastic backbend. The new redheaded one, Father Blake, had died near the confessional, and the arterial spray had even reached the racks of candles lit for sinners and prayers. Every inch of stained glass was covered with a thick layer of soot, and the pews—all terribly jumbled and splintered—were scorched.

Fat jolly Rosas, who had never liked me, was on the steps to the altar. He'd been flung over the crucifix, his guts spread in a tangle of gray loops and whorls. The crucifix itself had been torn down and mutilated, and in its place was nailed...

Bile burned my throat.

Gilberto was whispering. "*Aunque pase por el valle de sombra de muerte, no temeré mal alguno. Porque Tú estás conmigo.*" He took two steps to the side, leaned over, and heaved.

"*La primera Lanza* was here all the time." I sounded like I'd been punched. "For *years.*"

A long time ago, there had been a case involving a firestrike spear. Guillermo had lied to me then, but he'd been protecting an even bigger secret. *I can't let you break your oath,* Rosas had told him, and relations between me and the boys of Sacred Grace had been decidedly chilly ever since. I never played basketball with sleek dark Guillermo anymore, and we kept the exorcisms strictly business.

The altar had been torn to bits, something wrenched

from its depths. Of course, hide one of the most powerful Talismans on earth in plain sight. That had probably been Rosas's idea. My boots slipped in the blood and foulness on the steps. The stench of a battlefield was overpowering. No matter how many times you smell death, it never gets usual. It never becomes routine.

Rosas's face was twisted in horror. He'd died in a bad way. *Not so jolly now, fat man.* From the way he'd been flung, he'd probably been trying to protect Gui, buy him enough time to reach the altar and the artifact inside.

The very thing Perry was after.

It has been in my keeping all this time.

The case had also involved a wendigo and the Sorrows. Now I remembered that *Perry* had shown up during the hunt with the firestrike—the only weapon capable of killing the goddamn thing the Sorrows had been using to hunt me. I'd only had Perry's word that he'd gotten the firestrike from Sacred Grace. He'd told Saul as much, and since Saul had told *me* I'd taken it as truth.

Perry could not have stepped on this consecrated ground, could he? No. But he *had* been up to his eyebrows in that case, with Melisande Belisa, and neatly misdirected me. *Never assume* is the rule when it came to hellbreed, and it had been only a small mistake on my part. A tiny link in the chain, but enough.

Not to mention Perry had planted distrust between me and Father Gui. Which must have warmed his cold, dead hellbreed heart all the way through. If I hadn't assumed the firestrike was what the priests were hiding, I would have come back and torn the whole place apart until I found everything—and the Spear they had been hiding all along would have ended up in Galina's vaults, where

Perry couldn't lay his hands on it *ever*, world without end, amen.

It was all so simple, now. Somehow Perry had gotten wind of the Spear, hidden out here in the middle of nowhere. The other thing he needed was a hunter to wield it. I'd assumed the firestrike had been what Sacred Grace had been hiding, and relations between me and the priests had been decidedly frosty ever since. It was a pity, because Gui probably would have eventually told me, vow of secrecy or not.

We were, after all, friends. Or we had been. Had he wanted to tell me, any of those times he tried to talk to me and I ignored him, keeping the conversation to the exorcism at hand? Had the secret been burning in him all this time?

It didn't matter now. With the Spear right where Perry could keep an eye on it, all he had to do was wait for me to damn myself. He'd waited *years*.

And all that time I'd been oblivious.

Never assume, milaya. *Is shortest way to get ass blown sideways.*

"*FUCK!*" I screamed, and the word hit the walls, richocheting back to sting me. Gilberto crossed himself again, reflexively.

Little creaks and cracklings ran through the church walls. The building groaned, etheric contamination spreading as the murder and hatred boiled. *Wait. Wait just a second. Hellbreed can't touch it, and the ground's sanctified. So he sent Traders to open up the way and contaminate. What do you want to bet some of them are still here?* "Gil. Behind me."

He moved immediately, thank God. "You see something, *bruja*?"

"Listen." I kept both guns loosely pointed down. "They're still in the building, or at least, *some* of them are. Nine o'clock, there's a door. Move toward it, nice and easy."

The dogsbody growled and looked up, a quick inquiring movement. "Hey," I said, and its ear flicked at me. "Go with Gil. Protect him."

The hound shook its narrow head, then padded toward my apprentice. *Well, there's that, at least.* "Gil. Get out of here, go—"

Now we hit the stubbornness, at the worst possible time. "Ain't leavin you, *profesora*."

I would have kicked his ass for it, but the choir loft exploded and the church was suddenly full of hellbreed, its walls shuddering at the violation. A century of blessing and sacred belief rose to push the intruders out, but it was damaged now. The Traders had broken it with murder and suffering, and theft.

The blessing, crackling fine lines of blue, beat ineffectually at the damned as they swarmed. They hissed, jaws distending, their beauty sliding aside, and every single one of them was 'breed instead of Trader. Fast, brutal, and harder to kill. There were at least a dozen of them. They didn't look like they cared very much that Perry supposedly wanted me alive.

This is not going to end well.

33

Father Gui's body hit the altar with a meaty thump. I followed, blood slicking my lips and the knife sinking in past a hard hellbreed shell, twisting through the suction of unholy muscle. We slid down the wall, the gem singing in my wrist as it pumped etheric force through me, every muscle cramping and my breath a harsh ratcheting as I swore, again, obscenities interweaving with a chanted prayer in bastard Latin. The 'breed exhaled foulness in my face, but he was already dying, thin cracks of dusty corruption racing through his skin as the silver's poison spread.

Gilberto screamed, a high breaking note of rage, and fired again. The dogsbody made another one of those wrenching guttural noises, and my boots jolted down. I heaved the rotting body away, it fell on Gui's wracked and lifeless frame with a wet splorch.

Sorry, padre. Wish we could shoot some hoops instead. The dogsbody hunched, snarling, and I crashed into the 'breed crouching in front of my whey-faced apprentice. He was giving a good account of himself, but it was only a matter of time. The 'breed went down in a heap; I cut its throat with one swift motion and the dogsbody was on it too, jaws crunching with sickening finality. The 'breed exploded in a shower of brackish fluid, dust spilling from its veins, and I rose from the tangle, spinning the knife. "Come on!" I yelled, the knife sliding back into its sheath, and we were out the door before more of our pursuers decided to chance the inside of the church. The murder would echo here for a long time, eating further at the blessing in the walls until someone could get out here to clean it up.

I might even be the one cleaning, if I survived this.

"Need transport!" Gil yelled.

Well, at least he was thinking. "Don't *worry*!" We pounded down the hall, smell of chalk and incense, vestments hung on one side and the wine cabinet locked behind gilt-edged froufrou, my coat snapping and the silver in my hair buzzing and spitting blue sparks. It was dark in here, the lights flickering and buzzing. The sharp-edged charms Perry had given me were heavy, twitching as if alive. "Gonna have to steal a car!"

"Aw, *chica*." Gilberto coughed rackingly. He was keeping up so far, but soon his strength would start to flag. There was only so much healing sorcery could do, and both I and the dogsbody were moving with eerie speed. "You a real role model."

"Bite me, kiddo." Our footsteps sounded like one runner, until I left the ground in a leap that blew the outside door clean off its hinges. I rode it down, guns out, and swept as a howl went up.

The sun was low in the west, not setting yet but damn close, and clouds were boiling over what had been a blue vault. Greenyellow stormlight filled the alley; there was a basketball hoop bolted above the one-car garage at the dead end. The garage door was open, and I didn't have time to remember playing horse with Father Gui as an apprentice, both of us talking smack and the priest's three-pointers marvels of accuracy. He crossed himself after each one. Misha would be drinking a beer and watching, occasionally catcalling a point of advice that was of no earthly use whatsoever as Father Rosas sat next to him in a sagging lawn chair and glowered disapprovingly.

No, no time to think about it and feel the rage or the grief, because there was a car backed into the garage, pointed out at the alley. It was the church's only vehicle, the ancient Cadillac Ignacio had picked up for a song and I'd rebuilt and cherried out, long ago in the dim time after Mikhail's death. No time to remember working on it, Ignacio handing me tools and Gui asking me soft questions about what this or that part of the engine did. *"Get in!"* I yelled; there were lean shapes at the alley's mouth.

The key was in the ignition, and it reeked of Ignacio's cigars. Gil was coughing, gone cheesy-pale in a way I didn't like at all, and the dogsbody growled as the tools hung on pegboards chattered, the entire garage rocking like a ship in a storm as the church tolled its distress.

The shapes at the end of the alley were hellhounds, their eyes full of venomous, greenish glow. I twisted the key and was rewarded with a throbbing purr. The old girl still remembered me. *"This* is a car!" I barked. "This is the kind of car you steal, Gil! Good old American heavy metal!"

He slumped in the seat, but his quick brown fingers were busy reloading. "They don' look happy, *bruja.*" Another cough, but I'd snapped the parking brake and dropped it into gear. I floored it and the Caddy leapt forward like it had never intended to stay still.

"*Fuck* them!" I yelled, and we hit the massed bodies at the end of the alley with a crunch. The Caddy snarled, the dogsbody let out a yowl, and we were through as the sky muttered with thunder.

"Where we goin'?" Gilberto grabbed for his window, rolling it up, and I had a mad desire to flick on the air-conditioning.

Shit if I know, kid. But it hit me like lightning, Melendez's mouth shaping a spirit's words, and understanding broke through me like water through a bombed dam. It could have been intuition, or the gem in my wrist suddenly singing in a language I understood, or just the most insane option at this point. But as soon as it occurred to me, I knew it was right.

The speedometer's needle popped up past sixty and I stood on the brake, twisting into a bootlegger's turn, fishtailing as hellhounds boiled out of the shadows, their hides leprous with steam in the scabbed light. They closed around us like a wave, running, their obsidian-chip teeth champing between gobbets of poisonous foam, and Gilberto let out a short miserable cry as he realized they were *herding* us.

"Gonna play some baseball, Gil. It's the World Series, and I'm on call." My breath came in heaving gasps, and my cheeks were wet. The world was doing funny things seen through my left eye, jumping and twitching as the strings under the fleshly curtain were plucked and torn. "Listen carefully, and *don't argue*."

IV: Dies Irae

34

There was nobody on the streets. I wasn't surprised—
even numbskull civilians will stay inside when the sky
looks like a ripening bruise and the air is full of scorching
that feels like an ice bath. Now that we were going the way
they wanted, the 'breed hung back, letting the hounds nip
and harry us through the streets. I made a few attempts to
shake them, just because I don't like being chased. Mother
Mary on a pogo stick, how I *hate* to be pursued.

But there was nothing left to do, and Gilberto did *not*
look good. He clutched at the gun like it was a Grail, and
his lips moved a little as if he was praying.

It was a good idea, but I had no time.

"You hear me?" I finished, as we hit International Way
and the four lanes ribboned around us, every light turning
green as we sped through, tires smoking and the hellhounds pouring around us in a steaming wave. "No heroics, Gil. You get the *fuck* out of here and strike for Ridgefield. Leon'll take you in."

Gil's chin set stubbornly.

"Gilberto. You're a liability, not a help. You go, or I

swear to God I'll beat the shit out of you myself." It was a good threat. I even sounded like I meant it.

"You goin' in there to die." Flatly, as if he was talking about the nice weather we were having lately. "*Mi hermano*, he look like this, like you. Right before he got shot."

I almost winced. His brother was not a safe subject, the past reaching out its tentacles to strangle us all. "They can't kill me, kid." I sounded weary even to myself. "Perry needs me for this." *A Trader can steal a Talisman, but not wield it. Not for very long, anyway—but if he's using it to power the hellmouth...Still, I'm the Judas for the Other Side. I have to make it a little longer, right?*

It was *so* not a comforting thought.

Gilberto's chin set itself, stubbornly. "So I go in. Watch your back."

"No."

"*Profesora—*"

"No, Gil. You have your orders, goddammit."

"*Profesora—*"

"*No.*" I said it a lot more sharply than I meant to, and hit the brakes, slewing us sideways as International dove down to follow the river. The stadium was here, hulking like a giant animal over a bone, one of the places in the city where you can't see the huge granite Jesus on top of Mercy General. Sometimes I'm pretty sure it's an act of will that keeps that particular landmark from being visible in some pockets of urban real estate. "I'm counting on you, Gilberto. Don't let me down."

He mumbled something. I smashed the accelerator again, spun us into another turn, stood on the brake. "I can't *hear* you, apprentice." Snap of command.

"*Si*," he said, scowling. "*Si, profesora.*" Just like a good soldier.

Just like me, when Mikhail would tell me what was what. Would I ever reach the point where I'd trade Gil for my own mark, sell him to Perry to buy a little more time? Or bargain him into it out of love, believing that he could do what I couldn't and stop *el rubio Diablo* from spinning the wheel and landing a double zero?

I don't want to find out. It ends here. "Good fucking deal." We rocked to a stop, tire smoke rising in sharp-toothed shapes around us. The hellhounds flowed in a leaping circle, stormlight running wetly over their smoking hides as thunder rumbled again. "Gil..."

He stared out the window, sallow, pitted jaw working.

"You're my apprentice," I said, finally. "And you're a good one. You won't understand for a long, long time. But I love you, and I'm sorry. It's not your fault."

I hit the latch and was outside in a hot second, leaning down to glance through the back window. "Stay with Gil," I said, sharply, and the dogsbody settled into the backseat, whining. Every hair on my body tried to stand straight up, I heard hellhound claws skritching and scratching, and the splatter of foam from their panting mouths. The circle tightened, pressing closer, and I glanced up at the sky.

The clouds lowered, sickly greenish-black. Lightning crawled through their billows, occasionally lancing with a *crack* like a belt hitting naked flesh. I slammed the door, Gilberto already shimmying over into the driver's side. The Cadillac purred, a plastic rosary swinging from the rearview—maybe it was Father Gui's, maybe Rosa's—and Gilberto stared through the window, his dark eyes suddenly wet.

I told him what I wish Misha had told me, I realized, and swallowed hard. The hellhounds didn't draw any closer.

I stepped back once, twice. The engine revved, the tires chirped...

...and the hellhounds flowed aside at the last moment, leaving a clear path for Gilberto as the wine-red Caddy shot up Martin Luther, its engine singing in mingled pain and relief.

* * *

The Santa Luz Stadium and Convention Center was a squat, graceless concrete dome, pathways cut up and down its sides like ribbons of frosting on a particularly nasty soot-gray cake. Normally, a gigantic American flag fluttered atop it, waving like a stripper's pasty, but the three squat glass towers of the nearby convention center leered at an empty flagpole now, reflecting bright white flashes as the storm closed over Santa Luz. No rain, everything hot with that queer icy heat, the edges of my coat flirting as the wind teased them. My right hand touched a gun, and I felt very exposed standing here.

Almost naked.

I swallowed again, waited as the Cadillac's roar was lost even to my jacked-up hearing. "*Do svidanye,*" I whispered. My left hand had already closed around the whip's handle.

If they wanted me to go in there, they were going to have to work for it.

Unfortunately, the hellhounds took me up on the challenge. They moved in, heads down and snaking, a whole massed tide of them, and I gave ground. The whip flicked, breaking tough skin and loosing spatters of stinking ichor, but I didn't draw the gun.

I had no bullets to waste, now.

They herded me past the ticket booths—all their glass shattered, glinting back little fractures of lightning—and the crowd-control turnstiles, the aluminum tubes twisted back in weird contorted flower-shapes. Someone had certainly been smoothing the path for me.

The primrose path, Jillybean. All the way down to Hell.

When the dogs got too close I flicked the whip at them, and one or two screamed in high, childlike voices. Thunder was a constant roar now, and I *felt* the sun touch the horizon, beginning its slow nightly drowning. The city shivered, concrete groaning, and the wind from the river howled through empty parking lots, tearing at the edges of the dome.

Darkness rose from the corners of the earth, and the hellhounds herded me into a long, low corridor. I heard a mutter, the bulk of the storm shut away. They'd stopped steaming under the lash of daylight, but the press of their bodies made the air quiver with unhealthy heat.

The corridor curved, and for a long time it seemed like I'd be in it forever, the hounds pressing forward to nip at and drive me along, my whip flicking with a jingle of blessed silver every few moments to hold them back. I skip-shuffled along, my back to one wall or the other, and ghastly fluorescent tubes fizzed and blinked overhead. Chipped paint on the concrete turned sickly as the hounds brushed against it, and the little dapples of my sea-urchin aura showed up, punctuating the etheric bruising with tiny crackles.

The corridor terminated in a set of double doors, pulsing as the air behind them pressed close with a crowd-murmur. The hounds stopped, some of them crouching on their haunches, tongues lolling and yellow foam dripping, wriggling into cracks in the floor with subtle hisses.

He must really be excited. I bit back a bitter little laugh. *All this trouble, Perry, when you knew I'd show up anyway.*

One of the hounds hiss-growled very softly, its lip curling back from glassine teeth. I jingled the whip and the beast cowered back into the mass.

Gonna see what's behind Door Number One, Jillian? Oh yeah, you bet. Right now. I eased along the wall, keeping an eye on the hellhounds. *Right fucking now. He's been setting this up for decades.*

Be a shame to keep him waiting.

I pushed against the crossbar. The door opened, sterile white light flooded through, and the sound of a crowd belched into the hall on a tide of dry candy corruption. The hounds pressed further back, and for a moment I considered taking them on until I ran out of ammo.

But that would be a waste. I had better things to use my bullets on.

I braced the door wide and stepped out into the glare.

35

*W*hatever game we were going to be playing, it wasn't baseball.

The playing field was venomous green, usually Astro-turf but now transmuted into short fleshy spikes that twisted and rippled obscenely as the crowd-roar passed over them. The glare was amazing, a nuclear flash prolonged until it was a scream of whiteness, a world-killing light. I blinked, my eyes watering, and forced myself to scan.

The field was bare and green, an indecent hump in the middle with a low block of darkness placed precisely on its crest. The sound was immense, swelling through feedback and screaming, the roar lifting my hair and blowing it back as etheric bruising tightened and my aura sparked, every inch of silver on me running with blue light.

It halted, a sudden silence filling the vast dome, and that quiet stole all the breath out of my lungs, the way a sudden jolt at the end of a rope will. Training clamped down, my lungs shocked back into working and my pulse dropping as my right-hand gun cleared leather. A rush of warm air slid past me and toward the closing doors; they latched shut with the clicks of bullets loaded in a clip.

Perry laughed. He spread his arms and grinned with sheer mad good humor. "*Darling!* One appreciates punctuality in a woman, almost as much as one appreciates beauty. Then again, my dearest one, you are *so* worth waiting for."

He wore black. A thin V-neck sweater and narrow pleated trousers, a sword of darkness against all the glare. His hair was pale tarnished silk, and his eyes glowed hellhound-blue. The change from his usual white linen was a shock, too, and my busy little brain started worrying at it. What did it *mean*?

Just let it go, Jill. You'll find out soon enough.

Super-acute senses are sometimes a curse. My eyes stung, but I caught movement up in the stadium seats, behind the screen of glare. *How many? Sounds like a lot, but echoes, hard to tell. Jesus.* I kept the gun trained on Perry, shook the whip slightly to assure myself of free play. "Actually, *Hyperion*, I'm early."

"We can argue later, my dove. And Brother Michael?"

"He sends his love." An answering grin pulled my lips back from my teeth. "You're being an asshole, Perry."

"Oh, you wound me. I have kept faith with you in every possible way. I allow you so much more than I would ever allow another." He backed up a step, two, his wingtips touching the fat blades of not-grass with slight squelching sounds. "For example, it was necessary to allow you to betray me. Or whatever you thought you were doing, darling. I don't expect you to be anything other than what you are."

"Which is what, Perry? What do you think I am?"

"My unwilling ally, darling. My enfleshment, my entrapment, and my lovely, lovely doom. In the old sense, of course. *Doom* as in 'inescapable.'" He actually lifted a hand and blew me a kiss. A susurrus went through the invisible crowd, a breaker of whispered titters. "Come here, dearest. Come see what your suitor has created, all for you."

I shot myself in the head to get away from you, Perry. Don't pretend you've got my interests at heart. But sick knowledge impelled me forward.

I had to *see*.

The altar was long and low, made of black volcanic glass instead of a chunk of a hangman's tree. I took it in with short, sipping little glances, between scanning the rest of the stadium. It seats an ungodly number of people for Wheelwrights games and other foolishness, a real sink of taxpayer dollars from the seventies when everything was whiskey-a-go-go out here in the desert. Santa Luz fought like hell to get the stadium pried out of the grip of the Noches County seat, and the success was Pyrrhic when everything went over budget and repairs started coming due.

And now it was full of hellbreed and Traders, bright-eyed and staring, whispering at each other. Popcorn passed from hand to hand, and I smelled hot dogs and hellbreed. The place wasn't quite packed yet, but it was filling up.

This is not good.

My pulse settled down. The sudden calm would be ominous, because it meant I was ready for action. But Perry just smiled, and the scuffle of finding seats intensified.

It was the altar's surface that made my throat seize up and my stomach sink. Twisted runes—the closest you can get to Helletöng in written form—were scored deep into the volcanic glass, their sharp edges full of diseased blue hellfire. There was a chalice of heavy golden metal, full of clotted scum. Not gold, because pure elemental metal—copper, silver, gold—is always a bane to them. Silver works best, and the silver in my hair was sparking continuously now. My apprentice-ring was dangerously warm.

There were other things on the altar. Deformed claws, lumps of meat. Organs from their victims, a loop of hanging-rope, a knife of sharp alien geometry...and the Lance.

La Primera Lanza del Destino, wrenched from its hiding spot at Sacred Grace, lay on the unholy altar, curls of steam rising around it as it shivered uneasily.

A long, fluted cylinder of dark, stained wood, or a metal veined and carved to look like wood. It vibrated also, etheric force barely held in check, and its long, leaf-shaped blades looked too delicate to do any harm, both of them trembling like high school kids on a first date.

The world spun out from under me. I knew what it was, now. Hutch's books had shown me everything once I knew where to look.

The granddaddy of all Talismans, the one all other Spears are copied from, the Spear of Undoing. No wonder the Church had kept it so secret. It was older than the pagans, far older than the savior they prayed to, and it probably hadn't been anywhere near his martyrdom...but still. It was a Major Talisman, and you don't leave those lying around. Especially when they have a nasty habit of being able to *unmake* things.

"It's not going to work." My voice was a thin tremor from the dry cave of my mouth. "There's no way it's going to work."

"Oh, you're such a *pessimist*." Perry sighed. "We have

everything we need, my dearest. You and I will deal with my master, the hellmouth will remain open, and when the smoke has cleared, we shall be the undisputed rulers of a world remade in our own image."

Whose image? Not mine, you bastard. "Your master?"

"Father, master, whatever." He shrugged. "You didn't think I was *common*, did you, Kiss? I've taken an interest in your line for a very long time. And in Dresden, lo these many years ago, your predecessor Jack Karma and I had a meeting of minds. I gave him something he wanted, he gave me something I needed. And beautiful music was made."

This much, at least, I knew about. "Argoth. Your *father*?"

"One of many, darling. I told you, I am Legion. But *he* is very, very angry. You've barred him twice now. Ever since dear Jack sent him back, he's been aching and frothing to return and play games in this most fascinating of worlds. And to reclaim me, of course." He tilted his head, grinning at me. The silence was full of whispers, nasty mouthings, wet silk against sweating legs. "He thinks I'm going to help him."

"Aren't you?" I edged closer to the altar, but Perry resolved out of thin air next to me. The air tore itself apart with malevolent children's laughter. His fingers closed around my upper arm, slim steel bands, and I went very still, my left hand still on my whip handle.

"Now, now. Close enough for the moment. Don't be hasty." His fingers flicked, claws sliding free of pale narrow hardness, and leather tore. Perry grabbed my wrist, locking it.

He drew in a deep breath, his ribs crackling as they expanded. *"My children!"* he roared, and I almost flinched. His fingers bit down, and he shoved me back from the altar. *"Now is the hour of our glory!"*

"Glory!" A sea's foaming roil. The crowd went wild, arms lifted, claws and fists shaken. They howled and screamed and yapped, Trader and damned, all of them twisting under their screens of human flesh.

I stumbled back, using Perry's shove to get some space. Ran through the next few minutes in my head. There was just too much that could go wrong—

"Open the door!" Perry yelled, and the exotic thought that I was going to witness the creation of a hellmouth got me moving.

"The door, the door!" the crowd screamed back, and surged forward against the metal rails keeping them off the ten-foot drop to the stadium's floor. *"Open the door!"*

Thou Who, I thought, as my weight dropped back into my left leg, muscles tensing in preparation. *Thou Who hast given me to fight evil, protect me, keep me from harm.*

It was now or never. I exploded into a leap, aiming for the altar. If I could get my hands on the Lance—

Except it was too late. The gem on my wrist screamed, a high thin note like glass shivering into breaking, and Perry grabbed my ankle. He twisted, his fingers sinking into my boot with a sickening crunch, and hurled me across the field.

36

*T*ucking, rolling, the not-grass splorching underneath me and sending up a rank, juicy reek. I fetched up against the goalpost at the north end of the field, and the gigantic hollow sound it made would have been funny if the red rage of pain hadn't swallowed me whole. I was on my feet in an instant, whip shaken free and the not-grass suddenly sticky underfoot, gripping my bootsoles like an angry insect-eating carpet. The gem wailed, my ribs popping out with crunching wet noises, and I whooped in a breath as I jagged to the side, heel grinding down and my entire body a scream of agony. The whip struck across Perry's chest, silver biting, flaying his sweater and the white marble-hard shell underneath.

"*Lovely!*" he screamed. "*Just like old times, Kiss! Kiss me again!*"

Backing up, a glance shot at the altar where the 'breed made a circle, pushing the Traders in front of them. Slack-mouthed, their eyes bright with the shine of the dusted, the Traders pressed forward, and the deep thrumming all through the stadium wasn't just the blood in my ears.

That's where he's going to get the initial charge to break open the hellmouth. Traders. A whole lot of them.

And with that much ritual death, plus a Talisman to fuel it, he could keep a gap in the walls of the world open for a while.

It made a mad sort of sense, really. Innocent flesh breaks the walls between here and Hell better than anything else, but in a pinch other death will do. And if it's the death of the damned, it's the next best thing to innocent. Because none of the damned ever really thinks they're going to be the one.

Death is for other people, like payment and guilt. The damned believe they're *special.*

I suppose we all believe that, way down deep.

The gun spoke twice, holes blown in Perry's sweater. Black ichor flew, splattering, but not enough of it. Perry grinned, a death's-head smile, and leapt for me. I faded back, still firing, and the fact that I still didn't know nearly enough about exactly *what* he was rose up to bite me.

He produced hellfire in the blue spectrum, when anything above orange is seriously bad news. He wasn't an *arkeus* or a *talyn*, because he had always been all-too-disturbingly physical. And right now he was acting like the bullets were bee stings—a little irritating, certainly, but not putting him down the way a load of silver should.

He flashed through space with the stuttering, eerie speed of hellbreed, but I was one step ahead of him, leaping up and to the side as muscles pulled against flash-healing bones in my side and my ankle gave an almost-unheeded flare of sick burning pain. The squelching underfoot heaved, whatever had taken the place of Astroturf trying to throw me, and if I could just get my hands on the Lance and a few more seconds' lead time I could disrupt the altar and maybe take down enough of them to—

Perry hit me with another sickening sound, and I flew up into the bleachers, twisting and firing as blood burst from my lips. Red blood, no trace of black corruption. The gem screamed, pumping etheric force through me on a wave of bright white, and the cry was echoed by the crowd at the altar. Traders were being pulled down, hellbreed hands narrow and hard and clawed and hairy quelling their struggles as the mood inside the stadium tipped over into glee and terror.

The Traders had Traded, and now the bill was due.

He hopped up the bleachers towards me, black wingtips leaving wet black prints, the crowd had pulled away from this section and I suspected that was why he'd thrown me up here. He was *playing* with me, cat with mouse, and the knowledge filled me with welcome fury.

Do not get angry, Mikhail had always warned me. *Makes you stupid.*

I couldn't help it.

The Traders began screaming, and the stadium was an echo chamber, collecting the cries in massive sheaves and throwing them back down to earth. *Didn't count on being the sacrifice, did you? Serves you right.* I was up on my feet again, steel-shod heels chiming soundlessly as I found my balance in a wide aisle, Perry hopping up the steps in a mockery of dancing, his joints moving in sickeningly wrong jerks.

The stadium howled, concrete vibrating in distress, and Perry flung out a hand. Blue hellfire splashed up the seats to my right. I was already moving, flinging myself through a wall of superheated air, leather crisping and smoking, landing braced on two seats and pushing off, *twisting* in midair as my coat gave a snap like wet laundry, and my feet skidded across the not-grass, throwing up huge chunks of rotting foulness. Traders were dying in droves, the deep rumbling of Helletöng swallowing their screams whole, and a pale oval of brightness was spinning over the altar.

Jesus Christ! It was going too quickly—of course, he'd had a lot of time to prepare. The altar was heaped with harvested organs, and the Traders were falling at the hands of the hellbreed they'd Traded with, corruption-reek filling up the vast bowl space. The bodies fell, twitching, dust eating through them and spiraling up on hot drafts, spinning eddies of it coalescing and sprouting curse-wings. The baby curses flapped, squawking in 'töng, and glaring white light stabbed through me as Perry hit me again, driving me down into the not-grass. I choked, spitting to clear my mouth, my abused ribs giving another howl, and the knife was in my hand as we rolled to a stop, the blade dragging against his shell and biting in, silver sparking and hissing.

He jerked back as if stung, grabbed my wrist, and twisted, the knifeblade running with blue light, ichor sizzling on the metal. I punched him twice with my free hand, fist braced with my whip handle, black ichor flying. I spat again, tasting foul oil-soaked dirt, knee coming up as my heel stamped down, but he was too heavy and getting heavier, the physical world rippling around him as etheric force ran through us both. The gem was a wild high melody over the subsonic fright-train grumble of 'töng, and I was suddenly in the desert again, clawing my way up out of sand with the hornets buzzing and eating all over me, screaming and choking as ectoplasm and grit filled my mouth.

"Beautiful!" Perry yelled in my ear, even though I punched him again. His head snapped back, more ichor flew, and he was grinning through a thin black mask of it as his chin came back down.

I screamed, struggling, and the world skipped like someone had jostled the CD player it was spinning in. It came back, but only at a quarter of its usual speed, the curse-birds gaining strength and mass and slowly beating their wings and the screams of dying Traders running like colored oil on a wet plate.

Perry held my wrists. He was impossibly heavy, as if gravity had decided he was an exception to every rule. Ichor dripped down his face, and he blinked at me, first one mad blue eye, then the other. "Judith," he crooned, under the soupy feedback of the titanic noise raging in slow motion around us. "My darling. My *flesh.*"

Don't. Call. Me. That. Rage ignited, I heaved up under him, breaking my right hand free with another screaming twist. The knife flicked, biting his abdomen again. We rolled, the fetid green juice of the crushed not-grass sliding and slipping over us both like birth fluid.

The world snapped forward, catching up with itself, and I heard a familiar battlefield yell.

Thank fucking God. Relief then, hot and acid against my throat.

The hunters had arrived.

37

The tranced Traders were still dying, but now the hell-breed were dying too. I saw Benny Cross from Louisiana, his ferret face alight as he opened fire with both guns; Sloane from gray rain-drenched Seattle, the charms in his hair chiming as he swung two silver-plated *escrima* sticks, Leon from Ridgefield, his battered tan duster scorched and spotted with blood while Rosita, his modified rifle, roared. Thierry Parvus from Saskatchewan, dropping out of the sky like God's avenging while the copper charms on his boots' fringes rattled and spat, Emoke Kolada and Dmitri Roslan, John Blake and John Carver and John Gray and Jack Quint and Jack Hell, Louis Darmor and MaryAnn Bright, too many to list. Some of them I only knew from word of mouth, others I knew because I'd worked with them; a few had come to Santa Luz to help out once or twice and I'd returned the favor. Many of them I didn't know at all, but they were all hunters, elemental metal jingling and long coats swinging as they waded into the fray, their auras cracking with sea-urchin spikes like my own.

Their cries were a bright counterpoint over the rumble

of 'töng, and I could have wept. Because we do something the 'breed don't ever do: we work together. It means every hunter is worth more than their weight when it comes to holding back Hell's tide; even when there's a mass of them, every one of Hell's scions only thinks of his own advantage. The hunters moved in tightly disciplined bands, cutting through the crowds, and I saw Anya Devi, her beads running with blue light and Benny Cross at her back, heading straight for the altar.

If even one of us could reach the altar, we could nip Perry's little plan right in the ass.

Oh, God, oh God thank you—

Perry snarled, my fingers in his hair, and I slammed his skull against the yielding ground. It felt wonderful, so I did it again, realized it wasn't going to do any good just as he got his wits about him and heaved up, tossing me away. I landed catfooted, had my balance in a split second, and leapt after him.

He was heading for the altar. He was too impossibly fast, streaking through trembling, overloaded reality. Anya was bogged down in a knot of struggling 'breed and Traders, her guns literally blazing and her scream of frustration a rising hawk-cry of effort.

Don't worry, I'm on it, just keep going—

Another roar filled the stadium, and I didn't have time to blink or even really register the fact that Weres had begun pouring into the stadium through flung-wide doors, leaping gracefully and flickering between animal and human form, clustering dazed Traders and bringing them down, trying like hell to avoid the 'breed. Lionesses, tawny-armed and honey-haired, working together to take down their prey, other cat Weres simply, magnificently fought; the bird Weres flickered through their feathered changeforms and raked with long talons. If they could keep the Traders away from the ritual death meted out near the altar, just maybe...

But we were doomed, because Perry was faster than all of us. He cleared a thrashing knot of 'breed in a single leap, and hurled himself at the pale oval spinning atop the altar's black crouch. The curse-birds swarmed down, ripping past him in black bullet-shreds, and the oval became a dome of pitiless white light.

He couldn't touch a Major Talisman. But he didn't have to. All he had to do was get it close enough to the hungry orifice.

His foot flicked out, and he kicked the Lance directly into the incipient hellmouth.

The world exploded.

I was down and rolling as the shockwave passed over me, the fabric of reality bunching and twisting as it was torn rudely open. Bodies went flying, ichor splattering, and the noise was so big I moved in a bubble of silence as soon as it started, hot fluid trickles slipping down from my ears, kissing my neck. The pain was silver nails driven through my skull, a warm gush of blood loosing itself from my nose, but I was already committed to the leap. A collapsing hellbreed, his mouth a soundless scream of agony, folded as my boot kissed the top of his head, propelling me forward, my whip hand flicking forward and the gun in my other hand now.

Too late. The door was open.

Hellbreath streamed free, a wave of heat so fierce it was cold, and it was a good thing I was temporarily deaf. Surviving Traders fell, hands clapped to their ears, screaming silently. I had no time to think about how the Weres were handling this, I was too busy, bracing myself for the hit as a tide of half-seen shapes burst free of the hole in the world.

This wasn't a regular portal, a hair-thin millisecond gap in the world for something to slip through. This was a full-fledged hellmouth, the dome of white light an obscene abscess swelling, pushing against the altar's surface, hell-breed crawling out of the yawning light as Hell shoved them free.

I strained through air gone thick as lead, committed to my leap, as the mouth pulsed once, drooling hellbreed and the shadowy forms of *arkeus* like pus. Perry lifted his arms, braced against the flood of his kith and kin, and leaned forward. His mouth stretched, and the long grinding of Helletöng was a single word, rubbing through the deaf-noise and spearing every cell of my body.

The hole clotted, and for one second as I hung above him I thought perhaps it had closed of its own accord. But no, it was just heaving around something almost too big for it, and I must have known on some level. Because the gun was back on its holster before I hit the ground, my whip jolting free, and I dove for the altar as the hellmouth pursed its thin lips and vomited.

* * *

The gem on my wrist gave a hard, painful jerk. My whip uncoiled, silver jangling silently. My right-hand gun spoke, burning flooding my arm and the gem shrieking. If I hadn't been swimming in so much pain already, the sudden cramp might have brought me to my knees.

I opened my mouth to scream if I had to, but there was no *time*. The world burst out into hypercolor, even more vivid than the superacute senses the gem gave me. At the same time, everything slowed down, my hip popping forward because always, in whip and stave work, it's the hip that leads. Temporary deafness fraying at the edges as the whip stretched, blurring-fast, and the thing vomited through the hellmouth leaned back, its foot crushing against the wooden Lance as it shuddered on the altar's top. Ash rose as the Lance twisted, bits of it grinding away finer and finer as the hellmouth chewed at its stored-up power.

The *thing* that had come through was an amorphous bipedal shape, silhouetted against the glow—hellbreed are like Elder Gods, they do not dress when they are at home, but when they come over into the physical they need *some* kind of shape. There's a moment just as they're coming through where you can glimpse their alienness, and it can drive you howlingly, gratefully insane.

But I was already halfway there, fury rising inside me. A chilling, glassy sound broke out of my mouth, burning my throat. Even through the deafness I heard it, like murder in a cold room at midnight, and we struck—the whip and I—at the same time, with physical and etheric force.

And we got his attention.

The world went white. Landing, *hard*, throwing up a sheet of juicy foul green and clods of oily black not-dirt, knocking over hellbreed like ninepins, the jolt snapping bones with sweet pain, blood bursting free in scarlet banners. The gem screamed on my wrist, and a shock ran through me from crown to feet as it tried to patch me up and get me fighting again. Everything tilted sideways, and something damp kissed my cheek.

Rain. It was rain. The roof was crumbling, concrete chunks falling with silent, eerie grace, smoke thinning as water fell from the sky and lightning flashed again and again.

They had come.

They shone, sliding down through the gaps in the dissolving roof like cosmic firemen, clarity glittering on their armor and their wings. No guns for them—they had swords and slender spears, bows and knives, chains and flails. They moved among the hellbreed, winnowing, and Hell's scions were screaming in terror but still standing to fight.

They had no choice.

The clarity around the newcomers shone through the hellbreeds' twisting, stripping off their masks and the rotten apple-bloom of damned beauty.

He landed next to me, his hair a furnace of gold and his blue eyes alight, and leaned down. The gem gave a heatless, massive twinge all through my broken bones. His hand closed around mine and he pulled as if I weighed less than nothing, hauling me to my feet.

"This is the help we can give!" Michael the Caretaker said. The words cut through the deafness, laid right in the center of my brain. I was so far gone I didn't even feel a weary satisfaction at seeing the wings behind him, glorious white and feathered like a vulture's, spread wide, glowing like the sun. *"Human hands must end this!"*

Oh, I'll end it, I thought, and another cold, adrenaline-fueled little laugh burst out of me as Michael swung aside, his sword coming up with a sweet singing, cleaving the cringing air.

Perry fell back, snarling, and he had a sword of his

own. Its blade was tarry black, drinking in the light, but I promptly shelved him as a problem and looked to find the badass who had just stepped through from Hell.

I'd settle Perry's hash later. Still, if the caretaker wanted to save me the trouble, that was fine with me. I had other fish to kill.

38

The hole in the world glowed white-hot, and more hell-breed were draining through. The big one—Argoth, a nightmare made flesh now—crouched as he finished settling into form, a sheet of glaucous film tearing from the inside as he used his claws. He stood, naked, and my boots were thudding onto the squishy field, jolting agony through me like wine, laughing at the idea that I could be stopped by the blood I was losing or a little thing like the broken bones grating together, desperately trying to heal as the gem sang a descant of impossible, strained beauty.

I left the ground, sound coming back in stuttering bursts as my eardrums healed with spikes of wet red pain. Roaring, screaming, weeping, the cracks of thunder and wet sizzling sounds, hunters screaming their battle cries and Weres making a lot of noise, gunfire spattering—

Impact. Or not. I missed him.

He *twisted* aside, his mad blue eyes wide with delight, and the first shock was that he looked like Perry. Or maybe Perry was just a pale copy of this creature, a marvel of twisted pale beauty, his mouth a cruelly luscious crimson

slash, his ears coming up to high points poking through the
frayed mat of spun-platinum hair. Force transferred and I
was thrown, the whip handle biting my hands as it was
ripped free and the gem resonating to the chaos around me.
Landed again, all the breath and sense knocked out of me.
My body decided now was a fine time to just take a little
vacation. Just lay there and breathe for a second, except I
couldn't get any air in.

Get UP! But nothing would obey me, my hands flayed
and the broken bones healing but too slowly, everything
inside me straining and even my will—that trainable,
teachable thing that drives the body, that *makes* it obey—
wasn't working. What the mind requires, the body will do;
but the body has its limits. Sorcerous gem or not, I suspected I'd reached mine.

Well, maybe not *suspected*. More like, *found out*.

A shadow fell over me. My eyes rolled. It was Argoth,
standing with the Lance shaking unhappily in his pale,
beautifully shaped hand. It wept and strained to get away,
ash rising on a hot updraft, and he snarled.

He shouldn't have been able to touch it, but it was probably drained from holding the hellmouth open. Tracers
of ash ribboned back as the hungry mouth yawed, wind
screaming as it sucked, shrinking—but not fast enough. It
was gorged with incredible power, and it would close itself—but Argoth was *here*.

Perry could do all sorts of crap he wasn't supposed to;
why should I have expected his father, original, whatever,
to be different?

I noticed, with a variety of shocked, swimming amusement, that his long, amber-burnished fingernails were
buffed. *Well, if you're going to step out of Hell, you might*

as well make sure you've got a manicure, right? It was the merry voice of doom, caroling inside my weary skull, but the only thing I felt was exhaustion and a great drowsy sense of having let them down.

Wake up! Move! It was my own voice, shrilling at me. Usually when I'm hurt bad there's someone else inside my skull, pushing me.

But I had nobody left.

He lifted the wooden Lance, glare of lightning playing along the slick, ash-weeping blade, and a wide, beautiful-ugly, triumphant smile twisted his face. *Now* he looked like a hellbreed, the shadow of the thing freshly released from Hell's cold, screaming confinement rippling under his skin.

I braced myself to die again.

Then his head jerked back, black ichor spattering. And again. Bullet holes bloomed on his chest, and my head lolled drunkenly enough to see Gilberto, wide-legged in the shooting stance I'd taught him, making his triangle and aiming nicely, squeeze the trigger again. His eyes were bright and lively, he was covered in black stinking 'breed rot, the bandage on his arm was torn and flapping, and the Eye of Sekhmet glowed on his chest, sending up a curl of smoke that wreathed his sallow, young-old face.

He was *laughing*. Even as Argoth let out a banshee wail that dwarfed all other sound and spun the spear, the bullet holes closing over and sealing the hurt away. Silver wasn't going to put this bitch down.

The wall of sound hit Gil, and he tumbled over backward. But the dogsbody was already in the air, its blond hide streaked with spatters of smoking black, and it hit the baddest hellbreed I'd ever seen with a crunch I felt all the way down on the ground.

Now get up, Mikhail said inside my head, and I could swear...

No. I don't need to swear. I *saw.*

One of the winged things was near me, a familiar hitching limp as he eased his sore knee, that clarity blooming over him in a waterfall of light. Not the sterile white nuclear light from the hellmouth, but the white of a clean sheet of paper, a freshly bleached sheet, sunshine on sugar sand, joy and sunrise. He leaned down, his hair a mop of pure silver, and grabbed my arm. It was the same hand, hard and callused from daily practice and nightly hunting. The same long nose and narrow mouth, the same pale blue eyes with dark lashes, the same cleft in his chin and the same vulnerable notch where his collarbones met the breastbone. He didn't look tired, but there was still the faint shadow of knowledge in his eyes. His wings were iron-gray, like his hair used to be, and there was the scar along his jawline, now a thread of gold against his skin. And another scar on his throat, a thick, golden torq.

His mouth opened, but nothing came out. My teacher's voice whispered directly inside my head, even as his lips soundlessly shaped the words.

Now get up, milaya, *and kick bastard back to Hell where he belong.*

He gave me a little push, as if we were in the sparring room and I had to do it again, but faster and better this time. I stumbled, glancing down to find my footing, new strength pouring through me and the gem resonating on my wrist.

When I looked up, he was gone. The dogsbody landed

in a heap next to me, scrabbling weakly for a moment before going limp, twisted on itself. Its eyes fell shut, and it gave a little sigh.

Argoth grinned, licking his red, red lips. His tongue was purplish, shocking against the rest of his beauty, flickering between sharp white teeth. The world was tearing itself to pieces around us, but we stared at each other for a few heartbeats, and he lifted the warping, trembling Lance slightly.

I let out a long breath, my ribs finally healing fully with snapping crackles. The hellmouth pulsed behind him, casting knife-sharp twisting shadows, and the flood of Hell's icy heat lifted my blood-soaked hair. I lifted my filthy hands, and the sharp pinpricks of Perry's charms dug into my skull as they moved restlessly. The hornet buzz filled my head.

That's so strange. Now I remember being dead.

Then he was on me, the Lance moving so fast it blurred, still wicked sharp even through the shredding of ash rising from every surface, screaming its bloodlust and defiance. But I'd thrown myself forward, already inside the arc of his attack, and grabbed.

My right hand closed on the Lance's haft, and its chill jolted up my arms. Argoth had raw power, and a hellbreed's ability to twist things into obeying him. But I was a hunter, and I was human, and I had an edge when it came to forcing a Major Talisman to do what *I* wanted it to.

Or so I hoped.

Because after all, we made the Talismans. They're *ours*. They do not come from Hell.

My left hand clamped down over his, my fingers biting with preternatural strength, and we were face-to-face for a long, shattering moment while I drove him back. There was a warm wind behind me, and it smelled of peppery adrenaline and vodka, leather and musk and the warm smell of Mikhail's skin as he lay beside me in our shared bed. I *pushed*, and the wind behind me wasn't just Mikhail. It was my fellow hunters, Anya and Gilberto, and Monty and my cops; it was my city exhaling as dawn rose and shuddering as dusk fell, while I prowled its rooftops and alleys; it was the hornets buzzing and the spear singing a glassy bloodlust cry, the gem burning on my wrist and every inch of silver on me suddenly running with the same clarity that folded around the winged things.

And finally, it was Saul, his eyes dark with pleasure as he sighed into my hair. Saul cooking pancakes and yawning, his sleepy smile a reward all its own. Saul holding me while I wept, my own arms around him as we both shook, the promise of pain shared and halved in the darkness.

You will not survive, Michael had told me. *You will have to sacrifice yourself again to destroy Hyperion.*

All I felt, finally, was relief that Saul was safe with Galina.

I drove forward, legs pumping, and Argoth's face corkscrewed in on itself as he realized what I was about to do. He tried to let go of the spear, but I had his right hand locked too. The gem sang on my wrist, a rising tide of light inside my bones.

I pushed against him, close as a lover, his hot rank breath in my face and his teeth champing, spattering me with yellow foam.

Not so pretty now, are we.

I threw us both into the hellmouth. The silver I was carrying and my hunter's aura would disrupt it. The shock would shred my physical structure, but that was a small price to pay.

Wasn't it?

Mercifully, everything went black.

39

Confusion.

"Hold her head up." A familiar voice, but so tired, almost slurring the words. "Jesus."

Stutter-flashes of light. Rumbling as the storm retreated, cold rain lashing down. I was wet all over, and freezing. Every part of me burned with savage pain. Someone's arm under my head, sharp little charms biting into my skull. Heaving breaths; someone was moaning.

I'll bet there's a lot of wounded. Then, muzzy amazement. *Wait.*

"I'm not dead?" I actually said it out loud, my lips rubbery, sounding like a dumbfounded drunkard.

A short growl-cough of a laugh, one I recognized. "No. Not yet."

My eyes flew open. I tried to move, too, my entire body tensing, but Saul's arm tightened under my head. He was haggard and damp with rain, and the blood on his face made every part of me cold with fear.

"Relax," he said, gently but firmly. "Just settle down for a second, okay?"

"Galina—" I began.

"She's okay. Mad as hell, but okay. We're going to have to have a talk, Jillian."

I stared at him. There was crusted stuff in my eyes. I blinked. Lightning spattered through the clouds. The stadium's roof was a gigantic gaping hole. The whole place was peppered with huge chunks of concrete, as if the gods of urban architecture had decided to throw up over everything.

Monty is just going to have a fit. It was a good thought, a sane thought. It meant I was alive. Saul's mouth was drawn tight, and he looked fine. Bloody, but fine.

"You are never doing that to me again," he informed me. "I swear, Jill. If you even try I'll..." He ran out of words, his irises flaring with orange as the cougar came close to the surface. It retreated, and the rumble in his chest was a growl.

My lips were cracked. My mouth tasted foul. But I managed to get the words out, only slurring them a little. "Nothing. Could be worse. Than losing. You."

A flash of pain crossed his face, and it tore at my heart. I never wanted to hurt him. But he simply leaned forward, his other arm slipping around me as well, and pulled me close. We clung to each other, one bone-thin Were and a very tired hunter, and if there were tears on my cheeks nobody saw and I didn't care.

He was alive. So was I.

It had to be enough.

* * *

We didn't get to stay like that, though. "Jill?" Anya Devi, softly.

Saul's arms loosened. I found I could move. "Jesus," I moaned, and someone laughed.

"Always did know how to throw a party, darlin'." Leon's Texas drawl was thick as cream. He must've been tired. "Nice friends you got. Where you find them?"

"Oh, shut up." Anya sighed. "Jill. Please."

I got my legs working again. Saul helped. He hauled me up carefully, I still weighed more than I should. Denser muscle, denser bone, the gem sparking on my wrist, humming a low note of satisfaction. My skin crawled. I was covered in guck and goop and I stank to high heaven.

Everything stank. The not-grass was dying, lashed by cold water. The altar was crushed under a huge shipwreck-shape of concrete, a charred stick jetting up from its crest. After a second I realized it was a flagpole, and the char-tattered rags hanging from it were anonymous. The hellbreed and Traders were either dead or fled, but there were bodies *everywhere*. Mounds of corpses, and grim-faced Weres picking through them, looking for survivors.

Or looking for their kin, or for hunters.

"Did we..." I steadied myself against Saul's shoulder. *Did we lose anyone?* I couldn't say it.

"Some. Maybe." Anya was wet clear through, leaning on Theron. The Werepanther looked somber, but Devi just looked tired. "We'll deal with that in a bit. There's...something you should see."

Oh, Christ, what now? But I squared myself, wearily, and found I could stand. Not very steadily, but I could at least hold myself upright. I could even fight, if I had to.

Except what was left to kill?

I had a sneaking suspicion I was about to find out.

The Lance lay near the altar, twisted like the flagpole,

quivering a subaudible hum of distress and frustrated
anger. It was weak, very weak. All the force it had accu-
mulated was now spent, and all it could do was shake like
a whipped dog.

Dog. "Gilberto?" I whispered. "And the...the dog?"

"Gil's fine." Anya pointed. "See?"

My apprentice was bandaging Benny Cross's leg. Half
of Gil's hair was singed off, Benny was covered in all
kinds of crap, and the dogsbody slumped next to Gilberto,
hanging its narrow head. It glanced at me, ears pricking,
but it looked as tired as Anya. As tired as I felt.

Thank you. I didn't even know who I was thanking.
"Good deal," I rasped. "Okay. What's next? Point me at it.
I'll kill it."

"Good." Devi shook herself away from Theron with a
quick glance of thanks. "Because it's Perry. Sort of. And
if you don't ventilate that fucker, I just might."

40

At the northern edge of the battlefield, a few of the winged things had gathered. The rain avoided them.

They didn't turn as Anya and I approached, Saul and Theron hanging back with perfect Were tact. A few other hunters—Dmitri Roslan, Jack Quint, a short, hard-faced woman I realized was Belle de Sud herself, with her long brown fingers flicking uneasily at her whip handle, four or five others—stood in a loose semicircle, watching. Dmitri flicked me a salute, his usual grin absent; I returned it without thinking.

I couldn't help it. I stared at the wings. They were all white, some with flecks of brown. And *huge*, managing to look perfectly natural instead of a violation of biology. The clarity had faded to a slow gleam around them, no longer hurtfully bright. They faced something chained to the goalpost, glints of gold shifting as the blackened, charred thing moved slightly. A ripple of tension went through the winged, as if they expected him to break the thin golden bonds and start making trouble again.

Bitterness filled my mouth. Anya tapped at a gun butt, her face set.

The tallest of them half-turned as I halted next to him. It was Michael the Caretaker, and there was no shadow of scarring left on his face. His wings drooped a little, as if he was tired, too. His eyes were the same, though, bright and mild, that shadow of pain sending an answering twinge through me.

"You understand," he said, quiet.

I don't understand this at all. "Yes," I heard myself say, dully, a good pupil aiming to please. "Sacrifice."

Michael nodded. "You were willing, again, even when there was no hope. That creates a...new thing, you could say, in the Pattern." He looked back at the charred form, and his shoulders dropped again. "His father is dead. He is utterly flesh now, as he wished to be." A world of sadness in the words. "The choice is yours, to spare or to kill."

I didn't want to think about that yet. "Where's Mikhail?" My hands were fists. "I *saw* him. He was here. Where is he?"

Michael shrugged. One wing flicked, delicately, sending a clean breeze over my filthy cheeks. "Only the ones present are here."

"Well, no shit." Sarcasm gave me fresh strength. The gem muttered, etheric force trickling back through me. I needed food, and rest, and maybe a couple pints of something eye-wateringly alcoholic before I'd be anything close to my mettle, but right at the moment I didn't care. I was shaking.

But not with the weakness. No.

With *rage*.

He turned, this time facing me fully. "Love cannot be

forced. Love is only given, freely." A faint smile, but he
didn't look happy. Instead, it was that sorrow again. "Love
is only *proved*, though it asks no proof in return. This is
important, but it is not our task here. We are to witness
your choice." Again a wing dipped, indicating the blackened body, and I was forgetting I'd ever seen him without
the snowy feathered expanses.

My fists ached. "What were you doing down there in the
Hill's boiler room all this time, huh? Just waiting for this?"

"Witnessing." He nodded slightly, as if the question
was expected, weighed his answer, and added more.
"Serving the Pattern."

"Your Pattern fucking *blows*." It wasn't up to my usual
standards. I sounded more like Gilberto than myself. "It's
insane. It hurts good people. It's not fair."

"It is," he said gravely, "all we have."

He made a sudden movement, and another ripple went
through the winged things. But he'd just unlimbered his
sword from somewhere. It was a heavy broadsword piece
of work, too tall for me, with wicked finials on the guard
and a ruby the size of a fist at the end of the pommel. It
looked razor sharp, and its bright blade smoked with dappled light.

It looked a little like the sunsword. Well, the sunsword
was a toothpick compared to this, but still, you could see
an echo.

He presented me with the hilt. Anya breathed an obscenity.

"It is your choice," Michael repeated.

It was hard work to shake my right hand out. Even harder
to touch the damn thing. Warm strength poured down my
arm from the cool metal, and Michael nodded approvingly.

I probably looked ridiculous, stepping across the sludge-dying not-grass, gingerly and awkwardly holding a broadsword almost as long as I was tall away from me. The winged stepped back in unison, but the hunters moved forward, almost as if prearranged.

Is this part of his fucking Pattern too? The bitterness was all through me.

He'd been burned, terribly. Weeping cracks coated his charred flesh, but his eyes were still the same sterile blue. The dome of his skull without any hair to cover it was subtly wrong, and he seemed smaller. Of course, anyone's going to look small covered in fourth-degree burns and chained to a goalpost, right?

Even a hellbreed.

His lips cracked. Thick colorless fluid wept from them. "Kissssssss." Sighing, like a lover.

"Hyperion. *Perry.*" I swallowed hard. My palms might have been sweating, or it might have been the rain or the filth making the hilt slippery. The sword hummed, a thunderbolt contained. His own black blade lay in pieces around him, and Perry raised his burned-bared head and stared at me. "Or should I say, Argoth."

A shrug. More blackened skin broke, a brittle sugar-glaze. How he was still alive? "Only a part of him. A fragment. Insurance, originally. A doppelgänger, meant to be a placeholder here, in case the masters needed hands in this world."

It was my turn to nod slightly. "But you wanted more. Slipped the leash, made a deal with Jack Karma, and got the original locked away in Hell. Then you started planning how to get all of the original's power, all the other pieces of him." I coughed, tasted smoke. Thunder roiled in the distance, and the rain intensified. "But for that, you needed a hunter. Because you didn't just want all of your father. You wanted to be *real*. Anything above an *arkeus* isn't usually physical, it can be disrupted and once it is, goodbye and good night. The bargain with Karma and his line kept you here and gave you a simulacrum of flesh, and you could afford to settle down and wait for a hunter who could take on your poppa *and* keep you bolted to the physical world at the same time." *You followed Mikhail all the way from Europe. That's almost why he drew on you in the Monde that first time I saw you. Did he think he was free of you? Not likely. So what was he thinking?*

Would I ever know?

His tongue flickered, startling cherry-red. He studied me for a long time, and I let him. The sword quivered heavily, but my arm wasn't tired. It was building in me, the knowledge of what I had to do.

"I am flesh now," he finally hissed. "*Flesh*, my darling one. You made it possible. You killed the *original*, as you so quaintly call him. I am his heir, and we are linked. I am your other half. We're the same coin, my love."

Negation rose inside me. But I nodded again, slowly. He was at least partly right. I'd been mortgaging bits of myself to Perry for years, telling myself it didn't make me a Trader. It gave me the strength to police the nightside more effectively, and his mark on me had been the punishment I deserved.

For everything.

No. I couldn't afford to lie here. He was right. There was only a thread-thin edge between Perry and me. A coin's edge. He had waited for me for a very long time. Waited for the hunter who was, at bottom, *like* him.

We are the ones crying in the dark, and on our backs they build golden cities.

God help me, I understood.

"So what is it to be?" More of his brittle skin cracking as he shifted. The thin golden chains sent up threads of steam, whisked away by the cold wet breeze. "Cut me loose, and take your place as my keeper? Think of what you can do, with me your willing slave. Think of the battles you can win." Another wriggling motion.

He might eventually squirm free, I realized. But it didn't seem important.

"Or strike me down with that avenging sword— overcompensating a bit, aren't we? And damn yourself with murdering the helpless, whose only crime was to wait for you and love you?" Those white teeth were now grimed with thin pinkish fluid, darker lines accumulating between them. He writhed again. "I waited so, so long for you, my dove. Theirs is not the only Pattern."

There. That's what he's after. "No," I dimly heard myself say, through the roaring in my ears. "I suppose it isn't."

"We can make a new one," he whispered. "Just you and me. A *fair* one. You can mete out justice, and I will make it total. Just let me loose."

I stepped closer, boots squishing in the muck. "I suppose it isn't the only pattern." Louder now, clear and strong. "It's not even the one that *matters*."

Perry gazed up at me. "Let me free." So soft, all the promise in the world. "You will never be lonely, Kiss. Not so long as I am able to comfort you."

Oh, God. The problem wasn't that he said it.

The problem was that it was *true*. There was only a hairsbreadth of difference between Perry…and me. Or at least, the part of me that made sure I survived. The stranger who lived inside me, strong and ruthless where I was weak. And with him dead, I would be—down in the secret place where the animal of survival crouches, the part of me that was coldly determined to do what *had* to be done—*alone*.

Utterly alone.

The sword rose, thrumming, its blade suddenly pouring with white radiance. Perry bared his teeth, more skin crackling, and the golden chain burst with a tinkle. My right wrist flamed with cramping pain, but I brought the blade down with a scream. It cut, the goalpost singing before it groaned and tipped, smashing into the wet ground with a *plorch*.

Lifted and flung, my right arm on fire, torn out by the roots, every nerve screaming…and I landed, hard, my fingers forced open and the sword clattering away. Rustling filled the broken bowl of the stadium, and they took wing, spiraling up with a grace and authority that forced a dry barking sob from my aching, parched throat.

The last one bent over me, blue eyes dark with sorrow. But he was smiling, and he laid one warm finger to my lips. Warmth broke over me in a wave, white light filling my head for one long glorious moment.

Well done, he whispered. Or maybe it wasn't him. Maybe I just thought he did. Maybe I needed someone to say it.

In any case, there was a pop of collapsing air, and he vanished.

I lay there in the rain, fresh cold sludge working up through my hair and the tatters of my coat, with my right arm flung up as if to protect me.

My whole, naked, unmarked right arm.

41

We had Galina to thank. Pissing off a Sanctuary by attempting to burn down her house from the outside is not a good idea, and she'd done something Sancs only keep for emergencies—somehow opening a space down in her vaults for hunters to step through from other Sanctuaries. They'd been flooding into Santa Luz ever since I'd made that frantic phone call to Anya Devi, and with them working from the top and other hunters working from the bottom, as well as Galina's control over the wrecked physical structure of her house, they'd broken through before dusk.

It didn't take a genius to figure out something big was going down, either. With the sky going dark and hellbreed and Traders popping up everywhere and making for the stadium, you only had to have half a brain in your head to figure out where the big event was going down.

Montaigne was moaning about property damage. Anya filled out the reams of paperwork for a Major Paranormal Incident so we could get government funding. Flash floods had claimed a couple lives, whole sections of the barrio were burned down, the morgue was groaning at the seams from the citywide spree of murder, arson, and other hell-breed fun. Most of the other hunters had only stayed to help deal with the cleanup in the stadium—banefire and yellow tape, just to be sure, and the Lance reduced to cold, metallic ash scraped into an alabaster jar—and headed back to their cities.

We're not much on goodbyes. So mostly they just slid out of town after exchanging a few words with me or Devi.

A few stayed. We'd lost four hunters and six Weres. One of the Weres was Rahel, and, oddly enough, that was the thing I cried over, hunched next to Saul's bed with my face in my knees, snot slicking my upper lip as I shook and sobbed as quietly as possible. I bit the smooth, unmarked skin on my right wrist where a scar in the shape of a pair of lips had been pressed, where the gem had shivered free of my flesh. I was still stronger and faster than even the average hunter, but there was no mark on me.

It's not even the only pattern that matters.

A bunch of 'breed had escaped through the hellmouth. Things were going to be hopping all over—but at least we'd staved off the *big* catastrophe. Argoth was no more, and there hadn't been any other prepared hellmouths.

Just the one. Just Perry's lunge toward fleshly incarnation. With me as his linchpin and Argoth's power behind him, what would he have been able to do?

What *wouldn't* he have done?

Galina's house and shop were fully rebuilt in a matter of eighteen hours, growing up from the ground like a mushroom. You can't keep a Sanc down for long; even if Perry had succeeded in locking her temporarily inside her vault and making her mad. She stalked around muttering for a while, checking every inch of her house and making tiny adjustments while the walls shivered with redgold sheets of cascading energy.

We all stayed out of her way, except for Theron.

The dogsbody had vanished. One moment it was there at the stadium, the next...gone. I didn't mention it to Devi.

Gilberto was in the barrio with some other hunter apprentices and Leon Budge, helping the Weres rebuild. Mickey's on Mayfair had gone down in a three-alarm fire—more hellbreed work—but they would rebuild.

Saul slept through most of it, but every time he woke up I was at his bedside. Devi handled the rest. It was one more thing to thank her for. Every time I tried, though, she just rolled her eyes and waved an absinthe bottle at me, threatening to make me drink until I shut up.

I shut up.

When Saul woke, he ate. I carried tray after tray of food up the stairs, watched him fill out bit by bit, listened to his breathing.

I did not think about Perry. Or about wings. I didn't sleep much, either. Maybe I was afraid of dreaming.

Hello? I asked the silence inside my chest. *Who am I? Tell me who I am now.*

There was no answer.

Anya tapped on the door one long, drowsy-sunny afternoon. Saul was sleeping deeply on his side, his hair streaked with tawny lights. I held a finger to my lips and tiptoed to the door. Left it open a crack so I could hear him.

"You can take the truck," Devi said bluntly, her *bindi* glimmering. She pushed a bead-weighted strand of hair

behind her ear. "Get out, get away, get your head cleared
out. There's nothing you can do here."

I slumped against the wall, one hand on a knife hilt. She
was tense, I realized, and I left my fingers fall away. "I'm
a liability." Flatly, daring her to disagree.

"You need a *vacation*," she corrected. "You've done
enough for a while, and if you keep pushing you're going
to kill yourself. Or Saul. Or both, and I don't want to deal
with that."

I moved, restless. Looked at the floor. Our boots were
placed just so, both of us braced and ready for action.

"Mikhail," I said finally. "He was there."

Her chin dipped a fraction, the scar down her right
cheek flushing. "Maybe he was. *I'm* not going to fucking
disagree. I'm not even going to speculate who or what
those bird-things were. Nobody is."

At least, not out loud. Well, thank God for that. But I
shivered. "One thing."

"Okay." She didn't even ask *what*. Just agreed.

My heart twisted, I pushed down the pressure in my
throat. "The Monde." My throat was so dry. It was work
to get the sounds out. "Burn it. Banefire. Please."

"Of course. Jill." Her hand on my arm, brutally short
fingernails digging in. Her duster made a sound, but my
arms were bare; I wore only a T-shirt and a pair of spare
leather pants. "Perry's dead. Absolutely *dead*. He's not
coming back."

You promise? Because I wouldn't put it past him. But
she was a hunter, and I looked up. We held each other's
gaze for a long time, possibly an eternity. And I found out,
gratefully, that *I* couldn't lie to a fellow hunter.

"I'm afraid either way, Devi," I whispered.

She nodded. There was nothing else to say, so she didn't bother. She just let me fold forward until my head was on her shoulder, and the silent sobbing that shook me was like an earthquake. She stroked my hair, touching the sharp-spined charms he'd given me, and they didn't bite either of us.

Misericordia

*W*e left near dusk, stealing out like a pair of thieves. At least, we would have sneaked out if Galina hadn't packed everything for us and Theron hadn't cooked a gluttonous farewell meal, during which Anya stalked in reeking of smoke and nodded at me.

The Monde was gutted. I didn't even have to go check.

She stayed only long enough for a silent beer before vanishing again. Gilberto sucked down a couple beers, too, ate a whole pan of tamales, and informed me he was going to be working in the barrio with the Weres, not to mention training with Devi, until I came back.

"We still need to discuss you not following orders," I muttered.

He actually *winked* at me, and left with a couple bird Weres who didn't look at me. They were probably kin of the deceased, but they said nothing.

Weres don't talk about their dead.

I turned the key and the Chevy roared into life. Theron waved, then ducked back inside Galina's store, the bell tinkling and gleaming as the door closed. I dropped the car into gear, popped the brake, and pulled out slowly even though the street was deserted. Turned left at the bottom of the slight hill, and began threading our way toward the freeway.

When we reached Miguel and 147th, Saul let out a sigh.

"We'll stop over the state line for a snack." I kept my eyes on the road. "And, you know, if you get tired..."

"I'm *fine*, kitten." Slightly irritated.

"Here." I dug in my pocket. The new coat was stiff, and I was hoping I could go for at least a week without it getting ripped or blown off me. We were supposed to be embarking on a vacation, but there were a lot of new hell-breed around.

Trouble might find us.

I fished out an unopened pack of Charvils. "Congrats. Galina says you can smoke again."

"Thank *God*," he said with feeling, grabbing for it, and I surprised myself by laughing. It was a harsh, cracked sound, but it felt good.

The rearview mirror was alive with reflected sunset, but a shadow flickered in its depths. I stood on the brake and we skidded to a stop, Saul's right hand slapped down on the dash.

"Jill?" Quiet, but with a thread of a growl underneath.

I hit the seat belt catch and hopped out, the gun held low and ready. Scanned the rooftops, every hair quivering, my nape crawling with gooseflesh. Readiness settled over me, and it felt so good I could have cried.

A long lean shape flickered out of the alley to my right, and I sighed. Eased my finger off the trigger. "Christ."

Saul's door opened. "Is that what I think it is?"

The dogsbody's fur gleamed golden. It was rail-thin,

and it cringed as it trot-walked up to me, ears back and flat,
stubby tail tucked as far as it could go. When it got within
twenty feet, its front end came down, and it finished by
literally crawling on its belly. The ugly thing heaved to a
stop right in front of my boots, and I shut my eyes, listening to its quick wheezing breaths.

Sweat stood out all over me. I lifted the gun, just a little.

The dog whined. Softly. Saul was still and quiet, watching.

I could just bend down, put the barrel against the thing's
domed head, and pull the trigger. Easy, so very easy.

The dogsbody whined again, and shuddered. Its head
was on my boots.

No, Jill. It was my conscience, speaking loud and clear.
You don't get a chance to practice mercy every day.

My cheeks were wet. I forced my eyes open. The sun
was dying, and the usual wind from the river cut across
the buildings, laden with desert sand and exhaust. The dog
sighed, its eyes closed.

I slid the gun back into its holster. Cleared my
throat. Still, I sounded choked. "Put the gate down, will
you?"

Saul said nothing. His footsteps were soft, and the
screech of the tailgate covered up whatever he might
have muttered. I moved my toes and the dog looked
up, its eyes wide and dark now. Not blue, and not pale,
colorless crystalline. Relief tasted like thin copper; my
mouth was full of it. I swiped at my nose with the back
of my hand.

"Get in," I said harshly.

The dog hauled itself up. It shambled to the end of the
truck and made a graceless clumsy scrabble, its nails click-

ing on the bed as Saul slammed the gate. It settled down with a sigh, right next to the spare tire, and closed its weary eyes again.

I got back in and slammed my own door. Saul was a moment behind me. The engine idled; someone had done some tune-up on it. Probably one of the Weres, Devi wasn't a big car person and Leon held his own truck together with spit and baling wire.

The click of a lighter sounded very loud in the cab's hush. Saul inhaled and blew out a cloud of cherry-scented smoke.

"I'm sorry," I managed through the rock in my throat. "I can't—"

"I always wanted a hound." Saul grabbed his seat belt. I mechanically followed suit.

"I..." Everything I wanted to say balled up inside me, and he glanced over. A half smile curled up one corner of his mouth, and the pressure inside my chest eased. How the hell did he do that? Would I ever figure it out? "I thought cats don't like dogs." I dropped it into gear again, eased us forward toward Fifth Street and the freeway on-ramps.

"That's not a dog. It's a *hound*. Completely different." Saul snorted, took another drag. "Hope it eats Purina."

"Yeah." I braked for the red light on Fifth, we rolled to a stop. Traffic was light here, for once, and if we were lucky we'd be out of town in twenty minutes. "Saul?"

"Hmm?" He settled further, stretching his legs out.

"I love you."

I'm surprised he heard me, because I couldn't say it very loud. But his reply was clear and distinct.

"I love you, too, kitten."

By the time we crossed the state line he'd scooted over to the middle seat belt, I had my arm around him, and we drove on into the desert night.

finis

Glossary

Arkeus: A roaming corruptor escaped from Hell.

Banefire: A cleansing, sorcerous flame.

Black Mist: A roaming psychic contagion; a symbiotic parasite inhabiting the host's nervous system and bloodstream.

Chutsharak: A Chaldean obscenity, loosely translated as "Oh, *fuck.*"

Demon: A term loosely used to designate any nonhuman predator with sorcerous ability or a connection to Hell.

Exorcism: Tearing loose a psychic parasite from its host.

Hellbreed: A blanket term for a wide array of demons, half demons, or other species escaped or sent from Hell.

Hellfire: The spectrum of sorcerous flame employed by hellbreed for a variety of uses.

Hunter: A trained human who keeps the balance between the nightside and regular humans; extrahuman law enforcement.

Imdarák: Shadowy former race who drove the Elder Gods from the physical plane, also called the Lords of the Trees.

Martindale Squad: The FBI division responsible for tracking nightside crime across state lines and at the federal level; mostly staffed with hunters and Weres.

Middle Way: Worshippers of Chaos, Middle Way adepts are usually sociopathic and sorcerous loners. Occasionally covens of Middle Way adepts will come together to control a territory or for a specific purpose.

OtherSight: Second sight, the ability to see sorcerous energy. Can also mean precognition.

Possessor: An insubstantial, low-class demon specializing in occupying and controlling humans; the prime reason for exorcists.

Scurf: Also called *nosferatim*, a semipsychic viral infection responsible for legends of blood-hungry corpses, vampires, or nosferatu. Also, someone infected by the scurf virus.

Sorrow: A worshipper of the Chaldean Elder Gods.

Sorrows House: A House inhabited by Sorrows, with a vault for invocation or evocation of Elder Gods.

Sorrows Mother: A high-ranking female of a Sorrows House.

Talyn: A hellbreed, higher in rank than an *arkeus* or a Possessor, usually insubstantial due to the nature of the physical world.

Trader: A human who makes a "deal" with a hellbreed, usually for worldly gain or power.

Utt'huruk: A bird-headed demon.

Were: Blanket term for several species who shapeshift into animal (for example, cougar, wolf, or spider) or half-animal (wererat or *khentauri*) form.

A Note on Kismet

Hopefully, after six books, I have once again earned a little leeway to bore you, dear Reader, with a closing word.

Jill Kismet started out as a "what-if?" character. I was tired of paranormal heroes and heroines who had adversarial relationships with law enforcement. If there were things that went bump in the night, I reasoned, the cops (and other first responders) would be more than glad to have a specialist on hand to deal with them. I asked myself what that specialist might look like, what kind of person would be attracted to that type of job. How they would deal with the stress of the paranormal, what sort of enemies they might face.

However, when Jill strolled onto the page in *Hunter's Prayer* (which I actually wrote first) and began speaking, something much deeper than a "what if?" happened. *It's not the type of work you can put on a business card,* she said, and I immediately felt a galvanic thrill along every nerve ending I owned. The more I wrote, the more it seemed Jill had just been waiting for me to sit still long enough to hear her. (I didn't even know why she'd chosen the name "Kismet" until *Flesh Circus*.)

It is very unfair of me to compare characters, though such comparisons are all but inevitable. I'm often asked about Jill and Dante Valentine: if they're sisters, if they came from the same place. They most emphatically do *not*. Danny Valentine is a broken character. Jill is not broken—bent a little, maybe, but still whole. I think that is the critical difference between them, though they both have smart mouths and a love of weaponry, as well as a streak of sheer adrenaline-junkie grade-A crazy.

Hey, write what you know, right?

Writing Kismet took me through some pretty dark times. I won't deny that sometimes, writing a gruesome scene—the clinic in *Hunter's Prayer*, the scurf-hole in *Redemption Alley*, the Cirque itself, at Carper's graveside, the scrabble out of her own grave—I found solace in the fact that no matter how bad I had it, my character had it worse. I also can't deny that many of the issues I wrestle with found an expression in her. As I noted in my goodbye essay on the Valentine series, any story about the possible future—or even about an alternate present—ends up saying far more about the writer than anything else. The filter the story passes through shapes it, for good or for ill.

Oddly, the character who affected me the most over the Kismet series isn't Jill. It's Perry.

If I did not feel physically filthy, if I didn't crave a hot shower and scrubbing every time he wandered onto the page, I went back and dug deeper and did it again. As much as I loathe him, I ended up pitying him as well. That's the tragedy of hellbreed—they carry their punishment with them. As Milton remarked, *"The mind is its own place, and in itself / Can make a Heaven of Hell, a Hell of Heaven."*

Human beings are very good at doing this as well.

Other characters came from different places. Saul was, in my original plans, only on board for one book. He was supposed to be a cautionary tale about how people with itchy trigger fingers and vigilante complexes are hard to have relationships with. Nobody was more surprised than me when the two of them made it work. I am asked many questions about Saul, and I have always wanted to note that if Saul's and Jill's genders were reversed, the vast majority of those questions would never see the light of day. They would simply match a number of assumptions and be let go.

Gilberto surprised me too. I had no idea why he was so important in *Redemption Alley*, but he literally would not go away. It was only later that I understood why. Monty and the various Santa Luz cops—fighting the good fight, being Jill's backup, extending to her the rough take-no-prisoners compassion they give to each other—are homages to the silent heroes who, every day, respond first and do their best to keep other people safe. More than that, however, they are people Jill cares about. If there is a grace that saves her from becoming what Perry wants her to be, it lies in that caring.

Galina represents another type of courage—those who quietly and patiently guard and build. And dear, sweet Hutch, bulletproof in cyberspace and a weenie everywhere else, is probably the most gallant of the bunch.

Still, I had no Grand Statement I wanted to make with Jill. I had no agenda, unless it was to tell a good story in as unflinching a manner as possible. Jill's job is not to look away; in that, hunters have a great deal in common with writers. I firmly believe that if a writer is honest, if the writer doesn't punk out or look away, that their story will have the ring of truth, and it will reach the readers it needs to. I have done the best I could.

I am sad to say goodbye to Jill. But it's time. Other stories are knocking at the door. All that remains is to thank you, dear Reader. Without you, this would be pretty useless, right? So, thank you very much for reading. I hope you've enjoyed it. And I cannot wait to tell you more stories.

But there will always be a part of me in Santa Luz, watching the moon rise over the bad old lady herself, while rooftops lie in shadow and neon smears the street. There will always be a jingle of silver flechettes and the creak of leather, and the sense that someone is watching even the darkest corners of the city. Someone is out there to right the wrongs, someone is going toe-to-toe and looking to settle the score. In some part of me, Jill Kismet will always be on the job.

I wouldn't have it any other way.

extras

orbit

meet the author

Lilith Saintcrow was born in New Mexico, bounced around the world as an Air Force brat, and fell in love with writing when she was ten years old. She currently lives in Vancouver, WA. Find her on the web at www.lilithsaintcrow.com.

introducing

If you enjoyed ANGEL TOWN,
look out for

THE IRON WYRM AFFAIR

Bannon and Clare: Book 1
by Lilith Saintcrow

*Emma Bannon, Sorceress Prime in the service of the
Empire, has a mission: to protect Archibald Clare, a
failed, unregistered mentath. His skills of deduction are
legendary, and her own sorcery is not inconsiderable. It
doesn't much help that they dislike each other, or that
Bannon's Shield, Mikal, might just be a traitor himself.
Or that the conspiracy killing registered mentaths and
sorcerers alike will just as likely kill them as seduce
them into treachery toward their Queen. In an alternate
London where illogical magic has turned the Industrial
Revolution on its head, Bannon and Clare now face
hostility, treason, cannon fire, black sorcery, and the
problem of reliably finding hansom cabs. The game is
afoot...*

The door was swept unceremoniously open, and Grayson visibly flinched. Clare was gratified to find his nerves were still steady. Besides, he had heard the determined tap of female footsteps, dainty little bootheels crackling with authority, and deduced Miss Bannon was in a fine mood.

Her curly hair was caught up and re-pinned, but she was hatless and her dress was sadly the worse for wear. Smoke and fury hung on her in almost-visible veils, and she was dead pale. Her dark eyes burned rather like coals, and Clare had no doubt that any obstacle in her way had simply been toppled.

Green silk flopped uneasily at the shoulder, but there was no sign of a wound. Just pale, unmarked skin, and the amber cabochon glowing in a most peculiar manner.

Grayson gained his feet in a walrus-lunge. He had turned an alarming shade of floury yeastiness, but most people did when confronted with an angry sorcerer. "Miss Bannon. *Very* glad to see you on your feet, indeed! I was just bringing Clare here—"

She gave him a single cutting glance, and short shrift. "Filling his head with nonsense, no doubt. We are dealing with conspiracy of the blackest hue, Lord Grayson, and I am afraid I may tarry no longer. Mr. Clare, are you disposed to linger, or would you accompany me? The Palace should be relatively safe, but I confess your talents may be of some use in the hunt before me."

Clare was only too glad to leave the mediocre sherry. He set it down, untasted. "I would be most honored to accompany you, Miss Bannon. Lord Grayson has informed me of the deaths of several mentaths and the unfortunate circumstances surrounding Mr. Throckmorton's erstwhile guard. I gather we are bound for Bedlam?"

"In one way or another." But a corner of her lips twitched. "You do your profession justice, Mr. Clare. I trust you were not injured?"

"Not at all, thanks to your efforts." Clare recovered his hat, glanced at his bags. "Will I be needing linens, Miss Bannon, or may I leave them as superfluous weight?"

Now she was certainly amused, a steely smile instead of a single lip-twitch, at odds with her childlike face. With that spark in her dark eyes, Miss Bannon would be counted attractive, if not downright striking. "I believe linens may be procured with little difficulty anywhere in the Empire we are likely to arrive, Mr. Clare. You may have those sent to my house in Mayefair; I believe they shall arrive promptly."

"Very well. Cedric, I do trust you'll send these along for me? My very favorite waistcoat is in that bag. We shall return when we've sorted out this mess, or when we require some aid. Good to see you, old boy." Clare offered his hand, and noted with some mild amusement of his own that Cedric's palm was sweating.

He didn't blame the man.

Mentaths were not overtly feared the way sorcerers were. Dispassionate logic was easier to swallow than sorcery's flagrant violations of what the general populace took to be *normal*. Logic was easily hidden, and most mentaths discreet by nature. There were exceptions, of course, but none of them as notable as the least of sorcery's odd children.

"God and Her Majesty be with you," Cedric managed. "Miss Bannon, are you quite certain you do not—"

"I require nothing else at the moment, sir. Thank you, God and Her Majesty." She turned on one dainty heel and strode away, ragged skirts flapping. Clare arranged his features into something resembling composure, fetched the small black bag containing his working notables, and hurried out the door.

His legs were much longer, but Miss Bannon had a surprisingly energetic stride. He arrived at her side halfway down the corridor. "I know better than to take Lord Grayson's suppositions as anything but, Miss Bannon."

Miss Bannon's chin was set. She seemed none the worse for wear, despite her ruined clothing. "You were at school with him, were you not?"

Was that a deduction? He decided not to ask. "At Itton."

"Was he an insufferable, blind-headed prig then, too?"

Clare strangled a laugh by sheer force of will. *Quite diverting.* He made a *tsk-tsk* sound, settling into her speed. The dusky hall would take them to the Gallery, she perhaps meant them to come out through the Bell Gate and from there, to find another hansom. "Impolitic, Miss Bannon."

"I do not play *politics*, Mr. Clare."

"Politics play, even if *you* do not. If you have no care for your own career, think of mine. Grayson dangled the renewal of my registration before me. Why, do you suppose, did he do so?"

"He doesn't expect you to live long enough to claim such a prize." Her tone suggested she found the idea insulting. "How did you lose your registration, if I may ask?"

For a moment, irrationality threatened to blind him. "I

killed a man," he said, evenly enough. "Unfortunately, it was the *wrong* man. A mentath cannot afford to do such a thing."

"Hmm." Her pace did not slacken, but her heels did not jab the wooden floor with such hurtful little crackles. "In that, Mr. Clare, mentaths and sorcerers are akin. You kill one tiny peer of the realm, and suddenly your career is gone. It is a great relief to me that I have no career to lose."

"Indeed? Then why are you—" The question was ridiculous, but he wished to gauge her response. When she slanted him a very amused, dark-eyed glance, he nodded internally. "Ah. I see. You are as expendable as I have become."

"Slightly more expendable, Mr. Clare. But only slightly. Come."